To Brian.

Enjoy. Don...

Anyone get any ideas!

John

PROF. HARRIET

Lethal Alchemy: Power, Mystery, Survival

John Atkinson

Introducing Agent Frik

Acknowledgements

This could be a long list as Harriet is over a year in development. But it would not be here in your hands without help, contribution, and encouragement from my family and friends around the world. Each of you sustained me in the art of writing. Thank you from the bottom of my heart.

A special thanks to my beta readers and proofreaders, Jim, Tess, and Jonathan. Your eyes are better than mine!

Prof Harriet

First published in Ireland by Red Books Press, 2023
Red Books Press
Selskin House
St Peter's Square
Slippery Green
Wexford, Ireland

ISBN PaperBack 9781838215439

Dedication

I dedicate this book to all my fellow wrinklies hoping to find an elixir of youth.

CONTENTS

Chapter 1: Harriet meets Oxana in Seville 1

Chapter 2: Oxana makes a date with Enrico 11

Chapter 3: Harriet prepares her initial pilot findings 15

Chapter 4: Enrico meets his maker 20

Chapter 5: Harriet presents the pilot research findings 26

Chapter 6: Frik and Henri hear of a death in Seville 30

Chapter 7: Harriet taken to jail 33

Chapter 8: Oxana meets Cristiano 36

Chapter 9: Harriet interviewed in jail 39

Chapter 10: The Dublin team gear up 45

Chapter 11: Frik and Henri 48

Chapter 12: Gregor, Alexandr, and Sergei 52

Chapter 13: Cristiano interviews Oxana and lets her go 57

Chapter 14: Cristiano gathers information about Ricardo 63

Chapter 15: Harriet with Luz and Nancy 68

Chapter 16: Cristiano interviews Harriet 72

Chapter 17: Frik finds Oxana near another death 77

Chapter 18: Oxana back in Russia 80

Chapter 19: Irish diplomats get involved 86

Chapter 20: Frik arrives in Seville 88

Chapter 21: Oxana gets a new mission 95

Chapter 22: Frik, Harriet, Cristiano, Colin 99

Chapter 23: Harriet back in Dublin 108

Chapter 24: Oxana plans to move to Dublin 113

Chapter 25: Gregor gets the American money 119

Chapter 26: Harriet gets a new lab 127

Chapter 27: Oxana moves to Dublin 135

Chapter 28: Frik shares news of Oxana in Dublin 138

Chapter 29: Oxana in the lab 140

Chapter 30: Jack and Oxana 143

Chapter 31: Frik in Dublin meets Dr. Bowe 147

Chapter 32 Oxana gets her instructions 153

Chapter 33: Frik meets Harriet 158

Chapter 34: Oxana kills in America 167

Chapter 35: Cristiano makes a fuss 173

Chapter 36: Oxana leaves a clue 175

Chapter 37: Luv body found 180

Chapter 38: Oxana wants her cut 184

Chapter 39: Harriet talks to Frik about the patch 186

Chapter 40: Bowe and Dakota in Cuba 190

Chapter 41: Frik learns Oxana went to USA 194

Chapter 42: Two poisoned leaving Guantanamo 199

Chapter 43: The Pakistani men die 204

Chapter 44: Harriet sets up her new team 212

Chapter 45: Frik hears of Luv. Oxana in Moscow 217

Chapter 46: Oxana meets her father again 220

Chapter 47: Oxana earns a break from Harriet 227

Chapter 48: Circassians plan to deal with Russians 231

Chapter 49: Frik learns about twin spikes 236

Chapter 50: CIA share info about Gregor   240

Chapter 51: Harriet team plan to go to Sicily   243

Chapter 52: Circassians to Sicily   248

Chapter 53: Harriet and team fly to Sicily   254

Chapter 54: Oxana and father in Sicily   258

Chapter 55: Frik and Cristiano in Sicily   261

Chapter 56: Harriet and team meet the genetic expert   265

Chapter 57: The Circassians attack   270

Epilogue   274

CHAPTER 1: HARRIET MEETS OXANA IN SEVILLE

Oxana footsteps made barely a sound as she strolled into the coffee shop, clutching a largish, branded handbag to her chest. She walked with her head high and shoulders back. Harriet's eyes narrowed as she watched her closely. Oxana took two steps to clear the hissing automatic doors as they shushed closed behind her. Everything about her clothes, her posture, and her bouncy way of walking made Harriet think she looked much younger than expected. The three-page Curriculum Vitae, in the brown manila folder on the coffee shop wood-replica table, said she was forty-five years old. This person looked like her pictures, but younger—nearer to twenty-five.

Harriet stood up so her interviewee could see her across the crowded room. She had selected a softly lit corner of the coffee shop with some soft cushions as far away as possible from the noisy order counter and pickup station. It was a space where she hoped they could have a deep conversation without the overwhelming noise of other people, coffee grinders, and loud sanitised background music.

Harriet half raised her hand to catch the eye of her guest. Harriet was not the type of person to jump up from her seat. She did not wave frantically, calling out a name. She moved calmly and waved gently. The movement was barely noticeable to the other guests in the cafe. Harriet's mother had instilled in her an old-fashioned sense of being and acting like a gentile lady.

Oxana acknowledged the raised hand with a quiet head tip, a small smile, and a change of direction to reach the semi-private booth with its round table, bench seat along the wall, and fake timber chairs in a stainless-steel frame. Harriet quickly sat down again on the bench facing the door.

As well as looking younger than her age, Harriet noticed Oxana seemed to glide over the floor. There was no sound despite the dark but stylish high-heeled shoes. It reminded Harriet of a wild panther she had seen on a jungle safari—it too moved fast and without noise. Oxana did not rush across the white-tiled floor. She covered the few paces between door and table in the split second it took Harriet to sit down. Her strides were long, and she rolled forward like a golf ball towards a hole in a slippery green. As she watched her walk, Harriet wondered if she had had martial arts training. There was not much in her CV about sports activities or success. The CV had not mentioned her competence in martial arts or if she had skills in that area. Harriet scribbled a note on the page in front of her to ask her about her hobbies.

Oxana reached the chair and stood as still as a snowman. Her nostrils moved wider and then narrowed as she breathed in and out. Harriet looked up and received a half smile. Harriet was deliberate and slow in her movements as she stood up and extended her hand in greeting. She said, "I assume you are Oxana? Pleased to meet you. Please take a seat." Harriet sat again.

The grip Oxana offered was firm and her elegantly manicured hands had long fingers and were quite soft to touch. Then she carefully and silently lifted the chair back until it cleared the table. She sat down delicately, silently pulling the chair closer to the table. As she sat, she manoeuvred her bag, so it lay flat and tidy on her lap. She carried the entire process out in silence, and her movements were like a well-oiled machine. Harriet opened the thin manilla file on the table in front of her and she looked at a page with her handwriting in blue ink scribbled across the lines. Harriet began the interview by saying, "You are professionally qualified for this job. It is as if you planned and designed your career to highlight in your CV all the requirements of our research. It all looks perfect. I have a logistical question—do you have a visa to work in Ireland?"

Harriet's gaze remained fixed and engaged on Oxana's eyes. Once again, she felt surprise at the youthful face sitting in front of her. Her hazel eyes were bright and clear, with no wrinkles. The pale skin on her neck was tight and firm over her bones. Normally, stretch marks might appear as part of normal ageing, but not here. Since Botox became cheap and plentiful, a wrinkle-free forehead was not uncommon, but fine lines around the eyes and mouth were still common enough in women over forty.

Looking more carefully, Harriet was aware Oxana wore no makeup. She had the slightest colour on her lips. Colour from a lip balm rather than lipstick. Her olive skin looked like the sun enjoyed shining on it for many years.

"Well? Cat got your tongue?"

"Are you offering me the position?" Oxana spoke for the first time. Her voice held a tiny trace of an accent. Her cool and quiet tone again reminded Harriet of a panther not wishing to scare away its prey.

It was a deeper voice than she expected and again another surprise for Harriet. She had expected to hear a strong Russian accent. From her CV, Harriet knew Oxana was born and educated in Russia. Harriet could see this project would be her first major research undertaking outside of Russia.

Harriet listened again as Oxana spoke and could pick up a slight emphasis on parts of some words. She could hear the emphasis on the middle syllable 'off' in the word 'offering'. A native English speaker with a well-tuned ear may pick this up. But otherwise, her English diction was flawless.

"Yes, I am prepared to offer you the position. You will need a European work visa." Harriet said. "The work can start as soon as you can travel and move to Dublin."

"I don't have a visa. I can only apply for it when I have a

formal written offer of a project manager position from you." Oxana twisted her hair in her fingers as she said this. A flicker of doubt crossed her eyes. She said, "The grant of a visa should be a formality, but I must bring your official offer letter to the Irish Embassy in Moscow. The Irish authorities will expedite the application, as I understand the Irish government is keen to get holders of doctorates in advanced genetics to undertake research at Irish universities. There should be no problem. I expect a visa will issue three weeks after I apply. I will apply within days of receiving your formal offer. The offer is the first and important part of the entire process."

The waiter approached the table and pulled out a notepad and pencil. He didn't speak, but looked with raised eyebrows at the ladies and waited for them. As he approached, Oxana looked him up and down, taking in the black apron over his jeans and shirt. It was sagging around his midriff. The apron tie strings at the back were hanging loose and about to open. The front of the bib had streaks of white powder and grease marks plastered across his chest line. She concluded he had worn the same bib for several days and used it as a towel to wipe his hands.

The collar of his shirt was un-ironed and had several days of grime visible at the side of his neck. The shirt was once white but had aged to a stained yellow. His unshaven face had a five o'clock shadow plus a couple more days' growth. At best, he could be called scruffy chic. The disdainful look on Oxana's face said ugly-scruffy.

Finally, he moved and produced two one-page laminated menus for them. As he handed out the menus, Harriet noticed his fingernails had lines of black dirt and he had not trimmed them for several days. He said, "Can I get you something? Coffee, tea? We also have some fresh homemade pastries."

Harriet greeted the young waiter with a smile. She said, "An Americano coffee, please, with two shots of coffee. Please bring a jug of hot water on the side." She said to her guest. "Oxana, what would you like? It is my treat. You have come a long distance."

Oxana curled her lip in a snarl. "I don't need your fresh pastries. If you touch them with your filthy hands—they will be full of bacteria. I want a single espresso coffee and make sure you sterilise the cup. And wash your hands before you touch the cup. They are filthy."

The waiter's face paled under his brown suntanned skin in response to the hissed snarl. He scribbled their order on a scrappy notebook with a blunt pencil. Repeating the order back to them, he nodded, mumbled something Spanish under his breath, and scurried off. As he crossed the floor, he ran his fingers through his slicked-back, black, oily hair. They saw him looking at his fingers and shaking his head. He did at least go towards the sign showing bathrooms.

Harriet sat back and looked at Oxana more intently. This display of sudden temper and rudeness perplexed her. What was that about? Why had she abused him in the ad hominem attack and taken the young waiter's head off? He was only doing his job. The waiter should serve with clean hands and fingers, of course, that was to be expected. Harriet thought there were nicer ways to change his behaviour.

Oxana made a half smile and read the thoughts running through her future boss's mind, "You are wondering at my speech? I guess after a short lifetime of working in labs with microbes and genetics has made me super sensitive to dirt. There seems to be a connection between more coffee shops and lower hygiene standards."

Harriet listened with care and attention to this longish answer from Oxana. One of her worries was the quality of communication in English. She picked up slight modulations in her accent on certain words and parts of words as Oxana spoke. The first or second syllable always had a slight lift in emphasis and tone. But she had a good pace in her speech. She could move along without hesitations. There were no moments when she appeared to be searching for words.

"I agree. Standards are slipping everywhere," Harriet said.

"Last Monday, in a lunch café, I watched a young girl try to use a chef's knife to cut tomatoes. She didn't know how to hold the knife. She didn't hold the knife properly in her hand, and it was dangerous. The risk of cutting her own fingers was high. All her awkward out of control cutting made the slices of tomatoes and vegetables ugly, uneven, and fat. Chefs take great pride in correct knife work. People can learn that skill. There was no one to help her learn. That is such a pity."

Harriet continued, "I worked in bars and restaurants when I was a student. Many of my friends and I worked part time in kitchens. I needed the money to eat and live. We were fortunate then as managers of bars and restaurants wanted us. They trained us, too. Experienced chefs or managers showed us how to hold a knife properly. With cutbacks in staff and managers thinking automation was the answer to everything; they don't provide training anymore. The kitchen teams are so busy they have no time to mentor and train young students or trainees. The old master and apprentice working relationship seems to be gone. That is one reason I want you to join us. The ideal team comprises skilled people and people who can train others. You have impressive skills."

Oxana became quite agitated in her chair and said, "When the greedy capitalist managers in the West concentrate on making money, they don't hire good staff. They employ workers for minimum wage and treat them as slaves. As a customer, I feel we must step in and speak up. Our role is to enjoy a meal or cup of coffee, not to accept poor hygiene. If we accept poor service, we will only get more sloppy behaviour and dress. His uniform is a disgrace. He should use a fresh tunic every day, at least. Someone must make sure owners take care of their staff. The role of the customer is to point out when employers don't maintain quality standards. An acceptable way is to complain and call out poor service."

Harriet made a note of her comments on the page. As she wrote, she noticed she had earlier written the words 'Cork accent' on the page. The note reminded her, she had a concern about communication with the other team members. Many of them were from County Cork in the beautiful southwest corner of Ireland. She had a nervousness if the Cork contingent could communicate with the new recruit. They had a well-known reputation as the fastest English speakers in the world.

Besides the breakneck speed, they had their unique dialect and a sing-song accent. Working in such an environment could be a challenging mix for non-native speakers. Now, having talked to her and watched her correcting this waiter, she realised she would have to warn them about their cleanliness. They might not enjoy the tongue-lashing they would get from Oxana. She had little fear of the language barrier and crossed it off the list on her page.

Harriet leaned forward and said, "Can you think about my offer? Do you still want to join the team in Dublin for this research project? The contract for employment is a long, boring thirty-page document from the human resources section at Trinity College. It will guarantee your salary for thirty-six months from the day you start. The title is project manager. I wish to offer you the role. Will you stay for the full duration? I want to feel you are engaged in our project."

Oxana said, "but we have not spoken of terms or about living accommodations. I hear Ireland is full and flats are expensive and difficult to find. I enjoy living as close as possible to my work. If I have long commutes to reach work, then my energy levels drain and I will not perform my best work."

"This is a strange interview. I thought you would like to ask about my work to date, my successes and my failures. I thought we would chat about what I can bring to the project and my skills and abilities. But here you are already offering me the job. Are there no other candidates?"

The waiter arrived like a champion at a ceremony carrying a clean hand towel draped over his forearm, and with their drinks held high in the air on a shiny silver tray. The cups were white and rimmed with a blue colour around the top. This matched a circle on the saucers, which he placed in front of them with a flourish. Little shiny spoons sat on the saucer beside sugar cubes and a plastic wrapped biscuit. Harriet could see Oxana was checking his nails to see if he had washed them. The heavy, dark black grime was gone, but they were far from sparkling white and clean. He was still conscious of them and tried to keep them out of sight by serving the cups and plates with his fingers concealed underneath.

The waiter placed the cup and jug in front of Harriet with a flourish. He then lifted a napkin holder and two cakes on a white plate off the tray. A large green-blue fly buzzed its way out of the cakes. He swotted at it and placed them on the table between the two ladies. As he lifted the espresso cup off the tray, Oxana said. "No, thank you, don't bother. Take it back and don't dare charge me for it. There is no way I will put anything you touched near my mouth."

The anger and venom in Oxana's voice hit the waiter like a surfing wave. He reacted to this second assault and jumped back from the table. He moved his lips as if he was going to make a stinging retort. His mouth opened and closed as his Adam's apple bobbed up and down in his neck and his eyes flamed. He spun on his heel and sprinted back behind the counter. In a moment, they could hear a loud, non-flattering conversation about cows. The waiter seemed to have quite a deep knowledge of this subject. His colleague was in firm agreement and the tirade lasted some minutes.

"You were tough on him," Harriet said as she sat back in her chair and contemplated her younger colleague. The contents of her CV and the success she had in her career to date confirmed Oxana had super intelligence and a good intellect. Her doctoral studies had received top marks; but was she a tiresome woman? Would she be an impossible and intolerant person? Would she make friends or enemies back in Dublin? Would she behave like this with her team members?

"Do you think so? I am sorry." Her voice changed, and her face softened. "I think he will be a better waiter after my words. No? Do you agree? If my words encouraged him to wash his hands more often—wouldn't that be better for customers? No? Am I wrong? Maybe if he is clean, then customers won't catch the plague or a stomach bug from him."

"The plague, that's strong. It is not a likely outcome. What is more likely is he overreacts to your criticism and poisons the coffee of his foreign lady guests! We could convert him into a misogynist." Harriet said this with a hearty laugh as her nervousness took over. She felt uncomfortable with the conversation and wanted to reduce the tension. This hostility from Oxana stressed her, and she wanted to introduce a lighter note to their chat.

"But to answer your questions, I am not asking about your dreams and hopes. They are clear. Your work to date makes you a perfect fit for our team. You may know we are researching a technique to help telomeres remain strong as people age. The deterioration of these is the principal cause of physical ageing. We hope to develop a simple product to keep these telomeres healthy."

Oxana listened to these comments. She noticed Harriet had modulated her voice to speak more quickly and in a bit of a sing-song style. Oxana's eyes narrowed, wondering about this obvious test, leading her to doubt if her potential employer was a truly professional person.

"That is interesting. I know a good deal about telomeres. If you succeed, people can grow old gracefully with less physical illness, aches or pains."

"Yes, we think so, too. We have a nice and super-motivated team assembled. We will have someplace for you to live. The salary is about fifty thousand euros per year. We think you will like it. Many of our team members are from the funniest and friendliest part of Ireland. They speak fast and funny, very fast. I was worried if you would understand them, but now, I think your English is quite good. So far, you seem to understand me, and I am deliberately speaking fast to test you."

"Yes, I noticed you are speaking more rapidly than before. But do not worry, I worked as a translator in real time in another job before I completed my dissertation. English is the common language of research and universities. I can manage most dialects and accents."

Harriet said, "Yes, you seem to be perfect for us. I hope you will accept."

Oxana said, "I will give it good and careful consideration when you send me a written offer and contract. I like to check and double check all the details of your offer. The fine print I think you call it? As a manager, and an experienced researcher, the detailed way of working, dates of payment, tax matters, lines of responsibility, and amount of paid holidays and any other legal contract matters needed in employment in Ireland. When can you send that?"

The university needed Oxana; the project needed her, and most of all, Harriet needed her. Harriet looked at her watch and, startled by the time it told her, she jumped up, pushing the table back so the cups rocked in their saucers. She gathered the folder from the table-top and, extracting a card from her purse, handed it to Oxana, who placed it face up on the coffee table. "I am sorry to cut this short, but we will chat again soon, I promise."

Quickly shaking Oxana's hand, she raced out of the door, scanning the street for a taxi.

CHAPTER 2: OXANA MAKES A DATE WITH ENRICO

Oxana looked with wide eyes and open mouth at Harriet's retreating figure. She shook her head as she watched her run through the hissing doors and out into the street. The truncated work interview was a disaster. Oxana spent time and money to attend, and now she must rearrange it to be completed. Harriet left her business card on the table. Moments before Harriet glanced at her watch, jumped from her seat, with a look of panic spreading over her face and galloped out the door. Oxana heard her say, "I must prepare the keynote speech I am giving to the conference. I completely misjudged the time."

As she gathered her bag and stood, she said, "I know you will be in Seville for two days. Let's meet again. We can have a longer conversation about the project. I can answer all your questions. We want you to feel excited to come work with us and manage our project. We need you, and you have all the qualifications."

Harriet pointed at the table. "You have my business card. It has my private mobile number on it. Please call me after the keynote and we can arrange a new meeting. In the meantime, and to give you a quick answer to one of your questions—the university has accommodation onsite for you. It is very well-priced, and for university accommodation, the rooms are of better quality with nicer furniture and decoration, than in Russia. Your desk, the lab, the library are a few steps away. There is even a lovely café onsite for breakfast." With that, she turned and quick stepped out the hissing sliding doors.

As Harriet left, she paused, and glanced back through the doors of the cafe. She saw Oxana catch the attention of the waiter and gave him a big thumbs up. Her face held a big beaming smile, and she seemed to apologise to him. Harriet watched as he walked over, and they leaned close together in conversation. If Harriet had not seen and heard Oxana rip the waiter apart earlier, they would convince her she was watching a seduction scene. Harriet was standing too far away to hear them. The waiter straightened and nodded his head in agreement. The cafe doors closed behind Harriet and a taxi pulled up. She turned away from the cafe and switched her mental concentration and attention to the keynote which lay unfinished on her laptop.

As Harriet climbed into the taxi, her face was a mixture of puzzlement, sorrow, and panic. She knew the abrupt end of the interview was not professional. It was her fault—she made a mistake about the time. The day had not started well. The work and position were important. Harriet knew they needed another meeting and a more complete conversation.

As Harriet taxied back to her hotel from the café, her mind returned to the exchange between Oxana and their waiter. It was quite abrupt and rude. Maybe it was just the Russian way. Maybe she was tired. Harriet explained to herself that flying from Moscow to Belgrade to Madrid, plus a train to Seville, was tiring and stressful. Such a journey would make a saint snappy and irritated.

There appeared to be some aggression and rudeness in Oxana, yet her last behaviour suggested she was trying to be friendly and apologetic towards the unhygienic waiter. Harriet mentally moved on and cleared her thoughts. She switched to the presentation she must give in a few hours. Over one hundred top university lecturers and researchers in biogenetics would be there. She had to make a great impression.

Harriet hoped she would meet Oxana again in the next two days. During the conference, there were coffee breaks and conversations as people gather in the breakout rooms.

The opportunity to network was the reason many delegates attended. The opportunity to meet colleagues and competitors was a treasure to be savoured. It led to valuable collaborations and networks.

Harriet promised herself to look for Oxana in the conference breakout rooms. She was travelling alone and was representing her former University in Moscow. It was a common enough arrangement. Universities paid for flights and accommodation to be represented and receive a detailed first-hand report from a trusted source. Harriet was presenting a keynote speech to the assembled scientists from Europe. She also would meet members of the wider EU-funded project to compare notes and to set out an overall road map for the delivery of the research work.

Her immediate challenge was to design, arrange, write the text, and practice the slides for the keynote presentation. It was one reason also for the brevity of the scheduled interview with Oxana. Harriet's days were always full, with little spare time when events run over the allocation.

Back in the restaurant, Oxana looked at the waiter again, and her face brightened. Picking up the card left behind by Harriet, she took a pencil from the waiter's pocket and pencilled her number on it. "Call me", she said. She smiled at the waiter. She said, "What is your name?"

"Enrico, I am Enrico."

"You have a nice strong manly name. Enrico. I am sorry for how I spoke to you earlier. You deserve an explanation. The woman with me was interviewing me for a job at her university. She runs an important business in the university and I would work in her research labs. She demands everyone scrub their hair and skin clean. They have to work every day in spotless clothes. I had to pick on you to show her how tough I am."

"I am Russian, so we must portray a tough image. But we are quite soft and cuddly, especially with gorgeous Spanish men. Can I make it up to you, Enrico? Can we go out for a friendly drink and a local tapa later? After siesta? Please? Call me and pick me up at my hotel. I am all alone this afternoon."

Enrico took her offered card and looked at Oxana with a predatory glint. He stood back a half step and looked her up and down. Noticing her curves and her new friendly smile, he flashed his full set of teeth. "Tapas, drinks, with such a beautiful woman, of course. We can make a nice hook-up and forget all these harsh words. I will call you when I finish work, about five this evening?"

Oxana and Enrico carried on their conversation for several minutes. They were laughing at each other's words and smiling. Then he presented the bill. Oxana looked up, shaking her head. She made a rude gesture in the general direction of the door. The waiter laughed. She produced her credit card and hoped it would work. There were no euros in her purse and there were little guarantees about using Russian credit cards in Europe. Plus, she knew her account contained less than ten euros. She spent a good deal of her savings on two flights and to buy the clothes she was wearing.

"Great, Enrico", she placed her hand on his arm and brushed his cheek with the back of her hand, "I look forward to seeing you. Hasta luego, ciao."

Enrico watched her as she glided out of the café shop and through the hissing doors. She stopped as the doors opened, looked back, shook her hair, and beamed a big smile at him.

He tucked the business card into the inside pocket of his jeans and told his friends about his latest conquest. The cashier shouted stop and ran from behind the counter, shaking the credit card terminal. The green screen read in large red letters with a big X; declined. But Oxana was gone.

CHAPTER 3: HARRIET PREPARES HER INITIAL PILOT FINDINGS

Harriet looked at the expectant faces of the team as they assembled on the Zoom call. Six or seven eager faces looked at her from the lab at Trinity College in Dublin. The communications room buzzed as they gathered for this conversation. It delighted her there was a good broadband connection in her hotel room. Her assistant, Jack, set it up so she could present a mock-up of the slides for the conference and the team could help her improve them.

Jack was a treasure. His administration skills were of the highest order. Jack loved helping to get presentations set up. He believed in repetition. A presentation started with a summary, then the details, and finally a wrap up summary section. Repetition was his watchword, repeat, repeat, and keep repeating it until it was simple.

But it never was simple. The field of genetic research was fast-moving and complicated. Electron microscopes and techniques like chemical distillation did most of the work today. The scientists assembled the data and analysed the results. Researchers repeated the trial studies several times. They examined results from each trial and compared them. The researchers made a deduction or conclusion describing the outcome of the trial. This repetition and statement of outcomes was a key pillar of science—would another scientist get exact or similar results by repeating the procedure? How to capture all in a few slides?

Jack insisted there were lots of pictures in the presentation. He wanted people to talk about pictures. The audience were not attending the presentation just to read the text. They could do that anywhere. He wanted them to listen and understand. Jack had some rules, three lines of text per slide, very few words on every line. The presenters knew their job was to show and tell the pictures.

Harriet started on the first slide she had prepared. The team was leaning forward, checking every word and picture. They were looking for every opportunity to improve her keynote. All of them depended on the European Horizon grant of funding. Each one had a personal stake in her presentation and wanted to ensure it was a considerable success.

The European Union awarded them the research project the previous year based on a pilot. That was over and they were pitching for full award funding so they could complete their research and move on to publication and commercialisation.

The seven researchers knew her presentation and performance would affect their life outcome and path for three years. Harriet was working on the fourth slide when her phone buzzed beside her. She glanced at the smartphone screen and she could see it was a text message and it was a Russian number.

As Jack and the team were discussing font size and colour on the slides, she picked it up and read, 'what room are u, u left ur scarf in d café. I will bring it 2 ur room.' A smiley face completed the message. Harriet typed 204 using her thumbs, jumped up and propped the door so it stayed open, and returned to the desk and the meeting.

Harriet was just about finished practising her presentation rehearsal. They changed all the fonts and the background colours, and she was feeling very pleased with the team effort. She heard the bedroom door open, and on her computer screen, she could see Oxana's reflection as she glided with a scarf in her hand. The camera on the front of the laptop perfectly caught Oxana, as she put the scarf on the upholstered back of Harriet's bedroom chair. She turned and slid into the hotel hallway. The door clicked closed with a metallic sound. She was visible on the Zoom call for a split second.

"Who was that?" Jack said.

"That was Oxana, the Russian project manager I am interviewing to join us if the EU offers us extended time for our research."

"She looks very young."

"Yes, very observant, Jack. She does, but she is forty-five and has vast experience in genetics and research. We will be lucky if she joins us."

"Let's get our funding extension application in first though, eh?" Jack, as usual, was all business and focused on the outcome. "If you think she is an addition to the team, then great, get her onboard before someone else hires her. Good project managers are hard to find. The team could use a good project manager on this project. I have so many outstanding tasks queued in my project backlog I could float across the North Atlantic. Plus, I need help to finish a bunch of team tasks that are outstanding. I have dozens of files to rearrange as well. The administration people keep on changing the rules about filing."

The call finished shortly afterwards, and the entire team wished Harriet well. They assured her they would join the conference online and be able to jump in with any details if she became stuck. They also reminded her to reach out to them if there was a question from the audience that needed their support. Harriet nodded and thanked them all. She liked the atmosphere that surrounded this team.

The last six months working on the pilot project helped them bond as a team. Most were students studying and working towards a PhD in genetics. The research for the anti-ageing product would allow them to write a full thesis and receive the award for Doctor of Science. The field of biogenetics was new and everyone in it held very high university qualifications.

Business in this area was growing rapidly and all the main pharmaceutical companies funded huge research teams dedicated to using genetics to find new ways to cure old diseases or to solve problems in the biological space.

This team was working on reversing one aspect of ageing. There are telomeres buried deep in the DNA of cells. These reproduce with errors as they age. This causes the skin and organs of the body to shrink and shrivel up. The ageing process also weakened the normal human immune system. Anyone over the age of sixty had great difficulty building new muscle, and the strength in their bones declined. The point of their research was to reverse one of the well-known causes of telomere decline.

As well as Trinity College Dublin, several other university teams were working on other aspects of the project. The European Union allocated a huge fund to ageing, as the population statistics showed the population of Europe would age rapidly in the next decade. One outcome of this was citizens became more and more unhealthy. The EU delighted in citizens growing old, provided they remained healthy. Unhealthy and old citizens added an enormous cost to the health care and pensions in the EU. Trinity and other universities undertook research with EU funding to find products to help people age healthier. If they found these, and developed them to a commercial stage, then the European Union could avoid falling off a financial and health cliff.

The team had, she hoped, provided the EU with sufficient information and data during the initial pilot to earn the right to have their funding extended for three more years. It pleased her the EU was managing the funding directly as it prevented overlap between competing organisations. She remembered famous cases where two universities worked on the same project for years and published their findings within weeks of each other. This was a complete waste of brainpower and resources. The EU oversight deployed in this project ensured that error did not happen.

The conference delivered one secondary message—to share

what they were working on to minimise duplication of efforts. It worked for this purpose, but some used the opportunity to learn what the others were doing and try to sneak one step ahead. The first product approved and ready to launch reaped the rewards from the pharmaceutical companies.

Harriet enjoyed spending time in a long, hot shower. The hotel stocked, as usual, the cheapest of cheap toiletries, but she bought her own in the pharmacy down the street from the café where she met Oxana. As she showered, she thought about her again. Harriet put on her clothes with care and ensured all the buttons and zips were closed, and the clothes hung nicely on her.

She decided she was going to be an excellent addition to the team. She showed a level of honesty and commitment by returning her scarf. The scarf was a gift from her mother, and she loved its texture. Harriet was quite absent-minded and left her valuables behind frequently—once she left her rucksack on a train.

Picking up the room key, she gave herself one last check in the mirror, turned off the lights, air-con and, heaving a rucksack onto her shoulder, she headed down the hall to the elevators. Despite her earlier rush, there were three hours to spare before the conference started. As the weather forecast was good in Seville, she considered walking to the conference hall. She planned to ramble around the beautiful old city and enjoy the sights and sounds. If she passed a small Tapas bar, she could sit and listen to Spanish families chat and eat before making her way to the auditorium where the conference was being held.

Jack was sending the updated slides to the organisers, and she could listen to the early warm-up sessions before her keynote began. The six pm conference start was not unusual. Investors in California were just waking up to begin their day, and they were a vital part of funding for experimental products emerging from research carried out by attendees. She didn't expect to be back in her hotel room until after midnight.

CHAPTER 4: ENRICO MEETS HIS MAKER

Oxana clicked send and waited for Enrico to respond. She was still angry with Harriet for leaving the cafe without paying the bill. The credit card company automated refusal of her card was not a surprise but an annoyance. Enrico told her he paid the bill for her and hoped she would give him back his money when they met.

She sent him room number 204 and an invitation to join her for champagne with the promise of a nice dinner afterwards. Her phone pinged his reply, and she left her room to go down the fire escape stairs to Harriet's room two floors below. An earlier scouting mission showed cameras in the lift, but not in the hallways. Sometimes the interpretation of GDPR rules in Europe left security gaps. She didn't mind. Oxana watched Harriet leave the lobby of the hotel less than thirty minutes before. With her computer bag over her shoulder and wearing her presentation clothes, Oxana felt sure she was gone and would not return until later in the night.

Using the electronic key card, she took from the table beside the door when she returned Harriet's scarf; she checked the hallway was empty. She slid the key into the door and entered Harriet's room. She placed the key in the room switch and checked her surroundings as the lights and TV blinked on.

Harriet was messy, she thought as she saw her clothes piled on the bed and on the floor. Opening the minibar, she extracted the two small bottles of champagne. The cupboard under the TV revealed a couple of wine glasses, which she put beside the bottles on the desk.

Beside the glasses was a small hotel room safe. It was open, but Harriet's keys and passport were lying inside it. How careless, thought Oxana, as she picked up the passport. She opened it and found two fifty-euro notes tucked in the plastic protective sleeve. She put these in her pocket. They could go to Enrico to pay him back for the coffee.

She assumed the notes were some sort of emergency money. Well, she could make it so. She took out her phone and took a picture of the passport details page, getting the passport number and expiry date clearly in focus. Her friends in Moscow would give her money for these.

She looked around and opened the green wheelie suitcase. It held the usual change of clothing and some slippers. The clothes were cheap and not branded or expensive. Oxana touched them reluctantly, with some scorn. These are rough, and not nicely washed, she thought to herself. She checked the bathroom, peering at the brands of shower gel, shampoo, and lotions. She took care not to touch them.

Spotting the robe hanging on the back of the bathroom door, she quickly undressed to her underwear. She had selected a nice matching black lace bra and panties earlier as her plan developed in her mind. They fitted her perfectly, and she turned front and back in the mirror to see her curves were exactly as she wished them to be. She expected Enrico to knock on the door and she wanted his eyes to pop out of his head. Giving a last pirouette in the mirror, she checked her makeup and hair.

She folded her clothes into her holdall and opened the room door a crack. Turning the deadlock to stop the door clicking shut, she stretched out on the bed, seductively arranging the dressing gown to cover her body. She rolled her back to the door. She didn't have long to wait. Hearing the door open and feeling the draught, she rolled over facing the door. As she moved, she let her robe part to show her white skin and black underwear.

Enrico stepped into the room, his mouth fell open, as he saw her lack of clothing and how she draped herself over the bed. He quickly composed himself, and turning the latch on the door, pushed it closed. Holding out the business card, he read, "Dr Harriet Fischer, Professor of Genetic Development, Trinity College, Dublin, I assume?"

"Enrico", Oxana purred, "open the champagne like a good man and pour us a glass. We need to make a toast." Enrico threw the business card over his shoulder and jumped into action. He popped open the bottles and filled the two glasses with champagne in a flash. If he worked this fast in the cafe, he would earn a fortune in tips. Oxana took out the two fifty-euro notes from the pocket of her gown and placed them on the bed in front of her.

"Here, thank you for paying for the coffee earlier. It was embarrassing for me when my card did not work. Sometimes we Russians have difficulties in the West with simple things."

"It is ok," Enrico said as he sat beside Oxana on the bed. "It was only eleven euros, this is one hundred, it is too much."

"I know, but you can spend it on our dinner. But first, cheers."

They clinked glasses. Enrico took a deep swig, while Oxana took a tiny sip. Enrico put his hands on Oxana's leg, just where it met the gown. She wiggled her body on the bed and looked deeply into his eyes. "Mmm, Enrico, I was thinking about you all day."

She realised he hadn't changed since this morning, and he was still wearing the stained shirt with several pens and a tatty pencil in the pocket. She noticed his runners were old and decrepit and he smelled of the oil they used in the café. There was an odour of stale coffee, bread, and fried food.

"I know, you are thinking about me", he replied as he slid his hands up along her leg.

She wrinkled her nose, reached down, and caught his hand to stop its advance. "Wait," she said as she put her glass on the bedside locker. She leaned over him, brushing his body with hers as she took his glass from him. "Go to the bathroom and get undressed. I want you completely naked. There is also a hotel toothbrush there. Use it! I'll be waiting. Be quick."

Enrico moved from the bed and went towards the ensuite

door. "Your every wish is my command," he said. As he reached the ensuite door, he glanced back at Oxana stretched out on the bed. The gown fell open and showed far more than it concealed. "Hurry, you shouldn't keep a Russian lady waiting!" she said. He licked his lips and closed the door.

Oxana moved from the bed in a single swift motion. She took out a tiny vial of liquid hidden inside a stitched pocket in her bra. It was the size of an eye-dropper with a clear liquid inside. Opening the lid with some care, she poured all the contents into his champagne. It fizzed as she watched it dissolve into the champagne. The contents looked normal in a few seconds as the fizz faded. Sliding the vial back into its pouch beside her breast, she was standing beside the bed holding two glasses when Enrico came out of the bathroom. She scanned him up and down and saw with some surprise he had ignored her strict command and was not undressed fully. "Here," she said, handing him his glass. "Bottoms up!" As he gulped down the contents, she moved closer to him and took off his boxers. Taking her glass, he leaned forward to place it beside his on the bedside table. He sat on the bed as she slid his pants over his ankles. He grabbed her by the hair to pull her onto him when he stopped with a look of surprise in his eyes.

She watched as his eyes glazed over. Catching him before he fell forward, she pushed him back on the bed and lifted his legs off the floor, so he was fully on the bed. "Now, my little Enrico, perhaps you will learn to clean yourself up before you come to service a lady." Oxana's eyes stared intently as she stood watching the body. She took out her phone and started a timer.

Pulling two tissues from the box beside the bed, she wiped down the stem of her glass and poured the remains into his glass. She put her now clean glass back on the cupboard. Taking another vial from her gown pocket, she emptied it into Enrico's glass. The skull and crossbones and the word poison were visible on the label. The champagne fizzed again. Satisfied, she put the vial back into the pocket of the gown, having wiped it clean with some careful examination in the room's light.

Picking up Enrico's boxers and the business card off the floor, she headed into the bathroom, wiping the door handle as she entered. Inside, she looked at the card and her brow furrowed in thought. Deciding her next steps, she took his pencil from his shirt pocket. His clothes were strewn on the floor like a teenager's bedroom. Using the top of his pencil, she erased her phone number from the card. She rewrote 208 over it and smudged it with her finger. Carefully wiping the pencil and card, she placed both back into his shirt pocket and dropped his shirt back on the ground on top of the rest of his clothes.

A few minutes later, she came out fully dressed and carrying her nearly empty bag and the dressing gown. She threw the gown beside Enrico as he lay on the bed. Taking his phone from the bedside locker, she opened it and erased all messages between them, including her contact details.

Her timer now said six minutes. She knew she must wait four more minutes before the next step with Enrico. As she waited, she wiped the inside of the door handle, and taking the room key from its switch, she wiped it thoroughly before placing it back into its slot.

Looking around the room, her brain replayed everything. Her task was to leave the room as clean as possible. She was there earlier returning the scarf, so the police might discover fingerprints or hairs. But she had the scarf return mission as an excuse for any evidence they found.

Mentally, she checked off everything she touched in the last half-hour, and finally, she was content. She checked Enrico. She was sure the chemical was working. His ears and nose were shrinking. His fingertips too were less clear and on his upturned hand, the whorls and patterns of his fingerprints disappeared. She checked her timer. Nearly nine minutes. This was good. The latest batch of M278 was working fast—exactly as Gregor told her it would.

She checked there was nothing left in her glass. She picked it up and scrutinized it using a tissue to hold the stem of the plastic glass. She waited for the timer on her phone to reach ten minutes. She then made close-up pictures of his face, feet, and fingers. These pictures would automatically upload to the cloud where a team in Moscow would access them and study them. Picking up the robe, she covered his body and blew him a kiss goodbye.

She gave a last glance at Enrico, who continued his slow-motion decay to dust. His toes were shrinking. His ears and nose were more or less gone, and a fine powder remained. She slowly opened the hotel bedroom door. Satisfied the corridor was empty, she hurried out to the emergency stairs and climbed the two flights to her room. Opening her room, she went in and changed into clothes suitable for a business conference. At the lobby door, she spotted a taxi and regretting leaving the two fifty-euro notes with Enrico; she went around the corner to avoid the cameras while she hailed a taxi. Getting into the back seat, she asked the driver to bring her to the conference centre called Centro de Innovacion Y Technologie on the other side of the river in the Enterprise and education park. She needed to get there quickly to set up her alibi. She needed to get there before Harriet started her keynote.

CHAPTER 5: HARRIET PRESENTS THE PILOT RESEARCH FINDINGS

Harriet walked with an amazing feeling of well-being; her steps were light, and she swung her bag like a schoolchild going home to its mother with a great big A score on her report card.

Her presentation in the 'Centro de Innovacion Y Technologie' was exceptionally well received. The audience raised excellent questions, allowing her to elaborate on the work her team completed. The effort put into the presentation paid off handsomely. She spoke at length in response to the questions, and this showed the team's pilot in the best possible light.

Most delegate's remarks were comments from other professors about the excellence of her presentation. One of the more eminent professors said her research would become the baseline and foundation on which they could build their work. Many others agreed with this and applauded as he finished speaking.

She was delighted, and her tummy fluttered with excitement at the compliments coming towards her. She felt her phone vibrating repeatedly, and it held over ten messages from the team back in Dublin, complimenting her for her stunning presentation and for her responses to the attendees. They were all supremely confident with the presentation and felt the conference guaranteed the extension of funding. She felt good about it also, especially as the European director of the programme smiled and gave her a huge thumbs up as she left the podium.

As she worked her way to the back of the hall towards the exits, she spotted Oxana. She waved, and Oxana demurely waved back. Joining her, Oxana started eulogizing. "How amazing. Your work is so important, I hadn't realised. I hope I have not damaged my chances of working with you?"

Harriet was pleased and felt a small blush creep into her neck. This was a successful night. "Of course not Oxana, I said you were a perfect fit, and I meant it. Thank you for coming to the conference. Where are you staying?"

Oxana took out her plastic credit card sized room key and read 'Hotel Exe Macarena.' I think the hotel name is the name of a dance. It is about two and a half kilometres away or forty minutes by foot. It is the same as your hotel. Harriet seemed surprised to see the name of Oxana's hotel and took out her room key from her small black purse. "Snap!" she said.

"It is not a coincidence," Oxana said. "I booked in there after I dropped off your scarf earlier. I thought it was a pleasant hotel and I hope we can continue our interview tomorrow."

Harriet said, "Good-thinking Oxana. Yes, we can, but right now, I am starving and would murder a glass of white wine or a bottle! What do you say we walk and find a restaurant open along the way?"

"Lovely, that would be lovely, but it is very late, it is after midnight!"

"I know, but we are in Spain, so let us hope some chefs are still cooking. Spanish people are late owls. For them, it is not yet too late to eat. If the restaurants are all closed, we can raid the minibar. Or maybe they have room service in the hotel."

"Ok, let's start by walking. If it is too late, we can get a taxi. We could take one of those city scooters. I have the app for them."

"Uh, do you? Scooters are not for me. I get wobbles in high heels, never mind on a scooter."

The two women chatted about their life in research. They spoke happily of their future as they walked along the quiet, modern streets. They passed dozens of closed cafes and restaurants. Some patrons sat smoking outside them with staff putting away chairs and tables, but all the kitchens were closed. It was very late when they arrived at the hotel. Their last hope for a decent meal was the hotel.

The restaurant's double brown glass doors were at the back of the hotel lobby. They were firmly closed, and the lights were off. The A-board announcing the next day's lunch menu stood like a sentry in front of the restaurant door. Harriet made a face at the door. She crossed to reception and asked the night porter if there was any food available. A tired old man, who looked and acted in his demeanour like a retired police officer, told her, in broken English, the minibar in her hotel bedroom held drinks and the vending machine near the lifts offered snacks.

Oxana seemed restless. "Harriet, I think I will go to bed, and we can meet for breakfast. It is late and I am in a different time zone in my head."

Harriet was disappointed, but she was glad they had chatted as they walked home together. They exchanged ideas and stories on the walk, and Harriet grew in confidence Oxana would be a terrific addition to the research team. "Ok, Oxana, I will be up about eight am. I'll meet you for breakfast at eight-thirty?"

"Perfect, see you then, and again, congratulations and well done on your presentation. I hope you get some food. See you in the morning." Oxana entered the lift and pressed the fourth-floor button, having activated the security switch with her room key. She looked directly at the camera in the lift as it arrived at her floor.

Harriet waved goodbye and went to look for the vending machines. She wished a restaurant was open along the walk home. Now she lowered her expectations and hoped the minibar held champagne. She decided a celebration of peanuts, chocolate, and champagne would be enough for today. They could have a bigger, louder, and proper celebration back in Dublin tomorrow. For once, the vending machine worked as she collected a bag of cashews and a chocolate bar.

Her thoughts were still bouncing from idea to idea as she raced through the research work to be undertaken, and the research team she would be leading. If she could reduce the damage suffered by telomeres as they endlessly reprinted themselves, the work they did could create a new advanced starting point for others. It would be like starting a one-hundred-meter sprint from ninety meters. One professor even proposed it could add ten years to the average life span of humanity, and the potential to add twenty years to the human health span. She felt a happy tiredness creeping over her shoulders and gave into it and started for the lifts.

She pushed the button for the second floor in the lift and turned left when it arrived at her floor. Sliding her key into the card reader for room 204, the light blinked green. She pushed against the closer of the door, balancing her snacks and laptop bag on her hip with one hand. The hotel door opened under gentle pressure from her shoulder, and she paused as she could see lights on in the bedroom. She was certain she turned them off earlier, but maybe housekeeping cleaned and turned them on.

She entered and her eyes scanned her bed. When they absorbed the image, her legs collapsed under her. She heard screaming, loud screaming and realised it was her voice she heard. Scrabbling backwards on her behind, she dragged herself into the corridor. The room door clicked closed as she continued to scream.

Bedroom doors opened and hotel guests who were asleep moments earlier jerked open their doors and marched into the hallway. They approached Harriet with angry looking faces. She cried as she crawled on the floor, saying over and over in a high pitched, strange robotic voice, "there is a dead body on my bed."

CHAPTER 6: FRIK AND HENRI HEAR OF A DEATH IN SEVILLE

Frik heard the phone ringing as he woke from a deep sleep. He tried to focus on his bedside clock, and he thought it read 04:25. He rubbed his eyes as he sat up in bed and reached for the light and his phone. Through the open curtains he saw it was dark outside, and the windows were frosted in the corners. He sighed; it was typical weather for Munich in October. Some days were gorgeous, and some had weather cold enough to freeze alcohol. Looking at the phone number displayed on his screen, he could see it was the Head Office desk in Europol—The European wide Police agency.

Sliding the green button on the screen of his phone, nothing happened. He jabbed at the screen with his finger, but nothing happened. It kept ringing. He pushed and slid his finger repeatedly. Eventually, the phone stopped ringing. He looked at it in disgust. He hated touchscreens. Why didn't they manufacture it with one great big button to push? He thought about calling the number back, but an automated switchboard and an endless voice offering extension numbers to press in 3 languages lay in wait for him. No thanks, he thought—if they want me, they will try to ring again.

As ordained by some electronic gods, the phone again buzzed violently and nearly jumped out of his hand. This time it was the listed number of his immediate superior, Henri, in Europol. Henri was a good guy. He was French, and typically so. They had a relationship based on trust and respect. Frik knew Henri was like most French workers and enjoyed his time off. For him to call outside normal hours meant there was something extremely urgent.

"Hello," Frik said.

"Frik, are you awake? Are you still in Seville?"

"No, no, Henri. I am back home in Munich. I flew here yesterday."

"Such a pity. I might have to send you back."

"I'd like to go back. The weather here is terrible. A few days of sunshine on full expenses. I'm your man. What's up?"

"It's hard to understand the details now. We have received reports a young, healthy Spanish waiter is dead. The locals think it is murder. They found him decomposing quickly in a hotel room a few hours ago. An Irish professor booked the hotel room and found him when she returned from a conference."

"So, what's the problem? It's probably just a lover's tiff—Irish woman disappointed by Spanish man. It's not a best seller, Henri. It is hardly a matter for the great and mighty Europol."

"Yes, yes, so true. There are other strange circumstances here. The body has decomposed far too quickly. Something caused it to decay. There may be a biological agent involved. It may be a new and unknown agent. The decay may lead to a new criminal threat."

Frik knew police forces around the world expected a dangerous biological attack by organised criminals to happen within a year or two. There were rumours and tips from shady but reliable people. The criminals drug gangs operated high quality facilities with expert chemists working for them. They could brew up nearly any chemical concoction. Guns and weapons were the tools of yesterday. Secret chemicals, unknown toxins, quick-acting, untraceable poisons, were the future.

It was suspected and openly discussed in the police community that state agents from Russia poisoned a couple of diplomats on the streets of Europe. This caused uproar as the methods of killing used were difficult to identify. This made bringing the culprits to justice impossible. The criminals could spray, inject, or drop chemicals into a drink, making them hard to defend against.

Naturally, European diplomats were not happy about this and used their influence to ensure Europol took a more active interest in this area. Biohazards were easy to reproduce and easy to administer. Every day, police and customs find about seven packages containing Sarin, or some other biologically active substance in post offices and delivery centres around Europe.

So far, the police use of AI and algorithms was successful in finding new substances before they reached their target. Information campaigns ensured people did not open strange and unexpected parcels. The police set up hotline numbers for people to call. But crime, like viruses, evolved. Europol is now active and involved in the death of a waiter in Spain. Is this the start of a criminal campaign or the action of state actors? Who else was involved, and why? Frik was deeply sceptical; it was far too early in the morning to detect conspiracies. His instinct told him this was not a big biological attack.

"Ok, Henri, what do you want me to do? Will I go to Spain?"

"Go back to sleep, Frik. I called you as I hoped you were still in Seville. You could have gone to the scene of the crime. There might be something interesting to see. You could have met the investigation team as well. It's useful to have direct contacts in the investigation team if this develops. But for now, stand by. I know you have a few days of holiday left, so enjoy it. Keep your phone close in case I need to send you to Seville."

"Ok, Henri, I hear you—standby it is. The first part of the standby will be a layby—I am going back to bed. Stay in touch."

CHAPTER 7: HARRIET TAKEN TO JAIL

Harriet looked around her prison cell and felt dirty. A few hours ago, her community of scientists lifted her emotionally to the top of the world. Her keynote speech was a tremendous success with all the famous and highbrow professors in her field of expertise. She was looking forward to celebrating the news. Now she found herself locked in jail at a Spanish police station, and she was in shock.

When she opened the door to her hotel bedroom, she saw a bathrobe partially covering a shape. It could only be a human body. The smell was rank, foul, and overwhelming, and the disintegrating body looked like it had died and decomposed weeks ago.

What happened next was all a blur. She remembered crawling into the hallway outside her room. The police arrived, the hotel manager arrived, and the security staff from the hotel arrived. The security man arrived first and tied her hands behind her back, and tied her to a fire extinguisher bracket in the hallway outside her room. He sent all the other guests back to their rooms. She was sitting there in complete shock when the lady police officer cut her free.

Three police officers brought her downstairs, pushed and shoved her into the padded holding section of a police van. Outside the front of the hotel were five cars with flashing blue lights, and a big yellow and white ambulance parked outside. A crowd gathered behind the red and white plastic crime tape strung by the police between lampposts. She dropped her head when she saw a camera from a media team standing outside a large white van with the words Canal-TV on its side. The van carried a pop-up satellite dish on top. The police officer escorting her noticed her reaction and moved between Harriet and the TV cameraman.

The scene was chaotic and the number of people shouting instructions and questions in rapid-fire Spanish was panic-inducing. Mentally, her mind closed-down, and she developed a splitting headache. She struggled to put one foot in front of the other as the police escort used her arm to bring her towards the police car. When she was in the car, her escort got into the driver's seat and, turning on their siren, headed away from the hotel entrance at speed.

The arrival at the police station was a blur. They took her picture full on and her profile. They then took her fingerprints, inking every finger on both hands. The police officer prepared her for lock up by emptying her pockets and placing the contents into a clear, sealed bag and asked her to sign. She did not understand a word they said to her. They asked her to sign a sheet with a list of items. She refused.

The young police officer came back and told her she was under arrest. "What for?" was Harriet's response. The police officer exhaled deeply and shook her head. She scrambled for the word and it finally came to her. "Murder," she said. Harriet sank in some distress to the floor and her escort half carried her to the lockup cell in the police station basement. When she was sitting slumped forward on the narrow bunk, the police officer showed by putting his hands under his head, she should get some sleep. Reading from a card, she said the Spanish legal system would assign a lawyer and a translator free, and they would all attend a formal police interview at seven a.m.

The heavy steel cell door clanged shut. She was in a room about four metres square with a squat, stinking toilet in one corner, a sink with a single tap, and a narrow bunk along one wall. Covering the bunk was a thin blanket, but she wasn't cold. The smell invaded Harriet's nose. The officers turned off the cell lights, leaving a faint glimmer of street lights from the tall narrow window. Harriet shook.

CHAPTER 8: OXANA MEETS CRISTIANO

Oxana woke the next morning and dressed carefully in a grey business trouser suit. It did nothing to flatter her figure, and she did not apply any lipstick or makeup. A computer bag and a navy-coloured pair of low heels completed her look. She was ready for her second meeting with Harriet.

The hotel served breakfast in the restaurant on the ground floor. She took the elevator and stepped into a buzzing lobby filled with police, cameras, and men in white overalls. Through the revolving doors, she could see a cordon of red police tape in the street. She walked through the doors into the breakfast room. A young waiter took her room number, and she took a seat where she could watch the hustle in the foyer and entrance steps.

After breakfast, she approached the team at reception and asked if they would phone her friend's room. "I was supposed to meet her for breakfast at 8:30," she said. When she said the words 'Harriet Fischer,' the receptionist's eyes widened in alarm, and she jumped out of her seat and rushed into the office behind. A man in a suit, clearly a member of management, returned with her.

"You said to my colleague you have an appointment to meet Harriet Fischer for breakfast at 8:30? Do you know her?"

Oxana's face showed she was reflecting on her answer. "Yes, I met her briefly yesterday for an interview, but we are in regular email contact. She offered me a project manager's job at her University in Dublin last night. We were to talk some more about her offer over breakfast. Why do you ask?"

"She will be a dangerous boss, Professor Harriet, you should not accept any position from such a terrible employer. She has made a terrible mess in our hotel. Please wait here. I will get the police officer in charge. He will speak with you."

"Police?" Oxana spluttered.

"Yes, please wait here. Do not go away."

The manager drew himself up to his full height and gave rapid instructions to the receptionist. Oxana assumed he was telling her to watch her in case she wandered away. The manager was probably a reader of crime novels, and this was his chance to give the police a major clue to help them solve a crime. He approached and spoke to several police officers until they showed him into a room next to the bar. Knocking and entering, he puffed out his chest and put his head back. Oxana tried to stop herself from laughing at his pomposity.

A few minutes later, Oxana regretted not having dressed a bit more feminine. The bar door opened, and the manager emerged, followed by a fit, tall man with a full head of greying black hair and a crisp navy-blue jacket with four stripes on his epaulettes. He marched across the foyer in large shiny black shoes and the crisp seam in his trousers cut the air like a spoiler mounted on the rear of a racing car.

The manager must have a direct genetic link to Judas Iscariot as he stood stock still in the centre of the foyer, dramatically raised his arm and pointed directly at Oxana while mouthing, 'there she is'.

The policeman's face was clean-shaven and if he was working all night, he gave no signs of it. His blue eyes penetrated Oxana, and her neck flushed under his gaze. "I understand you are a friend of Dr Harriet Fischer?" he said in a rich baritone voice. His accent was heavily Spanish, but she suspected he was fluent in English.

"Who are you?" asked Oxana, with a tight lip. She knew she must be helpful, but difficult. But he was a hunk.

"My name is Detective Inspector Cristiano Martinez-Solenero. I am the chief investigator of the crime committed here yesterday. I am a senior officer in the national police force of Spain. My sergeant has arrested your friend on serious charges. We are trying to establish her movements yesterday. We hope you can help us."

Oxana felt a warm glow in her stomach. What a majestic baritone sound, what a masculine presence. He was a strong, handsome officer. She knew he would be part of her dreams for many nights to come.

"And do you propose to interview me here, standing in a public lobby where everyone can watch and wonder? I am not used to boorish behaviour, and I certainly don't wish to be seen talking to the police, no matter how important and high ranking they are, for an extended time. Tongues will wag. I have done nothing wrong, and I do not wish to have guests posting images and videos of me on social media and speculating about why the police are talking to me. I am happy to help the police in their investigation, but not in a public hotel foyer. Is there someplace private we can go? I must tell you also, she is not my friend, as you say. I met her yesterday for the first time."

The Inspector glanced down at the manager who was lingering nearby, preening himself like the best boy in class. "We will use your office. Please clear your desk. Now!"

The manager scurried off and the Detective inspector gesticulated for Oxana to follow him. As she passed in front of Cristiano, she could smell his cologne. Rich and citrus, it was quite a distinct aroma compared to the cooking oil smell of Enrico. She wondered what brand she would buy for him. Maybe 'Le Male'?

CHAPTER 9: HARRIET INTERVIEWED IN JAIL

Harriet must have fallen asleep eventually as she woke with the hard boards under the thin mattress pushing into her shoulder blades. She woke suddenly with a start and peered into the dank air around her. The torrid memories came rushing back. Memories of walking into her hotel room after a remarkably successful speech and there was a dusty mess lying on her bed under a white bathroom robe. A robe she used earlier when taking a shower and prepared herself to go to the convention centre.

She urgently needed to pee, and gingerly stepped over the hole in the ground in the corner of her cell. A raft of flies arose when she disturbed the water in the hole. She finished quickly and wished for a change of clothes. Even some new underwear would help. A faint memory of daylight glimmered through the overhead glass blocks. She was in a police station basement and the shadows of free people walking to work or school or their daily business passed across the walls of her cell.

She remembered they said they would interview her at seven. But about what? She was an innocent victim and had done nothing wrong. Sure, a dead decaying body was on her hotel room bed. The bed was perfectly fine when she left. There wasn't a dead body. She had a perfect alibi for every minute after she left the hotel until she returned after midnight from the science conference. Scores of people saw her during the evening, and maybe hundreds more watched her presentation online. It was an impossible nightmare.

The key scraped in the lock, and the cell door opened. Two police officers appeared. The first carried a fold-up trestle table, the other lifted a steel tray containing coffee and bread and cheese. A clean cloth had not wiped them in years, judging by the lack of shine and the grime on the surface. The officers set the table on the ground and placed the tray on it. They made no comment, and their faces were rigid. The officer handed her a plastic bag with an orange jumpsuit in it. A smaller bag inside the larger one held underwear and a washcloth.

They said nothing as they entered and delivered the items. They were like two robots on minimal electric charge, such were their slow, deliberate movements. This was not their first time performing this task. They acted like synchronised swimmers, smoothly closing the door, and firmly turning the key. She stood still at first. Looking at the bagged clothes, she decided she was not putting on the prison jumpsuit. It was orange. She fully expected to be released in a few minutes. She was glad of the underwear and quickly stripped and washed herself using the cloth and chilly water from the tap over the hole.

She redressed and tasted the coffee. It was cold, bitter, and disgusting, but she drank it and ate the bread and cheese too. She knew she must eat. Everything would depend on the next few hours. She urgently needed to get out of prison and out of Spain. She was due to catch an afternoon flight back to Dublin.

Harriet tried to keep herself calm. Sitting on the bed, she closed her eyes and took ten deep breaths, forcing herself to breathe out deeply. She felt extremely distracted and agitated, but she knew she must behave calmly. Her best chance was to listen, discover the challenges she faced, and address them one by one. Harriet needed to contact someone outside too, especially if they proposed to keep her in jail with these charges. She continued to breathe deeply. She was a scientist; this was illogical, and she would quickly get it sorted out.

She was not familiar with the rules of law in Spain. Harriet doubted if the rules she saw in the blockbuster Hollywood movies about phone calls and lawyers applied. Was this jurisdiction using Napoleonic law? Her mind jumped through all kinds of scenarios. What was Napoleonic law? She wondered if Spain might be a jurisdiction where the accused are guilty until proven innocent. But she spoke calmly and aloud to herself. Just wait, don't jump to conclusions. Gather the facts. Then make a plan.

As she was saying listen to herself, the door creaked again. This time, a young lady in civilian clothes entered. She was, Harriet thought, dressed in the smart casual way favoured by young professionals. She wore a skirt, a silk flowery blouse, and a pale grey cardigan. Harriet wished she could smell as nice as this young lady who had had a hot shower and washed her hair. The two prison wardens stayed outside. The smell of humid air from the hallway was welcome compared to the odours emerging from the rumbling hole in the ground of her prison cell.

"Hello, Harriet, my name is Nancy. I am your assigned interpreter this morning for the formal interviews and charges. How are you?"

Harriet carefully examined the young woman. She was barely twenty-four or five; she thought. Her English sounded ok so far, but she was so young. How could anyone depend on her? What did she know? Harriet resolved to listen and speak as little as possible.

"I am not great. The odious smells and terrible, dank, cramped conditions are not my idea of overnight accommodation."

"Ok, we will move to the interview room now. Are you ok to walk? They will have to handcuff you, but no leg irons for now."

"Yes."

Nancy shouted a rapid burst of Spanish to the officers, who opened the solid door again. One came in and put her wrists in handcuffs behind her back. The other officer turned and walked in front, along the corridor. Nancy gesticulated for Harriet to follow him, and the second jailor brought up the rear of the procession. Harriet thought it all quite bizarre that she needed to be handcuffed and escorted like this in a police station. She was hardly a dangerous criminal, was she? Why did Nancy mention leg irons? Surely it was a human rights abuse.

They climbed two flights of steps, and the effort winded Harriet somewhat. She was used to lifts and holding handrails as she climbed stairs. Without the use of her hands, she found the steps quite steep, and the builder did not design them for ease of movement. They ushered her into a large well-lit space with a sturdy steel table centred in the room. She could see they bolted firmly it to the ground. They arranged five chairs around it with three on one side. The prison warder pointed to one chair showing she should sit.

"Are they leaving my hands cuffed behind my back?" Harriet said in a low whisper to Nancy.

Nancy spoke in Spanish and the officer came forward and uncuffed Harriet. He then cuffed her left wrist to a centre bar in the middle of the table. Harriet sat down. She was pale and sweating slightly after the effort of climbing the stairs. Her nerves and the bright lights in the room added to her temperature. She noticed a tape recorder on the table and a mirror; she presumed two-way along the wall in front of her. It was just like a scene from a bad crime movie, she thought, except she was the starring criminal. Her racing heart did not slow down.

The prison wardens withdrew, and the door closed. Nancy looked at her.

"Ok?"

"No, I am not ok. What is going on? I'm filthy and did not get a shower. I am under arrest, and spent the night locked in an appalling cell. Strange men have pushed me and shouted at me in Spanish. I'm sitting here handcuffed to a table like a common criminal. No one has explained what laws I broke or what is the process. I feel dirty and violated. I am doing my best to hold it together here, but…"

"I understand, I do. I have experienced this confusing situation two or three times before. Your court-appointed lawyer will arrive in a few minutes and explain it to you. Well, he will explain it and I will translate it."

"When will I be able to leave? I have a flight this afternoon."

Harriet could see Nancy was a bit surprised at this remark. She thought carefully and firmly said, "the lawyer will explain the laws and procedures. He may help to get your flight cancelled."

Harriet slumped into her chair and her head sagged deep into her shoulders. This girl, Nancy, did not expect she would leave here today. She knew she must call someone. She needed to hear a familiar, friendly voice, someone competent who could work to get her released. Jack, she thought, I need to talk to Jack. He will turn the diplomatic wheels to get me released from this scary hell.

The door opened and a tall, legally dressed lady walked in. She looked as if she just walked out of an executive beauty salon. Someone professionally applied the makeup on her face and her hair was extremely well-styled. Harriet estimated she was about fifty to fifty-five years old. She looked at Nancy, nodded, and then greeted Harriet in Spanish. She smiled and Nancy translated. "Good morning, I am Luz Maria. You can call me Lucy. They have appointed me to represent you today."

Harriet replied, "Buena Dias, Lucy," and used up about fifty per cent of her Spanish.

Lucy continued to talk at what seemed like breakneck speed. Harriet observed as they spoke and she witnessed a professional woman working thoroughly, and so far, competently, but with no emotion or opinion of the character of her client. Harriet reminded herself to listen and to be nice to this woman. Her future might depend on it.

Lucy paused, and Nancy asked her something in Spanish. Then she turned to Harriet.

"Ok, this is the information we have. The police will interview you in about half an hour. They suspect you of murder. They found a body on the bed of your hotel room. He was naked. Your business card and room number were in his shirt pocket. There are no signs of forced entry. They found the bedside locker with two open bottles of champagne standing on it. There are also two fifty-euro notes on the bed. These have Irish serial numbers."

"The police are working on the assumption you invited him to your room. You had a few drinks together, and then there was a lover's tiff and you put poison in his drink and killed him. Maybe he tried to extort money from you? The police will follow this line of enquiry in the interview. These are serious charges. The evidence against you is strong. They suspect no one else and have paused the investigation pending the hearing. If it goes to trial and they find you guilty, the mandatory sentence for murder is twenty years in Spanish prison."

CHAPTER 10: THE DUBLIN TEAM GEAR UP

The team at Trinity College were talking at nineteen to the dozen. Jack sat back and listened and soaked up their good energy. They watched Harriet make her presentation the night before. It was a good presentation, and they knew it. Harriet sent a couple of messages saying it looked good, and she hoped they would get the funding extension within weeks.

Jack knew how important it was. While the conversation bubbled in their lab, he opened the spreadsheet to show the one million euros they received were rapidly running out. His figures told him there was less than twenty thousand left in the bank. It was enough for about ten more days at the present rate of spending.

Each of the team worked on a subvention from the college to this project and the lab, its equipment, research materials, and payment to administration for heat and light—all consumed money like water sinking into an underground cave.

"Ok, ok", Jack spoke to the chattering group. "Settle down. It was a good night last night. Harriet is pleased and there are some email messages this morning. They are incredibly positive and are giving excellent reviews."

"Yeah", they cheered. "Well done, Harriet. A super presentation."

"I will pass on your congratulations to her, and you can do so directly yourself. She is due back in Dublin this evening. She will probably go home to rest and charge up her energy after the journey. I am sure we can meet her in the morning to plan our next steps."

"Oh, not until tomorrow", the ladies said. This news disappointed them, as they wanted to hug the returning hero as soon as possible. The idea of waiting until tomorrow was not part of their hopes and dreams.

"Yes, tomorrow. So, in the meantime, can we go through the normal routine, please? We need a morning stand-up review to go through what you're working on and, most important, what's blocking your progress. The rest of the world, well, that is a bit of an exaggeration, is expecting our work to be complete so they can start their projects. They have decided our work will be the baseline. We need to tidy up the pilot, write it up, and share it with our colleagues."

One student asked, "Does this mean we are getting a project manager?"

Jack looked at him and tried to avoid being sarcastic, "You are well aware, James, Harriet was interviewing a Russian woman for the role of project manager. She told me they met, and they were going to talk again. I assume that was last night or today. So, Harriet advanced her selection of a project manager over the weekend. The grant of the second tranche of funding will allow the process of appointment to complete."

"How is the funding released? What do we have to do?" Nancy, a quiet but brilliant PhD student, asked.

"Great question, Nancy. You all need to put a project summary report in the next two weeks as a sprint deliverable. We need to get all our progress reports together and submit them to the EU Horizon group. I know it was prepared for Harriet's presentation last night, but you need to add in all the tables, graphs, charts and as many nicely coloured outcome results as you can. The EU like weighty documents. Let them see pretty pictures. Remember, the funding extension is for three years and will be over five million euros. They will take the grant of such a large sum of money seriously and will poke and push at every piece of information we give them. The big prize here folks is you will all earn your doctorates in three years. With those under your belt, you will be in pole position for the commercial world to employ you as fully fledged research scientists. There are plenty of pharmaceutical companies here and overseas looking for professionally qualified researchers. OK? Questions? Now get to work, we want to make Harriet proud!"

CHAPTER 11: FRIK AND HENRI

Frik spotted Henri heading outside for a smoke with a coffee cup in his hand. He liked Henri and walked after him. They had good chats about policing and remained true to their initial dreams—they could make a difference in society. If nothing else, he could tease him about his unhealthy smoking habit.

They worked in the same section of Europol for three years. Their respective national police force seconded both to help and act as experts to advise and support other police forces in resolving terrorism threats and actions. This normally was tracing suicide bombers and dealing with the fallout when cars plough into crowded pedestrian streets. There was also the non-media end of things where the revolutionaries try to raise money to fund their activities.

No matter what their plan, revolutionaries are like ordinary people who live somewhere, who eat three meals every day, take a drink, sleep, pray, and move around. They remain part of families and enjoy their friends. Most stayed in regular contact with their families.

The stupid use of mobile phones and emails by revolutionaries proved a successful way for police to catch and follow up suspects. A central body like Europol was good at holding and sharing this information with other police forces and was successful in getting criminals off the street before they struck, killed, and maimed innocent civilians to make their point.

"So, Henri, the mighty French football team, lost again." Frik always started with football. They shared a common interest in their respective national teams and with the European Cup only a couple of months away, there were plenty of qualifying matches being played. Last night the French team drew 1-1 to The Netherlands.

"We did not lose. Can you not read a scoreline? I thought you Germans were good at simple maths!" was the reply from Henri. He knew Frik was trying to rise him and get him to react.

"Ah Henri, to be beaten by the Dutch, the orange Wurst munchers, is such a shame for your country team. What was the score when Germany played them? Let me think, three German goals to nothing from the Dutch. I think that was it."

Henri snorted. That match was one Frik regularly brought up. He was milking it now as the score was four to nothing. Henri refused to join in and sucked a deep lungful of air from his cigarette.

"Ah, you don't want to talk about it. I can understand. Talking about garbage is not the French way! Let us change the subject and talk about something more pleasant. Dead bodies and murder. Tell me, how are things in Seville? Are you sending me there or not? I want to buy more sunscreen if you are. The weather is lovely there."

"No, they have arrested an Irish woman for the murder of a Spanish waiter. The initial emails and reports suggest a lover's tiff."

"An Irish woman eh, a lover's tiff. That sounds so French. Is she a redhead? They can be quite interesting. No? If it is just lover's tiff, then it is of no concern to us here in Europol. We do not deal with love, do we, Henri? Why did it raise a red flag here at all?"

"Well, our AI cop in the box looked at the reports and noted the victim was rapidly decomposing. Extremely rapid decomposition were the exact words. The computer matched this feature to a murder a few months ago in Vilnius in Lithuania. They found a former British diplomat, possibly MI5, beside a skip outside a hotel in a badly decomposed state. He was a dropout and an alcoholic and the British washed their hands of him. But, like our Spanish waiter, he was alive and kicking a few hours before."

"What do you mean—decomposed?"

"I mean decomposed, decayed, broken down, rotting, turned to dust. The Spanish waiter seems to have decomposed, and so fast and far, it looks like, on initial reports, the post-mortem is still pending, he was dead about nine weeks. The body was turning to dust. Yet we know he died in the hotel room. We know for a certain fact he was alive earlier the same day."

"The dead British man in Vilnius showed a level of decomposition usually observed after five weeks. The post-mortem report described how his internal organs, plus his fingers, toes, and ears remained only as dust. It was more typical of a body in a rubbish bin for five weeks rather than one which was only two or three hours dead. The report triggered a local police investigation to check the correct name tag was on the correct body."

"Ah, that is strange. Maybe they ate bad, how do you say it, Escargots? But what has it to do with terrorism?"

"Well, it is a biological thing, no, decomposition. So, if it is happening faster than normal, then the question is why? Is it some new virus or bacterium? Does it kill? Who has it? Why do they have it? Should we do something about it? Why are there two similar cases in countries in Europe? Are they connected? Police have a suspicious nature. We expect the worst when something out of the ordinary happens. Our AI systems inherited our suspicious bias."

"And have we shared these reports with our American friends?"

"Yes, they probably get the reports faster than I do. But we don't see what is happening at their end of the world. They don't reciprocate their information. Maybe it is nothing, maybe it is something. Time will tell."

"As usual, we sit and wait, eh?"

"Just so." Henri said, as he doused his cigarette in the coffee dregs and dropped it into the bin. "Come on, let us go back to work. There must be bad people out there for us to catch."

"I would like to read the reports when they come in. Can you share the files with me?"

"Yes, I will, but why?"

"Oh, I don't know, instinct. Or maybe I just want to avoid eating in bad French restaurants!"

"Ah, you play with the oxymorons again. Go to work. We can talk again soon."

CHAPTER 12: GREGOR, ALEXANDR, AND SERGEI

Gregor looked out over the roof of the buildings in Moscow. He was content. A few parts of the plan were coming together. The pictures from Seville were splendid. Oxana successfully tested M278 on another of their targets. This was a better version by far than the earlier version M275 and seemed to increase the speed of decomposition of a body by a factor of two.

He sensed the door open in his office, and he heard the voices of two of his closest lieutenants, Alexandr and Sergei. Normally, they worked in an office many floors below. Their official title was financial accountants, but their actual role was far more significant. They were his closest allies and handled all the shady work he needed done to keep the company successful. The company existed in the Russian economy but was developing into the wider global market.

Today, he called them into his office for an update. This was the only room with the only computer in the world with the information and results of their biological products. There were two, and oddly enough, the chemistry was similar in both products. One was a product M278, which stopped people from living and caused their bodies to turn to dust in a few hours. The other was an anti-ageing product, Rattler, to reverse the signs and effects of ageing. He hoped they would be as content as he was when they saw the results of Oxana's work from yesterday.

He took his seat between the two men and pressed play on

the console on his desk with his well-manicured hands. The gold rings on each of his fingers contrasted with the single letter tattooed in blue on each finger. The curtains closed automatically, and a large white projection screen dropped from its well-hidden storage position in the ceiling. Oxana sent five pictures yesterday, and they were now displayed as a multi-image grid on the screen. He pressed a button on the controller, and they enlarged and switched to a single image. He looked at the two men as they stared intently at the pictures. He silently scrolled through the five images and switched back to grid view.

"Gentlemen, good morning." He started formally. Despite their years of working together and the number of secrets they knew about the work his company was doing, he maintained a formal boss-employee relationship with them. He paid them extremely well, and they received other benefits as well. The money and their history together through many years on the battlefields of Afghanistan created a deep understanding and, most importantly, a deep unquestioning loyalty.

"Oxana sent us these pictures from Seville last night. She took them within ten minutes of administering M278. Another traitor to Russia exterminated. This time she got the target to drink it in champagne. A unique vintage!"

The three men chuckled at the idea of vintage French champagne being the chosen method to give the victim their biological killer.

"The enhanced version is quicker to act than its predecessor. You will remember the earlier version took several hours to act after death? Well, this version acts more or less immediately, triggering decomposition within minutes of death."

The two men nodded in memory and the large sale they lost to a client needing rapid results. Hours can pass slowly when escape plans depend on the disappearance of the victim's fingerprints and dental records.

"Oxana will be back in Mother Russia tomorrow. We will call her in for a full debriefing. How is her father? The grand chess master, Karpov?"

"He is fine, living the high life in the dacha. He is playing chess from time to time, indulging in vodka, and perfecting his reputation and skills as a grumpy old man."

"Good. When was Oxana allowed to visit with him last?"

"It was quite a while ago. She wanted to see him for his birthday, but we sent her to Vilnius. She was being difficult about administering M275, the earlier version, to a stranger."

"Ah yes, I remember. I thought with all the excellent work she did, perhaps we might let her visit her father for a day and a night? Would that be good? Will it help our plan?"

"Yes, I can set it up. She usually is quite difficult for a few days afterwards, though. But we have managed her before. She insists she wants to work for us as a partner and there is no need to threaten her father with harm."

Gregor said calmly, and with some steel, "I prefer to hold the pieces. Her father is where we want him to be, and she knows that. He is a treasured citizen of Russia and a prestigious retired grand master. If she wants his good health and reputation to continue, then she will have to work with us. I will make sure I am there during her visit."

"What happens next? Is the product developed enough for our customer?" This was the voice of Alexandr. He was perhaps the longest-serving employee and fought with Gregor in Afghanistan before the generals turned chicken and pulled out. So many of their comrades died unnecessarily there.

Gregor never forgot these and the embarrassment they caused to the Russian army reputation. After the war, he entered civilian life and as he built his financial empire under the new political regime; he set about making friends in strange places. He burned with a quiet hatred.

"Ah yes, our potential customers, yes, they are keen. They have, as you know, a problem with the twenty remaining prisoners in Guantanamo. Friendly countries in the thrall of the USA won't grant them safe passage or residence. The only people who want them are their families in their home countries. They do not wish to send them home as they might become heroes and lead a fresh wave of attacks against the United States. The soft power they get from sending them home is substantial, but the risks are enormous. This is the third President to promise to empty the black op camp of theirs in Cuba. It is a festering sore to them. They are keen to see our solution in practice."

"And the money?" this time it was Sergei who spoke. He was also a veteran of the Afghan war with Gregor and Alexandr, although he was a few years younger. He lied about his age at sign-up and was a volunteer, unlike his conscripted friends. He joined them when another of their colleagues died walking on a land mine.

He demonstrated an insatiable appetite for money, as he was part of a large and poor family. He had zero morals or scruples and lived to earn enormous amounts of cash. If this did not pay out soon, he planned to go back to the Army as a mercenary and make money on the side selling arms and munitions.

"The money is good. Many, many, millions of dollars in accounts in Bermuda, Malta, Cyprus, and Turkey. Plus, transfers of ownership of companies owning properties in Chile, Austria, and France. Do not worry, my money-hungry friend, this will be a huge payday, even after we pay all the development costs and bribes."

Sergei smiled and then his face grew dark as he said, "I want a box filled with dollars as well. I do not trust these numbers on a screen, one touch of a key by a person with access, and poof, the money disappears. Who would take my complaint about it? I want real money in a great enormous trunk, like a steamer trunk. Lots of fifty-dollar bills. That is what I want, houses and villas and yachts and fancy cars—and a steamer trunk filled with cash!"

The two men laughed, and Gregor tossed a glass paperweight at his younger friend, who caught it expertly. "Do not worry, my dear Sergei, you will be rich beyond your wildest dreams."

"But first, we must arrange a demonstration for the clients on American soil. So far, the CIA has seen our work in Vilnius and Seville. We impressed them sufficiently enough to go to the next step."

"Oxana will begin work in Dublin and from there she can reach all parts of the USA in a few hours. The flight frequency between Dublin and the USA is as good as London or Frankfurt. The client has arranged for her to be issued a US passport to ensure there are no obvious checks or tracking applied to her entry. Of course, the CIA will track her movements as she lands and departs, but that is good. She won't be able to defect and leave her loving dad behind for our care and attention. We will not have to communicate with her or them directly. They can use their monitoring systems to watch and track her. We can relax in the sun, knowing they are doing all the work. I like this as less communication means less chance of being caught or something going wrong. There is nothing to trace back to us."

Gregor opened a bottle of vodka and poured each of his friends a shot. They downed it to the chorus. "Our revenge will be sweet."

He refilled their glasses. The bottle would not last long.

CHAPTER 13: CRISTIANO INTERVIEWS OXANA AND LETS HER GO

Oxana took her seat opposite Cristiano in the plain, functional office of the hotel manager. Cristiano stared at him until he left. Oxana lowered her eyes and lifted her chin, enough to admire the handsome police inspector. He was gorgeous. She thought of ways to ensure she met him again, preferably off-duty and preferably near a hotel room.

"So, please tell me your name- your full name," began Cristiano when the door closed behind the manager.

"My name is Oxana Karpov. It is my family-name. I was married for six years, but he was not a keeper. Are you married?" Oxana she could see by his reaction she moved to a personal conversation too quickly. She would have to play a waiting game. She might have to freshen the bait to land this tough fish.

"Ok, Ms Karpov, is it ok if I call you Oxana?"

"Yes please, I insist on being on first-name terms with all the desirable, handsome policemen in my life." Again, Oxana bit her lip and kicked herself metaphorically for this overly forward comment. Once again, she watched the shadow of annoyance cross his face.

"Indeed. Now to the matter in hand, you say you know Dr. Harriet Fischer. Please tell me how you know her and your movements with her yesterday."

"Well, I am interviewing for a research project job in a Dublin University. Russia is an expensive, unloving, and hard place to live these days. She is leading a huge European funded research project into aging. It is an exciting field. My background is in biology and genetics, and I have many, many high-level qualifications."

Cristiano raised his hand, "Ok, I am sure you are amazing, but can we concentrate on Dr. Harriet, please? When did you meet her?"

It's like a chess match, Oxana thought. I make a move; he blocks it; I make another move; he blocks it. He is very defensive. Once again, she regretted the formality of her clothing. If only she put on something a bit more feminine.

"Ok, Detective Inspector, I like to set things in context. I met her for coffee yesterday morning for the first time. We were supposed to discuss my application for the research job. But she cut it short. She said something about having to get ready for her presentation. It surprised me when she rushed off before we finished, as her keynote was much later in the evening. She was giving the final keynote of the conference."

"At what time was this coffee?"

"It was about eleven thirty. We left at about noon, twelve o'clock. As I say, it was short."

"So, about thirty minutes. Did anything strange happen there?"

"No, nothing much, except…" Oxana had a quick brainwave.

"Yes, except?"

"She seemed distracted. As I went into the café, she was in deep conversation with the waiter. He was a filthy person with black under his fingernails. His clothes were dirty, not like you, nice and clean. I couldn't drink or eat anything he touched. I saw her give him her business card. I reacted badly to him, I am afraid. I simply cannot stand unclean staff in a cafe. My reaction to him annoyed her. She felt I was being tough on him. I thought I was going to flunk the interview. Tensions ran high, so I spoke to him when she left to make sure he knew I was not serious."

"And were you not serious?"

"About the dirt, yes, but I was afraid he might know Harriet somehow. The world is a small place. They seemed to know each other. If he said something negative, then Harriet might employ someone else. I need that job."

"And you saw her give him her business card?"

"Yes, well, it was the size and shape of a business card. He put it into his jeans pocket."

"Ok, so to summarise, you met her for the first time for thirty minutes around 11:30. This was to be a job interview, but she cut it short."

Cristiano made notes in a hardcover notebook using the most elegant gold pen Oxana had seen in years. His hand movements were fine and his fingers were delicate. Oxana felt a warm glow in her stomach, but forced herself to concentrate.

"Yes, I was certain I damaged my chances when she didn't ask me anything about myself. But when we met again later, she was warm and friendly."

"You met again later? You didn't mention it before. Really Ms Oxana, I need to hear everything. A tiny scrap of information can be a missing piece of the jigsaw I am putting together here. When was this second impromptu meeting, and where?"

"After her keynote. It was a wonderful success, her keynote. Normally I avoid such feel-good, sycophantic events. I prefer to go out in this beautiful city to a pleasant restaurant or to walk along the streets soaking in the atmosphere. But my old University paid me to come and collect the papers presented and make notes of the speakers and the universities they represented."

"Yes, interesting, but you have wandered off topic again. Please, can you stick to answering my questions? I asked about when and where. You said you met her again at the keynote."

"Yes, she forgot her scarf in the café, I think deliberately, and I sent her a message asking where she was staying. By chance, it was the same hotel as I was in. So, she gave me her room number, and I returned her scarf to her."

"You were in her room! This is another time you met her. At what time, consider the time, this is important."

"I don't have to think about the time. I have it on my phone." Oxana took out her phone and scrolled to her messages.

"Here it is. At 12:20, I texted to ask her where she was staying. She answered at once. At 13:40 she sent me a text thanking me for returning her scarf."

"Thank you. This information is extremely helpful. I will get a copy from your phone. My detectives will take your phone for a brief time later."

"No, that is not possible. I cannot be without my phone. My father is an old man and I need to be available at all times. I could send the messages to you. What is your number?"

Oxana was enjoying this cat and mouse.

"Please make a screenshot of the conversation and here is the business card of my lead detective. Send it to him."

Oxana smiled to herself, blocked again. My, he is defensive! What does a girl have to do to get his phone number?

"What happened in her room?"

"Nothing really. She was on a call on her computer. You know Zoom or Teams or something. There were about 6 or 7 heads showing on her screen. They seemed to work together. I assumed it was her team in Dublin and they were working on her presentation."

"Ah yes, and did you say anything to her?"

"No, nothing. She waved as I entered and left. I placed the scarf on the back of her chair. Oh, maybe there was one thing odd?" Oxana bit her lower lip and paused.

Cristiano leaned forward in the chair, "yes? One thing?"

"I thought I heard a cough in the bathroom, but it could be on the screen too. Or next door, the walls in your hotels are really thin."

"A cough, from the direction of the bathroom in Harriet's room?"

"Yes, but I am not sure. As I say, I was only there for a minute. A quick in and out."

Cristiano made a note and circled it with a flourish. He looked back at Oxana.

"Was that it? I still need to hear about your contact with Harriet at the keynote."

"Oh yes, well, I went to the conference from the beginning to the end. It was boring as old boots. I prefer more excitement. But I wanted to be seen to be there. I was to collect information for my old university. I hoped Harriet might offer me the job if she saw how keen I was. It was a waste of time as I did not see her until she rushed in to take her place just before her keynote started."

"You say she rushed in at the last minute?"

"Yes, I don't know where she was, but she gave a great keynote. I congratulated her on it, and we walked back to the hotel together afterwards."

"You walked back with her to your hotel! Ms. Karpov, you seem to have spent a great deal of time with her yesterday. What time was this?"

"Of course, I don't enjoy going on my own to hotels after dark. Let me see, I guess we got back about one am. Maybe it was a bit earlier. I know Dr. Harriet was starving. I ate dinner earlier before I went to the conference, but she said she hadn't eaten. She walked back, as she wanted to find a restaurant. But they were all closed. That is how I know it was so late."

"What bridge did you cross?"

"I don't know, but there was a cycle lane on one side and a walking lane on the other. We walked in the cycle lane. Does that mean you will have to punish me?" Harriet giggled to herself. She was really pushing her attack now, but she felt a strong need to try something unusual. They were getting to the end, and she did not want him to just leave. She wanted another meeting with him. He was not responding to her.

"Ok, we will check the CCTV cameras on the bridge."

He didn't take that bait, either. He just ignored her attempts to flirt. She thought he would make a great chess master or a poker player.

"What happened when you got back to the hotel?"

"We parted ways, Harriet and me. The receptionist said the kitchens were closed, but there was champagne in the room in the minibar and some peanuts and things in the vending machine at the lift. I went to bed. I didn't want to watch her drink champagne and eat peanuts. We made an appointment for breakfast at 08:30."

"It was, overall, a very boring evening for a Russian girl in Seville. Harriet went to the vending machines, and I could hear her pushing buttons as the lift to my room arrived." Oxana threw caution to the winds. "I'm in Room 421 if you want to check anything."

"Thank you, yes, my officers will look. I must go now. Dr. Harriet is in jail, and I will interview her. Thank you for your help. I may need to contact you again."

"Any time, but you know I am returning to Russia later today? But for you, I am sure I could delay the flight."

"Ah, I did not. One moment!" Cristiano took out his phone and made a call. In rapid Spanish, he gave orders to the person on the other end. He hung up.

"That is my lead detective, Jhon, please wait here, he will be with you in five minutes. He will take your screenshots and your number in case we want to talk to you again. Thank you for your help."

"Ok Detective Inspector, will he give my number to you? I would prefer to talk to you. You have such a lovely voice and eyes. I feel safe with you. I think it is important, no?"

"Yes, Ms Oxana, thank you again. Please wait here."

Oxana watched him imaginatively as he stood up and left the room. His movements were powerful and masculine. His fingers were long and made elegant strokes on the page as he wrote. She tried. She really hoped he would call her, and soon.

CHAPTER 14: CRISTIANO GATHERS INFORMATION ABOUT RICARDO

Cristiano sat in the back of the police car as the driver screamed across the city with a full siren blaring and blue lights flashing. He wondered about Oxana; she was quite obvious in her seduction approach. He was happily married, but the overt nature of her approach was flattering. But maybe that was the way of all Russians. She seemed well educated and certainly spoke excellent English, but he felt there was more going on than she was letting on. He had a sense she was hiding information about herself. He had good instincts about people. His years in the police enhanced these. With Oxana, he felt there was something deeper than her shallow, flirtatious seduction attempts.

He wondered how she achieved her success in life. There was no evidence of any hiccup in her progress. She seemed to get it all without trying too hard. Either she was really brilliant, which he doubted, or someone was clearing the path for her. Maybe there was a powerful family or organisation taking care of the minor details and made her progress seem more than it was. She was interesting, in a cheap sort of way. He felt the information she gave him was true. He would get it all double checked to be sure.

He looked at the notes he made during her interview. He drew a timeline in his book.

Harriet was out of the hotel in the morning- sometime around 11:00 until about 12:30 when she returned after the truncated job interview with Oxana. She was on a call then to several people in her room on her computer. Why did Harriet book such an abbreviated time for the interview? Why had she done it before the big presentation? Surely, she must have wanted to have spare minutes to fix or adapt the critical conference presentation? Why did Harriet complicate her day with a morning interview?

Then there was an unknown window from 12:30 until 20:00. Apart from the brief interlude when Oxana returned the scarf, and heard someone cough in the ensuite, he did not know where Harriet was during that time. But it was a long time window, more than long enough, to kill someone.

At 20:00 she was at the conference and then was very visible as she gave her keynote speech. She was talking to many people in the moments after her presentation, and Oxana walked her back to the hotel.

It was after midnight when she returned to her room and discovered the body. The police arrived around 00:30. Cristiano could see there was plenty of time where there was uncertain or no information as to the whereabouts of Harriet. There were considerable time gaps.

It was easy to jump to the conclusion she stayed in her room. It was possible Enrico was in her room after he finished work for siesta at 13:00. He may have finished early. His café colleagues would cover for him if he bragged about a 'sure thing'. The rendezvous could have gone wrong. But it would be really difficult to imagine she killed someone and then had gone and given a brilliant presentation to a scientific community! But why kill? Even with the opportunity, why? And how? The body was a few hours dead at most, but it was in an advanced state of decomposition.

He would meet his team before he interviewed Dr. Harriet. A few more hours in jail would not do her any harm and might help him ask better questions. There were a few holes in the time-line and his detective's work would fill these in. The obvious killer would emerge.

The car arrived and Cristiano went straight to the briefing room, where three of his detectives were standing at an incident board holding the information as it came to hand. He greeted them all and shook hands with them one by one. As he did so, and as he always did, he looked at each man and woman to see if they were alert. He liked to see what was going on in their eyes. He took immense pride in his team and wanted to make sure they worked well together.

"Ok, fill me in, please. Where are you all so far?" Cristiano kicked off the meeting. As was custom, Maria, a twenty-year veteran, was first up.

"So far, we know the victim was Enrico Almeria-Martinez. He worked as a waiter in the café Solara. He was working there for about the last four years. He was 34 years old, divorced with one child, a girl. He pays some money towards childcare, but she lives with his ex-wife, her mother. He shares a three-room flat with two other waiters. We do not record him as the owner of any vehicle. We arrested him about ten years ago for possession of a small amount of cannabis. There was an application from his wife for a barring order, but she never activated it. Otherwise —he is invisible to us, there is no other police record."

"Good, thank you, Maria. I have some information Enrico may have known Dr. Harriet, the woman we hold in our police cells here. We found him in her room. Can you and Michel check with his bosses, other waiters, his roommates if they heard of her before? Also see does he have a laptop or PC in his flat? He may be on some of those dating sites. Maybe he met Harriet there, and this was the face-to-face meetup. I will ask her myself later, but I want to check, as she will probably deny knowing him. A witness suspects they knew each other for some time."

Turning to his next officer, Cristiano said, "Michel, what do you have for us?"

"The body was in a severe state of decomposition. The time of death is impossible to confirm. It looks like it was 9 weeks ago.

Which of course is not possible as Enrico worked that morning and we have him on CCTV walking into the hotel at 16:30. He rode the lift to the second floor, and we assume he went into the room then. There are no cameras in the hallways—only in the foyer and in the lift."

"His clothes were in the bathroom. They appear to be the clothes he wore to work. They are old and in urgent need of a wash. His shoes were almost through their soles. They were a cheap pair of black sport shoes. A business card with the room number was in his shirt pocket. It was the card of Dr. Harriet Fischer. Someone handwrote the room number. We can look for handwriting matches with suspects, but it is only a few digits, so we are unlikely to get a reliable match. Enrico had a pencil in the same pocket."

"Someone, presumably the killer, covered him in a hotel dressing gown. It was white, but not anymore. There are no signs of a struggle. There were two brand new fifty-euro notes on the bed. The serial numbers show they came from the Irish central bank printing press."

"There was a single glass containing champagne beside the bed. It was half-full. The other glass was empty. There was an extraordinarily powerful smell of a poison from the liquid. We found a vial with skull and crossbones in the dressing gown pocket. Both have gone to the lab for testing. The vial was empty. Maybe he committed suicide? Why would he have poison with him? Maybe Harriet had poison with her and wanted to make it look like suicide?"

"One other thing, Harriet's passport was in the safe, but she did not lock the safe. Why would a woman come to a strange hotel in a strange city, put her document in the safe and then not lock the safe? It is another strange thing in a series of unusual things."

Cristiano made a couple of notes and then stood up.

"Ok, excellent work so far. It seems Enrico was not there earlier than 16:30. Double check the cameras again, please. Look from about 12:30. This alleged cough in the ensuite needs to be checked. It may not be someone at all. It may be someone on the screen or in another room."

"I am going to interview Harriet now. Will you come with me, Maria? The rest of you keep on building a picture of the victim. See if anyone else went into the hotel and to the same floor between the time Enrico went in and say 19:00. Get the hotel room cleaned out, oh who is on fingerprints?"

"I am", murmured the third detective.

"Good, get onto Jhon. He is still there and get him to collect fingerprints from a girl called Oxana. He will know who she is. She was in the hotel room after midday, so she may have touched something."

"Otherwise—keep going. When forensics and site investigation teams are done, remove the police cordon and give the hotel back its room. Bag up all of Harriet's clothes and passport and put them in the evidence room here. I suspect she will be our guest for a few more days. We don't want the tourists becoming afraid of visiting our city. If the press asks, we have a suspect in custody. That's it, but remember, so far, we have no motive for this crime. We do not have a weapon either. It is a strange case."

"We have a body and a time of death. We have three possibilities. Enrico killed himself in her room. Harriet killed him. Someone else killed him. So far, none of them make any sense and we cannot prove any of them. Maybe she will confess and make all our lives easier!"

CHAPTER 15:
HARRIET WITH LUZ AND NANCY

Harriet looked at Luz Maria- her lawyer and Nancy- her interpreter. She felt completely overwhelmed. She was depending on these two complete strangers for her immediate freedom. She felt completely out of control. She desperately wanted to be back home in Ireland. There, she knew people who would represent her. Plus, the language would not be like an elephant in the room. She could listen to her accusers and answer them directly.

"Luz Maria, please tell me what is going to happen this morning. Why are they so late? They said they would start at seven am. I have a flight this afternoon. I have to get to the hotel, get cleaned up, pack and get to the airport. What is happening? I have done nothing wrong."

Luz Maria looked carefully at Harriet. She saw a woman who was well to do and quite intelligent, but perhaps not street-wise. She would have to shock her a bit to get her to face the terrible reality of the situation she was in.

Setting her jaw firmly and looking Harriet straight in the eye, she said. "Look here, my English is not good. The police accuse you of murder. Murder of a Spanish man in a Spanish hotel. This is quite, quite serious. The evidence the police have is overwhelming. They found the dead body in your hotel room. He was lying on your bed naked; his clothes were in your ensuite. They also found your business card in his pocket. The business card had your room number hand-written on it. There are two new Irish fifty-Euro notes on the bed with him. The man is dead! Don't you understand? Dead—in your room. So, the police think it is an open and shut case and you killed him. They are only trying to answer the why and how. They believe you did it. They are just gathering evidence to prove your guilt in front of a judge. No one else is being investigated, only you."

"You can forget planes going to Dublin or anywhere else. They will hold you here for at least three days and then, or maybe before, they will charge you in front of a judge. The judge will examine the evidence they produce. If the judge agrees, the court will send you to jail pending trial. If you wish to prevent this, then you need to have some compelling arguments about how you did not kill Enrico. As you are not Spanish, there is no likelihood of bail, as the judge will assume you will run back to Ireland and hide."

"You are in deep trouble, Dr. Harriet, and I am trying to understand why you don't see that."

This long speech from a clearly annoyed and upset lawyer shook Harriet to her core. She could hear the tension and feel the anger in her solicitor.

"Ok, I am sorry, it was stupid of me. But I know I did not kill anyone. I do not even know anyone here called Enrico. How can I prove it? What is the prison sentence for murder?"

Luz Maria looked puzzled at this question. She thought to herself, is she confessing? If she is innocent, why is she asking about the guilty sentence? "The sentence is a mandatory 15 years, with a maximum of 20 years."

Harriet looked at the floor and said, "I didn't kill anyone. Yesterday was one of the most important days of my life. I made a significant keynote presentation to an international community of scientists. I interviewed a woman for a wonderful job. I sketched some birds in a square here in Seville. It was a lovely day. I didn't kill anyone! Surely, I get a phone call? Can I tell the Irish consulate I am arrested?"

"Yes, you will get a phone call. Just one. Think carefully who you call. I will ask the police, if they have not done so already, to inform the Irish embassy they have one of their citizens under arrest. They will send someone to talk to you. But they do not interfere in legal cases except to ensure the police follow the correct steps. I also do that for you. Believe me, the police will take care and ensure they have everything checked and double checked. This is a serious crime. They will not be making mistakes. Cristiano is the man in charge, and he is extremely diligent and thorough."

"But they are, they are making mistakes, they assume I did it! I did not."

Nancy listened and observed the lawyer, Luz Maria, who was quite competent in English. She found no need to interrupt or to help her find a word. She could understand Harriet's frustration, but there was no point. She needed to figure out the best solution. If she did it, then she needed to look for mercy or mitigation. If not, she needed to find some reasons to explain away all the evidence.

Luz Maria cleared her throat and looked at her notes. She said, "Can you account for every movement of your day? The police will ask you, especially they will want to know where you were at the time of death. That is the critical time for you to produce a strong alibi. You say you did not do it. They believe you did. There is evidence to support their belief. They want you to show them it was not possible. They want you to prove you were someplace else with witnesses and show them you have an alibi. I will keep asking them to prove you were in the room at the time of the death. They may do so, or they may not. They have evidence from many sources, like cameras and room keys."

"I can't, I went out for a walk in the afternoon. To clear my head and get ready for the presentation. There was a great deal on my mind. I just rambled around the old town enjoying the sunshine and the people and the lovely shops and squares."

Luz Maria looked at Harriet with steel in her eyes, "you will have to do better than 'rambled around' if you don't want to spend twenty years here rambling around a small prison cell. I need you to think and retrace every step you made. Somebody must have seen you. There must be cameras where you walked. We will need every detail."

Harriet wished she was a million miles away. Yesterday, she just wandered around the city without a care in the world. She stopped on the side of the street for over an hour with her sketch book drawing a picture of a bird on the cobbles. There was no date, and she spoke to no one. They would argue she sketched the bird weeks or years earlier. She could not prove it. No one stopped to look at her. The time she spent wandering was simply missing, and she could not build a full alibi.

CHAPTER 16:
CRISTIANO
INTERVIEWS HARRIET

A uniformed police officer opened the door of the interview room. A tall, elegant man swept in, followed by a younger officer. This very well dressed, perfectly shaved man sported a full head of black, neatly cut hair.

Luz Maria, the lawyer, knew him and greeted him in Spanish. He kissed her on both cheeks and smiled into her eyes. Nancy received a firm handshake as Luz Maria introduced her. Harriet's heart sank. They all know each other, they all work together. They are all Spanish. She meant nothing to them. She felt she would not receive a fair hearing from these representatives of the Spanish legal system.

Finally, they all sat, and the man spoke. "Good morning, Dr. Harriet Fischer. I apologise for being late. There are many people making many calls for my attention. Is that the correct way to say it in English?" He looked at Nancy, but Harriet answered.

"It is not, but I understand what you mean."

"Ah, good. I see. So let us be formal. We have a very serious matter to discuss. I will try to speak in English to you. Nancy is here for any clarification. If there is something I say wrong, or if you don't understand, we can try through translation. Ok? I want you to feel as comfortable as possible. But, and this is most important, I want to hear about your day yesterday, every detail."

Harriet looked fully at him and into his deep liquid-brown eyes. She noticed he was a powerful man with a firm but friendly face. All the girls in the room, including the unknown officer, seemed to hang on his every word.

"Let me introduce myself. My name is Detective Inspector Cristiano Martinez-Solenero. It is quite a long name for non-Spanish ears. I hope you realise we always have the name of our father and mother as our last name. This style of family names gives us quite a mouthful to be remembered. It is just one of our traditions. For this interview, may I call you Dr. Harriet? You can certainly call me Cristiano or Inspector, as you wish."

"Ok, Inspector, can we please get on with it? I have a plane to catch, and I did nothing wrong. My lawyer, Luz Maria, tells me you think I murdered a man. I want to assure you I did not, and never would murder anyone. Everyone who knows me knows I am a scientist and a pacifist. Murder is not something I am involved with."

Luz Maria spoke. "Chief Inspector, I want to assure you my client is innocent. She is a woman of impeccable character and of high standing in the academic community in Ireland and in Europe. She was speaking at a major scientific conference here in Seville and to lock her up in this tawdry prison cell on suspicion is quite unacceptable. I insist you release her on her own bond immediately while you find the person responsible for this terrible act of murder."

Harriet was a bit surprised but pleased at the strength of Luz Maria's words. These words quite animated Nancy the interpreter, who sat, nodding her head vigorously.

"Yes, Counsellor, I understand your concern for your client. Quite correct you are too, to make these points. However, I also must think of Enrico, who is dead, and his daughter, his estranged wife and, of course, his mother and father. How would it look if I released the person most likely to have killed him on her self-promise she will be a good girl? The most likely thing is Dr. Harriet would return to Ireland. She said herself, she has a flight to catch. That would involve me in a great deal of legal paperwork to have her extradited back to Spain. No, she stays here for three days at least. We provide this offer of hospitality in the laws of Spain."

"So no, as you know, we are investigating your client. I will continue to do exactly that unless your client wishes to confess and save us all some time and effort?"

The two women both spoke at once, and Inspector Cristiano let them talk for a moment, and then held up his hand.

"Ok, let us get to the chase as they say in the movies. I hope it is the right idiom. I have a dead body in the hotel room of Dr. Harriet. There is no forced entry. We know she met Enrico while she was having coffee in the morning at an interview with Oxana." He checked her name in his notes. "Karpov. We know Harriet's business card with her room number was in Enrico's shirt pocket. We also know there is a glass of champagne with poison in it. Finally, we have two Irish issued fifty-euro notes on the bed. Enrico was a poor man. He was young and good looking in an exotic Spanish kind of way. They did not pay him well as a waiter and he wore tired old clothes which were past their best. He has many expenses with a young daughter and an estranged wife."

"Dr. Harriet apparently arranged a liaison with him. Maybe they met online. Maybe it was a paid liaison, and this theory explains the one hundred euros cash on the bed. Something went wrong, and she killed him with a poison. She works in science and is the head of a University lab. She has easy access to chemicals. To us, it is open and shut case. It is sad, but it is simple."

Luz Maria was writing frantically and showed her writing to Harriet. Her page contained the words, *you met the victim Enrico in his workplace*, scribbled in large letters with six exclamation marks behind.

Harriet thought of writing something but changed her mind. She said, "I met Oxana for coffee so I could interview her for a job. Yes, that is true. But I did not know the waiter, and it is the first I heard he is the victim. I think I will not say anymore now and will seek to consult more deeply with my lawyer. I did not murder anyone. I will have to prove it to you. What time did the murder happen? I will prove I was not there."

The chief inspector seemed surprised how his information affected Dr. Harriett. His instincts told him she was telling the truth. But it made for a large mystery. If she did not do it, then who did? He wrinkled his brow and considered what to do next. He consulted his notes and asked his colleague a question before responding slowly and carefully.

"To answer your question, we have CCTV of Enrico crossing your hotel lobby at 16:25. He entered the lift to the second floor, and we have him exiting the lift at 16:28. We assume he walked to your room, entered it. You probably placed a towel in the door to prop it open or you turned the dead lock to prevent the door from closing. Your key card opened the door at about 15:45. So we know you were probably in the room. We also know you entered your room about 12:00. This was after you came back from the interview with Oxana. We then have you again using your card to return to your room after midnight."

"So, we know you entered the room at 15:45. Enrico entered about 16:30. Then you were next seen arriving late and flustered at your conference at 20:00. So, you killed him sometime between 16:30 and 20:00."

"That is when I was rambling around the old city. I was sketching a bird, and I lost track of time. Then I lost my way walking to the conference centre and in the end I was practically running to get there. I was late and yes; My face was red, and I was flustered as I am always on time. I was not late for my keynote, but they wanted me to check the setup, the microphones, and all sorts of technical stuff. Plus, there was a meet and greet for some of the other speakers and key attendees at 19:45. I was late. I thought there was enough time to get to the meeting, but it is easy to get lost in a big, strange city."

The chief inspector was very doubtful about these answers. It was not a simple case, after all. He stood up, "Dr. Harriett, thank you for this information. We will hold you pending our investigation. We can do so for up to three days. You may make a call and we will transfer you to a proper women's prison where you can shower and dress in clothes the authorities in Spain will provide for you. We have informed the embassy of your arrest and detention. They may be in touch directly with you. I will chat again to you soon when I learn more about this matter."

Harriet sobbed. She was going to prison. That was all she heard. They were not letting her go home. She was stuck in this nightmare. She barely heard the conversation as the inspector left, kissing her lawyer again on both cheeks and shaking hands with Nancy, her interpreter. Harriet slumped forward in her seat and cried.

CHAPTER 17: FRIK FINDS OXANA NEAR ANOTHER DEATH

The computer pinged and the number one appeared in red over the shared folder icon. Frik opened it. The Spanish police posted an update into the cloud folder they shared with Europol. This gave Europol access to the Spanish files across the entire network of Europol offices. The computers and their high-tech artificial intelligence scanned these and other shared files for trends or similar patterns. The international nature of crime made the sharing of information vital for crime solving. The Spanish police could grant access to other countries' national police and crime fighting agencies.

Frik scanned through the update to see if there was any more information on the biological cause of death. He took a keen interest in the post-mortem's outcome, mainly to understand the cause of the rapid decomposition of the body.

So far, there was nothing but an update on suspects and people helping the police with their inquiries. Frik noted the Irish university professor was being detained for the three-day period allowed under Spanish law.

Scrolling down through the file, he scrutinised the comments by the police inspector assigned to the case, Detective Inspector Cristiano Martinez-Solenero. The inspector recorded the help the Spanish police received from a Russian lady, Oxana Karpov, and the fact the Irish professor was pleading innocence.

The Spanish update did not definitively state the exact time of death. It did not identify the precise cause of death, either.

The initial work suggested it would be difficult to conclude these details because of the rapid decomposition of the body. The good news was the freezer in the morgue stopped the decay. The coroner noted the wallet and information found at the scene identified the victim, rather than fingerprints or dental matching. The implication was clear. It wasn't possible to identify the victim from fingerprints and dental records. The result of DNA testing was still awaiting finalisation. The Spanish police took a sample of the victim's hair from his home to match with the body.

Frik read some more and was about to move onto another case when he scrolled back to Oxana Karpov. Why was her name ringing a bell in his memory? Frik knew it was the family name of a famous Russian chess grandmaster, but something else was bothering him about the name. He heard or read it some place before and recently.

Frik closed the file and returned to the main search page of his computer and entered the name Oxana Karpov. From his experience, he knew that this type of search would be very slow. He could not offer more parameters to narrow down the search for the computers. Plus, he knew this was a Russian lady, so the computer indexing based on passport or citizenship would not speed up the results. If it was an EU citizen, he could put in their nationality and the search would speed up dramatically.

Resigned to waiting, he stood up from his desk to fetch a coffee. With luck, there might be some nice cakes in the canteen. It surprised him to hear his computer ping. The ping meant a match occurred, and the details returned to his screen. He sat down again and opened the file.

The report highlighted where he read the name before. The police in Lithuania interviewed Oxana Karpov, a Russian from Moscow, about the decomposing body of a beggar found there. She was not a suspect, but they found the victim close to a hotel where she was staying. The police interviewed Oxana and dozens of other guests of the hotel. They tried to find someone who interacted with the beggar in the previous day. She was not a suspect and she stated she did not notice the beggar as she went about her shopping trip to Vilnius.

Like most of the other hotel residents, they walked past him or simply ignored him. The police found no reason to ask any more questions of her.

Frik sat back and his years of police work were telling him this was too much of a coincidence. There were two rapidly decomposing bodies in two cities in Europe, and the same Russian lady was near both. Frik knew the chance of such a coincidence happening for legitimate reasons was very low.

Frik picked up the phone and called Henri. He didn't waste any time in idle chitchat. "Henri, I am going to Seville. I think there is something off about the dead body there."

Henri laughed, "ok Frik, I know you just want to get some sunshine. I hope I do not see your face on the TV when Seville FC plays against Bayern München at the weekend. If I do, I will refuse to pay your expenses!"

"No seriously Henri, there is something up. I found the name of a lady who stayed in a hotel in Vilnius close to another victim. This same lady is in Seville as well. Both victims displayed rapid decomposition after death. That is too much of a coincidence for this police officer. I will have to investigate."

"Ok, I will send the information to the Spanish police you are on the way. Send me the name of the investigating officer so I can inform him, and he will add you to their team. Remember, you are a consultant advisor. Do not step on the toes of the locals."

Frik quickly typed a message to Inspector Cristiano in the chat section of the shared folder. *Good morning, Inspector. Liaison officer Frik here. I am part of the Europol terrorist investigation team. Thank you for your update about the Enrico killing. I have information which will help you. I am flying down as soon as possible. My boss will send my paperwork to you today as well. Please put a watch on Oxana Karpov. She has appeared on our records here in a similar case.*

Frik pressed send on this somewhat cryptic message and planned for his earliest departure to Seville.

CHAPTER 18: OXANA
BACK IN RUSSIA

Oxana walked into the shabby international arrivals lounge in Moscow Airport. She noticed the state of disrepair of the lights, walls, and floors. Some things never change, she thought. It was still a large, bright, and airy space designed by international architects. But a level of decrepitude had descended on it. These were only further highlighted by bits being modernised. There was more high coloured plastic on some signs over the shops than on the original shop fronts. Shiny plastic was the new architecture. In places, there was modern LED lighting. These made the other lights and signs look even more dated and old-fashioned. She noticed more signs were in Chinese than she remembered.

The airport and its fittings did not wear the glitz and glamour of other capital city airports. As she travelled, many airports were more like ultra luxurious shopping centres than a hub for planes and travel. In the modern airports it was easier to find a shop selling luxury watches than to find the gate to board the plane. The airport in Moscow would soon be described as drab.

At least here there was no queue in check-in or security. Only a few flights landed daily from Europe since the special military operation in Ukraine. She went through the airport quickly. She presented her Russian passport to the non-smiling immigration official, and the officer stamped it after a cursory glance.

The next step was to collect her baggage with the gifts she brought for her father. She hoped they survived baggage handlers. She always tried to bring chess books and new electronic gadgets to her father. But someone sometimes intercepted them en route. She routinely put a bottle of vodka into the bag in the hope it might satiate the needs of the baggage inspectors. Or at least sufficiently interest them so the rest of the contents passed though intact. It was a crude plan but realistic in a world where basic pay was not enough for hard working airport staff and baggage handlers to enjoy a middle-class life. They saw nothing wrong with augmenting their meagre wages with some visitor trinkets. She kept her fingers crossed in the hope some books might get through the strict censor as well.

The luggage carousels worked swiftly, and her bag was quickly dumped onto the floor by a porter. She trundled through the rest of the process and customs officers waved her through without stopping. Her bag felt lighter than when she packed it, so maybe their colleagues in crime inspected it already. Passing into the public side of the airport, she looked for her pickup driver.

The man holding the handwritten sign with her name on it was as cheerful as the immigration and custom police. He scowled when she nodded her head in his direction and turned on his heel for the exit door. She pulled a large bag which left Dublin far heavier; she suspected her vodka bottle had been removed. The bag felt heavy again as he hurried to the secure section of the cars in the pickup space. She struggled to keep up with him as her bag bounced through the cracks and over the steps. The small wheels would not survive this treatment for long, she thought. There was no chance of finding a trolly as the driver was setting a ferocious pace as he marched towards the car. As she walked, Oxana frowned, as she could plainly see the building could do with a bit of love and attention. The direction signs were all out of kilter, and the smoking areas were full of cigarette butts. Waste bins showed heavy black marks where fire raged in them. Either there were no cleaning crews or no one to make them do their job. She hated dirt.

Despite the heavy load, broken paths, and rapid walking pace, she felt her pulse rising at the thought of meeting her father again. It was nearly a year since she last saw him. The occasional

Skype call since then did not replace being beside someone and being able to see them breathe as they spoke. The last years of Covid restrictions taught her that contact, one on one and face-to-face contact was important for the human psyche. To hear and see the entire person with all their body language signals was most fulfilling. The head and shoulders shot of people on screens simply did not replace direct contact.

Her driver led her to a huge BMW jeep, bypassing a long line of Ladas and Hyundai cars. Gregor's business must be doing well financially. It was quite a recent model, with modern colour and finishes. Like most Russians, Oxana possessed a keen eye for cars and types. The type of car, its age and condition were quite a status symbol for the Russian people. Taxi-drivers waved as he walked past, hoping to score a fare. He shouted at the driver to pop open the back door and then opened the rear passenger door for her. As she struggled to lift her bag, he pulled an unhappy face, picked it up, threw it into the jeep, and with a stern, 'quickly'. He slammed the back door as soon as she was in and jumped into the front seat.

They spent the next 20 minutes driving like a car on a racetrack, as he told the driver to go faster and weave in and out of the traffic. He was like a man possessed by a demon or a longing to check out the effectiveness of the air bags in the car. Oxana held on and could hear her bag sliding from side to side in the back as the driver swerved and steered around cars left and right.

The car finally cleared the heavy traffic and climbed the hill to the leafy area where the dachas of the politicians, the rich, and the crooked, lined the roads. There was no sign of dilapidation here with the roads newly tarred and lines painted. The local state services retrofitted most of the streetlights with modern LED heads. More of the entrance ways were ordained with electronic gates rather than the old-style security man with a dog sitting in a square hut with a heater and pointy roof. She wondered if the availability of men to do these jobs was falling. Certainly, with wars and emigration, the international bodies suggested finding a young man to sit in a hut all day and do practically nothing as a career was becoming increasingly difficult. But it was the way of the entire world. Everyone wanted to make a difference, she thought.

The road stopped climbing and passed over a pretty bridge with a gentle river underneath. Just after the bridge, the car turned into the drive of the dacha where her father lived. The original Soviet-era owners built it as a summer house for their reward as good and loyal officials of the Communist party. Gregor bought or obtained it, probably through nefarious means, several years ago. They made various improvements to allow year-round use. This was becoming common in the dacha belt around Moscow. They now occupy the original summer houses every month of the year, including the bitterly cold winter months. Standing on one thousand square meters, green spaces surrounded the house with trees and shrubbery. A small brook babbled along at the bottom of the plot.

The tradition of dacha owners was one where they came out to the houses from the city for the summer. They planted and grew their own vegetables on the plot and enjoyed the cool and natural atmosphere. These practices long since stopped for the wealthy owners and they concentrated more on low ornamental shrubbery and hedging to create a pleasant atmosphere, but also to allow good security in case of attempted kidnapping or robbery. Many owners clipped and tidied their plots to within an inch of their life to supply picture perfect images for family and friends as they enjoyed summer events and barbeques.

After the electronic gates swung open, Oxana spotted several cameras at car height as they drove up the avenue to the house. Fixed notices declaring danger from high-voltage electric fences were visible along the drive from the gate to the front door. Just before the house, a heavily armed guard on patrol with an Alsatian checked the car as they approached the inner gardens. The heavy and muscular build of the man seemed out of place for a quiet countryside dacha.

What was he protecting—Oxana wondered? Why such heavy

security? Was Gregor keeping people in or out? Oxana doubted if the cause of this visible, heavy security was her old father. She felt uncomfortable at the idea this was her father's forever home. It seemed to be more like a prison.

She saw her dad out on the terrace in a wheelchair with a blanket over his legs. He looked terrible. His face was pale, and he looked older than his 70 years. His face was unshaven, with scraggy white hair thinning from the back. He smiled when he saw her and raised a hand to wave. Why was he in a wheelchair? She panicked, jumped out of the car and ran up to him. Throwing her arms around him, she started crying. "What happened, Nana, why are you in a wheelchair, is anything broken, are you ok?" A flurry of questions tumbled from her as she looked him up and down, touching his arms and hands and face checking they were all intact and not covered in layers of plaster or strapping.

"I am fine, simply fine. I had a silly fall the other day, nothing to worry about. I just tripped on a step. I wasn't watching where I was going. It takes longer to recover at my age. Do not stress yourself, Dochka, I will be fine in a day or so. Let me look at you! As gorgeous as ever and looking as young as a twenty-year-old. How do you do it? It is so great to see you! Are you travelling alone?" he asked as he looked back towards the car.

"Yes Nana, I am all alone and before you ask—there is no man, Nana, no man is good enough for me! You trained me to be too fussy. They must live up to your high standards. Come! Let us go inside. You look cold. Is the heating on?"

"Yes, yes, it is as warm as toast. Come in, come in. We can have a small drop of schnaps to take the chill out of our bones. I have tea and some delicious smoked fish as well. I know you like that!"

"Gorgeous, but no alcohol for me today. It is too early, and I must meet Gregor and the others later. But let's have tea and yes, I love smoked fish. I bet there are some pickles about too. I miss this food in Europe. They eat so much garbage there now. Chips with everything. Even with pizza. I must get you, my gifts. They are in the bag in the car. I've some new chess books and some gadgets."

Oxana went outside. The car was still there with the back door opened. Her bag lay inside. She looked around for someone to help her. There are no gentlemen around here, she thought as she hauled the heavy bag out and across the gravel to the steps and up the front door. She made a note to compliment Gregor on the quality of his welcome when they met later that day.

CHAPTER 19: IRISH DIPLOMATS GET INVOLVED

Colin Delaney listened to his immediate superior, the second secretary, as he detailed his tasks for today. Colin was not too fond of the boss, nor of the work he did in the Irish embassy in Madrid. He spent most of his days talking to silly people who lost passports in swimming pools or had their wallets stolen when they fell asleep on the outdoor patio after too many happy hour cocktails. It was not the life he expected when he signed up to work in the Department of Foreign Affairs. He believed his work would involve high diplomacy and helping to prevent famine and war. The reality of organising coffee breaks for trade delegations and emergency passports was far more mundane.

Still, as he listened, he thought this new task sounded interesting. There was an Irish Professor from Trinity college under arrest in Seville. They were investigating her for suspected murder. The second secretary asked him to travel there to meet her and to collect information and to see if there was anything to be done. He was to stay until they formally charged her or released her. The Irish diplomats knew the arrest would be on the front page of the newspapers back home and they needed to issue the standard response—*the Irish embassy is aware of the situation and is providing diplomatic support to our citizen.*

He heard this type of statement on the radio during the morning news in his early life, and thought it implied a heavyweight response. He imagined an entire army of diplomats leaping into action. It disappointed him to learn it was just him, and he was to go by economy train, and he was to keep all receipts and be sure not to offend the police.

He was to bring their standard embassy goodie bag, comprising crisps, some crackers and cheese, a few stamps, writing paper and a pen from the embassy. His job, and his boss repeated this over and over; was to ensure the lady in question was given a lawyer and a translator. He was to remain there until he was certain the authorities would charge or release her before the three-day deadline permitted under Spanish law.

He remembered the parting words of the second secretary, "you want to be a diplomat, this is your first real chance. Do not mess it up. If the Spanish police think this woman killed someone, then she probably did. They are fantastic at their work, and very thorough. Give her the goodie box, ask her if we can call anyone for her, check she has her professionals appointed, wait, and see if they charge or release her, and then get back here. If you do any more than that, you will issue replacement passports to hungover tourists for the rest of your career. Do not talk to the media and ring me every day at noon. Keep your expenses down."

His boss reminded him, "Money does not grow on trees, watch every penny."

Colin headed back to his flat to pack a small bag and get on the next train to Seville.

CHAPTER 20: FRIK ARRIVES IN SEVILLE

Frik was pleased to see the uniformed police officer with his name on a screen waiting for him as he came out of Santa Justa train station in Seville. The last time he was here, he needed to find a bus and ended up going in the exact opposite direction to where he wished to go. Having a police car and driver would facilitate speedy travel.

The man greeting him, however, spoke no German and Frik spoke little to no Spanish. English was the common language of the officers in Europol so the 15-minute drive to the police station was relatively quiet. This officer spoke surprisingly poor English. They did not use the siren as this was not an emergency.

Frik remembered some streets from his recent holiday there. He loved the city with its ring road, the river trail, the old fortress, and the new enterprise area across the river. The city planners installed bike lanes on all the important streets. The city was a pleasure to tour. The sun was, as usual, shining nicely and he relaxed in the passenger seat and gathered his thoughts. He observed the crowded streets and the gesticulations of the people, which gave an impression of anger and hostility, though it was just the Spanish way of talking and sharing gossip.

Outside the police station, the car stopped, and the driver indicated Frik should get his bag and go into the building. Frik went up the steps and into reception. The receptionist rang another officer who came out to meet him and in broken English told him he would lead him to the Inspector in room 12.

They marched down a long dark corridor with Frik in the rear. Frik loved the sound and smell of police stations. The air of expectancy hung heavy like a fog on a lake. There was always a tension and at any moment he expected a door to burst open and officers gallop to a crime scene. The doors remained closed, but there was a bustle when you walked by a larger room where a few officers shared desks, phones, and banter.

The door to room 12 opened, and he entered to find an immaculately dressed inspector. He stood up. "Welcome Agent Frik, to our humble station here in Seville. I hope your trip was pleasant?"

Frik heard of the Spanish style among formally trained and career police officers and suddenly regretted his informal attire of jeans and a polo shirt. But he had important work to do. He needed this man's help to catch a murderer.

"Thank you, Inspector Cristiano. I recently was in your lovely city on vacation. I passed a very pleasant and safe week here in the old town. I assume they have sent my Europol papers to you and you know my role here?"

"We are always pleased to welcome tourists from Germany and other countries. The role of Europol is not new to me, although I have not worked directly with an agent such as yourself. I hope my English is good enough for our meeting. Should I get an interpreter?"

"No inspector, so far it is fine."

"Agent Frik, a small administration matter. As police officers here, we have strict rules about firearms. You came from the German police force originally, which is an armed service. May I ask you formally if you are carrying a firearm?"

"No Cristiano, if I may call you that? We do not. As Europol agents, we carry information, and good computers with access to many databases and data analysts. We look for connections and for similarities in events to see if we can find threads. These threads can lead us to help you prevent crimes or to solve crimes. We do not feel the need to use firearms to do our work. Most of our work takes place in meetings like this with senior officers like yourself."

"And what are you doing here? Solving or preventing?"

Frik looked at the inspector. He was clearly highly intelligent and was asking questions that were unexpected. It was almost as if he was trying to identify what was going to happen next and then be ready for it.

"No Inspector, I am not sure, I think solving, but perhaps also preventing another crime. The solving of one crime is never the end. Perhaps when you see what I have brought, you can decide. We in Europol never impede a local investigation. That is your prerogative. We just bring information and data we think, and we are sometimes wrong, might help you solve your case or prevent other similar cases from happening. My work is in the bioterrorism area. So that differs from what you might expect of a traditional ultra-national agency. We forecast many state actors and heavyweight gangs will use bioterrorism as part of their ways and means to commit crime and enrich themselves in the future."

"Bioterrorism, eh? That sounds quite ominous. Let us see what you have. I will ask a couple of my colleagues to join us. The more heads looking at new information, the better."

With that, Frik set about connecting his laptop into the overhead projector. He prepared a couple of slides on the plane and included a CCTV video to show the police here. He was clear about what he hoped would happen, but he needed the local police to decide the next steps, and he hoped they reached the same conclusion.

Two immaculately dressed officers came into the room. Their uniforms fitted them perfectly, as if tailored. They carried their police hats smartly under their arms. Frik could see the effect Cristiano made on his team as they emulated him in their dress and self-presentation. Frik's confidence grew and he was certain he could work and work well with this team.

"These are two members of the investigation team, Officer Angela, and Officer Jhon. This is agent Frik from Europol. He has rushed down here to solve the murder of Ricardo using his laptop and some databases."

Frik looked surprised at this unexpected note of sarcasm from

Cristiano. But he pressed on, shook hands with the officers, and presented the slides on the screen.

"I will try to be as efficient as possible; I am German after all. I want to show you some information about a murder in Vilnius in Lithuania about two months ago."

Frik explained the slides one by one. "This is an area outside a church in Vilnius. You can see a beggar man on a sleeping blanket, well wrapped in army style clothing and with some sort of woollen blanket around him. They killed this person on a snowy night. I should add the detail that begging is illegal in Vilnius. The only begging that is allowed is around churches. That is why the police did not take him away earlier in the night. He was in the geographic protection of the church. When the mayor tried to outlaw begging, the citizens forced him to change the law to recognise the long-established tradition of giving alms around churches and religious buildings."

The pictures showed a wide angled view of an old church with a few people passing by. The area was reasonably bright, and there was a cup in front of the man.

"CCTV took these pictures about an hour before the murder. They are from the camera located at the front door of the church. The next 5 pictures will show a lady giving the beggar a hot chocolate drink. He smiled and enjoyed it. It was, as I have said, a bitterly cold night in Vilnius. She was a resident of the hotel you see in the background."

"The next picture shows the man slumped into his blanket. It looks like he may have fallen asleep. This is about ten minutes after he received the chocolate."

"This next picture is more interesting as we see a lady again approaching him. We think it is the same person who gave the beggar the hot chocolate. This time however she is wearing a different scarf and hat. She is careful to keep her face down, but she moves the blanket off his hands and face and takes pictures with her phone. The chocolate cup is on the ground on its side, but it is now empty. You can see she takes a note out of his cup. It looks like a ten euro note. She was not only keen to kill him, but to rob him, as well. It all happens in a few seconds and then she is gone."

"The next picture shows the crime scene when the local police got involved. It was the next morning, about 10:00, when the social workers check on the known rough sleepers. They bring food and warm blankets and try to get the beggars to move into a hostel. They found our beggar friend or what was left of him. He was disintegrating into a pile of dust. His name was Ahkmed Pooliopis. At one stage he was part of the British secret service, but personal addiction problems developed. As you can see he is now dead."

"In Vilnius, the death of a beggar is sad, but not unusual. The police would not respond quickly, and they would only appoint a small team to investigate the death. However, the speed of decomposition of the body was a surprise. The officers on the scene were certain he was dead for days. When the post-mortem was done, and the police assembled these CCTV pictures, they realised it was a murder and whatever the weapon; it led to rapid decomposition of the body."

"The team got some extra resources, and they filed and uploaded this and a series of videos to Europol. When our AI and then our analysts looked at it, the computer picked up the rapid decomposition and matched it to your case here with Enrico. This similarity in rapid decomposition of a body shortly after death was a key unique aspect. This is what we do in Europol. We find connections and threads which may not be obvious."

There was silence in the room as they all absorbed the information Frik presented. Jhon spoke first. "The lady with the hot chocolate. You seem to think she was involved?"

Frik acknowledged the officer's question and said, "Yes, we do. The computers give it a probability of eighty percent. It is extremely likely the lady who is taking the pictures is the same as the lady who gave hot chocolate to the beggar. There are approximately fifteen minutes between the incidents, and the pictures are not great, but let me show you the image of her face. The local police checked other cameras in the area and uploaded the images."

Frik clicked forward one more slide. A grainy picture of a youngish-looking lady in a wide-brimmed hat appeared. Her face was long, with shadows showing high cheekbones. She seemed heavily made up with her lips and eyes highly differentiated with lip pen and mascara.

"That is the best enhancement we can make. It is from a camera further down the street from the church. The camera in the church porch took the earlier images. The time stamp and the clothes are correct for the woman taking the pictures of the corpse. It matches the time it would take to walk to there after taking the pictures. When we found this image, the computer increased the likelihood of a match from forty to eighty percent, as I mentioned. It satisfied us it was her as she walked away from her victim."

Cristiano cleared his throat and said, "the woman could be Oxana Karpov."

"Really, Do you think so? That is why I flew down here." Frik asked.

Cristiano turned to Jhon and in rapid Spanish said, "call the hotel immediately and see if Oxana Karpov is still there. If she is there, then send a car to the hotel and pick her up. If not, find out when she left and call security in the airport to see if she has left. If not, get them to hold her. The hotel will have her passport details. Get them and send them to immigration. Maybe we will get lucky."

Frik waited until Cristiano finished. "Ok, what's happening now, please?"

Cristiano turned back to Frik and said, "I think your photo is a Russian lady who came here to be interviewed for a job by our primary suspect, Dr Harriet. The corpse was in the room of Dr Harriet. The victim, Enrico, had a business card and room number for Dr Harriet in his shirt pocket."

"I spoke to Oxana for several minutes as she was to meet Harriet for breakfast. She spent quite some time with her on the day of the murder."

It was Frik's turn to be quiet as he absorbed this. Then he disconnected his laptop from the overhead projector, switched windows on the screen, and typed rapidly. He spoke aloud as he did. "Oxana Karpov, Russian. I will see if she has passed through European immigration yet."

The screen reloaded after he hit the enter key. In a few seconds, the screen filled with a selection of passports of people who matched the name. Frik selected filters for Russian and for recent arrivals to Seville. The screen returned a thumbnail of one folder on the screen, and he clicked it. Several images and columns showing dates and times through airports around the world filled the screen. The last entry said it all.

Frik turned the computer to Cristiano- "We are too late. Look, you can see here. She passed through immigration in Seville late last night. She is on the passenger manifest for a connecting flight, leaving Serbia for Moscow. She is bound to be in Russia by now. She has escaped. Your confirmation of her identity is the breakthrough we needed."

CHAPTER 21: OXANA GETS A NEW MISSION

Gregor summoned Oxana to meet him in his office. She had to comply. She enjoyed her time with her father, but she knew far more important things would have to be done. They were taking care of him, but he was really their prisoner. For the moment, there was nothing she could do. Gregor and his henchmen put her in an impossible situation. She must do as they wished, or they would simply put her father out on the street, or worse, kill him.

She shuddered as she imagined him with no home and no sense of pride. She gritted her teeth and once again promised herself to try as hard as she could to find a way out of this mess.

Gregor looked up eventually from the screen. "Ah Oxana, how wonderful to see you here in your home country. How is your father? I hope you enjoyed your visit. As you can see, we are looking after him very well. After he fell, we paid for therapists for him, and we bought him the best of the best wheelchairs so he could move about. It is important for our fathers to have their independence, no?"

"He is fine, Gregor, but we both know he is not independent. He is a prisoner here. He cannot escape. If I do as you ask, then he will stay here, otherwise I expect you will throw him out on the street."

"Oh, Oxana, you must think we are cruel and heartless. We like your father. It is of great prestige to us to have a former world champion grandmaster in our care. His picture is always a popular part of our corporate sales brochures. Our marketing team like to have him involved as part of our corporate social responsibilities. Our customers love the fact we have adopted him. You know how hard we work to help the elderly."

"Yes Gregor, if you were in Europe or America, they would make you a saint. Regarding the elderly, how are you getting on with developing the anti-ageing treatment? I am taking tablets every day for two years now and it is a pain. They give me indigestion. Have you found a new delivery method?"

"Oxana, youthfulness suits you! Does the entire world not tell you that you look twenty years younger? It is working. Yes, there is the inconvenience of daily tablets, but so far there are no major side effects. Our laboratory did amazing work. We have named it 'Rattler'. What do you think?"

"Rattler?" asked Oxana. "Why on earth? That is a snake. Is it snake oil or some sort of reference to poison? I think it is a terrible name."

"Good, I am pleased to hear you don't like it. Your specialities are not in naming products but in applying them. We have tested it in focus groups, and it is easy to remember. It is easy to say. Marketing think it will become a coffee hour topic of conversation—'where do you get your Rattler?' 'I think Rattler is the best beauty product since face masks'—and so on and so on."

"The name Rattler, of course, is from the idea of the Garden of Eden where there was perpetual life until a snake intervened. We want to use the snake image to show we have mastered what the snake did to us then. It's a delightful story, isn't it?"

"No, it's daft. It makes no sense to me," Oxana said.

"Anyway, Rattler is to be offered for pre-order in the next few weeks to the rich and famous as a treatment to reverse their ageing. Who wants to look at old rich people? No-one. We have changed the delivery system. You are a significant help to us there. We listen to you. We developed a patch you put on your skin for three days every month. We call it The Rattler patch. Isn't it funny?"

Oxana looked at Gregor as a snake looks at a rodent before eating it.

"We have improved the methods of production in the factory,

as well. As a result, we can make more product faster. These bio-engineered products are hard to produce. The biochemistry is quite tricky. But now, we are specialists in the field. Thanks to human test subjects like you, we are years ahead of the rest of the world."

"So, you want me to test this new patch? I am out of tablets, and I see my skin is already showing wrinkles around my eyes. I am using more makeup than ever."

"I solve your problems, dear Oxana." Gregor reached into his drawer and pulled out a small snakeskin box about the size of a cigarette packet. "Here you are, the first ready to go version of Rattler. Simply put one patch on your arm or thigh or stomach for three days each month and hey presto, you will be wrinkle free. We guarantee you will look twenty to thirty years younger within a month."

His two henchmen came into the room then and took a seat. They both lit foul smelling cigarettes and stared at Oxana like she was a piece of meat they could BBQ and eat bone by bone. They opened the vodka bottle standing on the table and poured each other a shot.

"Ah, good morning, gentlemen. Perfect timing. Oxana and I have finished our earlier business and now we can get onto the next step in our campaign to make rather a lot of money. Our product, M278, is field tested successfully now thanks to the work of Oxana in Seville and earlier in Vilnius. We have a rich State actor prepared to buy ten of the treatments. They have rather an embarrassing mess in an illegal prison camp in Cuba. They think our product will help them tidy their mess up rather nicely."

Oxana paled as she watched the men pour vodka and drink toasts to each other. It was all about money in the end. They were just ruthless criminals dressed up in fancy suits, living in dachas, driving nice cars, and making charitable contributions. She wished and wished she could find some way to break free of their clutches. But it always came back to her father. Plus, now the anti-ageing Rattler treatment. Only thugs like these would call it such a name.

Gregor put down his now empty glass for a refill. "So, Oxana, agents of our client have a problem, and we are going to help them. In exchange, we are going to be extraordinarily rich. We will move your father to a nicer place, and he will have a full-time assistant to help him with dressing, eating, walking. He may even have time to write his memoirs! I might hire a ghost writer for him. We will have to veto any comments we dislike and hold copyright, of course. But won't that be fantastic?"

"Yes, it will, but there is always a but with you, Gregor. What is it this time?"

"Nothing too complicated, Oxana, just a small trip to America. They want a demonstration of M278 on their own soil, so to speak. They have seen your work in Europe, but they are fussy. They want to see how their own police force reacts and how the FBI investigates after the M278 does its work. I am not too worried. They are paying a twenty million euros down payment on the work, and several million for each of ten more treatments. An invisible fatal bio-poison, disappearing bodies, and invisible agents is worth a great deal of money. Who knew?" Gregor and his two friends clinked glasses and laughed.

Oxana sat back in a mixture of horror and bemusement. She was wrong about them. Greed was too small a word for them. Now, they were beyond greedy. She watched as they emptied the vodka bottle.

"Can my father get the extra help now? He is in a wheelchair and is struggling to get dressed. Surely you can do that for him?"

"It all takes time, but I promise you," Gregor smirked, "once you are safely back from America, he will get the extra help."

"But first," Gregor continued, "we need to set it up. They need to transfer the money and name their target and how you are to deliver the treatment. We wait for them. You can stay here with your father until then and enjoy your new Rattler skin!"

Oxana listened as they laughed. She got up and walked out the door. There must be another solution to this mess she thought.

CHAPTER 22: FRIK, HARRIET, CRISTIANO, COLIN

The phone rang on Cristiano's desk. Frik paused mid-sentence and indicated he could answer it. They were getting to know each other better and, as part of Frik's training, they were always told to make sure they got on well with the local police force.

Cristiano listened and hung up after saying goodbye.

"There is a person here from the Irish Embassy. His name is Colin. He wants to see Harriet."

"That was to be expected," commented Jhon, "Will I find her lawyer and set up a meeting room?"

"Yes, please." Cristiano replied. Turning to Frik, he asked, "What should we do now? What are the next steps?"

The question pleased Frik. He felt Cristiano trusted him. He hoped his response could lead to a major break in the case.

He said, "Ok, thank you for asking. I know you want to solve the local crime. It is terrible someone murdered a citizen. Europol want to help with this. We also want to help solve the crime in Vilnius in Lithuania. So, my answer will address that matter as well. I would like Harriet to be released today, in fact, now. But I would like her to agree to proceed and hire Oxana. We have her in the same place at the same time as two murders. We do not have any hard evidence she did it, though. It is better for us if she is in Europe. We cannot arrest her in Russia. We need her back here. If she is working in Dublin, we can keep a close eye on her as we gather more evidence."

Silence greeted this plan. The two other Spanish police officers coughed and swayed from foot to foot. Angela spoke up, "That is good for Europol, but we have not solved our murder. It stays here as an open crime. We dislike failure in this police force. We pride ourselves on our ability to solve crimes."

Angela continued, "I understand what you want, but try to see what we want. Plus, maybe she is a psychopath? Do we want to bring her back here to kill more Europeans? Let her stay there in Russia, she can kill whoever she wants there! Why don't we just prevent her from coming to Europe ever again?"

Frik looked carefully at Angela, "yes, you are correct, we all want to solve the murder. But at the moment, there is no evidence."

Cristiano spoke, "We do not even have her fingerprints to prove she was in room 204 here. We will find the evidence in the coming days. Working with our colleagues in Europol and Lithuania, we will catch her. There is always a trace left behind. We need time and patience. As long as she is in Russia, we can never arrest her. I think Frik has a good plan. It is not perfect, but it solves some problems for us all."

Frik spoke again, "If we just block her access to Europe, then the deaths remain unpunished. She could just change her name and come in on a new passport and visa. If she stays in Russia, Enrico will never have justice. But if we have evidence and she returns to Europe with the same passport, then we know where she is, we can arrest her, fingerprint her and check against the crime scenes."

Cristiano stood up and paced. "This is a good plan, but it is slow. There are many ifs, buts, and maybes to it. But we have no choice at the moment. We need to get this Oxana woman in for questioning. She seems to be involved. But the poor CCTV picture in Vilnius and the lack of any evidence here is a big problem. She may not be the murderer. I agree with you Frik, let us at least get her into Europe where we can arrest her when we have more evidence. In Russia, she is out of our contact."

Officer Jhon stuck his head around the door. "I have found her lawyer, plus I asked the wardens to get Harriet dressed and up here. She will be ready in ten minutes. We will be in room eight."

"Thank you", Cristiano said. Turning to Frik, he said, "there is one weakness in your plan. Perhaps Oxana won't come to Ireland now. Perhaps Harriet will not ask her. Maybe she has decided not to go ahead with the appointment?"

"Yes, you are right. That is a risk. I think we might use our embassy person to aid us. Can we talk to him now?"

Cristiano pressed a button on the phone and, speaking in rapid Spanish, he gave instructions to whoever was on the other end. Cristiano impressed Frik with his decision making and clear style of command. What was most impressive was all the officers in the station seemed to like and respect him. Seville police were lucky to have such a high-quality officer on their side. Europol was always looking out for new people, too.

Harriet heard the keys rattle in the door as a warden unlocked it. Another female warden came through carrying all her civilian clothes and a new clean set of prison underwear. "Here, put these on. You are going upstairs for an interview again. Quick now!"

This interruption puzzled Harriet. Why did they want her to get dressed in her own clothes? Why the sudden interview? She thought she would not hear from anyone until the 72 hours were up and they would charge her. The police inspector seemed convinced of her guilt. She turned her back on the watching police officer and changed into the clean underwear and her civilian clothes.

Police officer Jhon, surprised Luz Maria, Harriet's lawyer, when he asked her to go to Inspector Cristianos' room. There must be developments in the investigation, she thought. She knocked on the closed door and opened it when she heard, "Come in."

"Ah Luz Maria, this is Frik, from Europol. He has helped us with our investigations into the murder of Enrico. Your client, Harriet, will join us for this meeting in a few minutes. I am glad you are still here. We were afraid you may have left for the day. Before that, a member of the Irish diplomatic team from Madrid will join us. He has come over to meet with Harriet, who is an Irish citizen."

"Thank you, yes, it is lucky I am still here. I am pleased to meet you," she finished as she shook hands with Frik. Europol, she thought, here in Seville, so fast, helping with a murder investigation. It is getting stranger and stranger, she thought to herself.

Colin was sweating profusely in the waiting room of the police station. The train from Madrid was easy, with wonderful air conditioning and a nice café. But after Santa Justa station he was on public busses and in the heat of the city. At the station, they took his details, and he was still sitting in the smelly, sweaty waiting room with all kinds of civilians. He was considering making a complaint when a lady police officer approached and beckoned him to follow her.

She knocked on the door and gestured for Colin to enter after they answered it with, "Come in." Two men and two ladies were inside. A fine tall man in an impeccable uniform came forward and shook his hand. "Ah, you are Colin from the Irish embassy, so sorry for the delay. I was gathering a few people to meet you." Cristiano quickly introduced the lawyer Luz Maria, Frik from Europol, and police officer Angela. Colin tried using the memory trick of putting each person into a room and associating their name with something in the room. As he did so, he handed out his official business card with the embossed gold harp in the top left corner. The harp featured on all Irish Government and state documents.

"It is a pleasure to meet you", Colin said, "but I am here to see an Irish citizen, Harriet Fischer. I must report back to the ambassador directly on the situation and when she is to be released." He blushed as he said this, as it was pushing the matter more than his instruction from his boss dictated. Cristiano did not miss it, "well as you know the police have arrested her and the charges are murder. So, we will follow Spanish law, and not the desires of the Irish embassy in this matter. But you will see her shortly. That is being arranged as we speak."

Frik stepped in to speak. He sensed the Irish man was quite inexperienced and could cause an un-needed row with an excellent police officer. "Yes, Mr. Colin, everything is being done to the best of the ability of the police force here in Seville. As you can see, Harriet has a lawyer appointed, and Luz is with her at every interview, including this upcoming one."

Colin realised he over spoke, "of course, of course, I did not mean to imply anything. If she has committed a crime, then yes, we will always support the Spanish police. I mis-spoke, sorry. It is just I came here to see Harriet and instead I have a committee meeting." Cristiano gave the junior diplomat a break, put a friendly note into his voice, and declared, "following our investigations and with Europol's help, Harriet is to be released without charge in the next hour or two. We have a few more minor questions of a tidying up loose ends nature to ask her. Then we expect to release her. We have sent for her, and she is presently preparing to join us in Room 8 where we will inform her formally of this. You are all welcome to join us if you wish. But please act as observers and say nothing to Harriet until I finish my questions."

Luz Maria gave a silent "yes," under her breath. Colin said, "thank you, this is wonderful news. It will please the ambassador to hear this news."

The door opened and a police officer entered and said, "we are ready in Room 8 whenever you are."

Cristiano said, "you are all welcome to join, please follow this officer. He will lead the way. After you." He pointed with a sweep of his arm to Luz Maria and then Colin and then Frik. They all trooped out into the heat of the hallway, each with their silent thoughts, and up one flight of stairs to Room 8.

The police officer, Jhon, knocked and opened the door. Seated and handcuffed to the central bar of a steel table in the middle of the room was Harriet. A lady police officer stood silently inside the door. Harriet, despite being dressed in her own clothes, looked terrible. Her hair was unbrushed, and she wore no makeup. There were large bags under her eyes, and the sag of her chin showed she had not slept. She had spent some time crying. Her red, bloodshot, puffy eyes looked at them one by one as they entered.

When Cristiano saw Harriet's handcuffs, he growled in Spanish at the police lady who jumped and opened them at once. "It is my turn to apologise. It is protocol to have every prisoner secured. I should have asked for the order to be overridden when I gave orders for Harriet to be brought here." He went to a table in the room's corner and took a packet of wet wipes to Harriet. She used them to wipe her hands and her eyes.

As he handed them to her, she noticed again what a fine specimen of a man he was. She could smell his cologne as he placed the box in front of her and she could see a line of muscles under his shirt with some colourful tattoos.

Inspector Cristiano introduced everyone again to Harriet, emphasising Colin was from the Irish Embassy in Madrid. She seemed grateful for all the attention. She sensed something changed, and she looked carefully at Frik when Cristiano said he was with Europol. What was he doing here and was it something Europol was interested in?

"So, Harriet," began Cristiano, "I have a couple of questions. Where did you meet Oxana on the morning of the conference?"

"I don't know exactly. It was at a café she suggested. If I could see my phone, I could look it up. I used Google maps to get to it, so it will be in my history. She sent me an email suggesting it. Something like Café Sailor, or Café Sola. I am not good with names, especially when I do not think I need to remember them."

"You say Oxana suggested it? That is interesting. When you were there, who served you?"

"I don't know," Harriet replied, "but Oxana was quite rude to him. She said his fingernails were dirty and she refused to drink the coffee he brought. She made a bit of a scene, to be honest. I found it embarrassing, but she was right, for a waiter, he was quite dirty."

"What happened then?"

"Nothing really. She was rude and became upset with the waiter. I stopped the interview and arranged it for another time. I knew she would be at the conference I was attending later that day. I felt she could not give a good interview there when she was so upset. I gave her my card so we could meet again. She could have emailed me as before, but a call is so much easier when you are trying to make an appointment. By coincidence, we were staying in the same hotel, and we walked back together after my keynote speech finished. But you already know that."

"So, you gave her your card and then went back to the hotel?"

"Yes, I forgot to pay as well. It was a strange, distressing first meeting. It was all a bit off-putting. I thought she was exceedingly difficult towards the waiter. But later she was charming. I was going to offer her a job—when the funding came in. We need a project manager for our research."

"And when is this funding due?"

"We don't know. Probably in the next few days, the conference went well. All the decision makers were there. We lodged the application paperwork with them. It should just be a rubber-stamping task, so I expect the news will come out in a few days."

"And will you offer Oxana a job, then?"

It extremely impressed Frik how Cristiano brought the subject around to the real purpose of the conversation. None of the others could suspect this was his plan from the start.

"Yes, she is the best qualified, and she is available. We had a lovely chat after my keynote address at the conference. I feel we can work well together and she will be an addition to the team in Dublin. I decided the rudeness with the waiter was an aberration caused by jet lag and stress."

"Ok, that is all I wanted to ask you. Thanks to the help of your legal team, the embassy and Europol, we are releasing you now immediately, and without charge. I am sure your lawyer and Colin here from the embassy will help you return to Ireland. We have brought your bags from the hotel; they are downstairs in the evidence room. You are free to go."

Cristiano stood up, and Harriet cried with emotion. She looked from one face to the other to make sure she heard him correctly. There were smiling faces all round. She was free to go. She grabbed another tissue and blew her nose. Cristiano and Frik stood up to go. Cristiano said, "the Spanish police thank you for your cooperation in helping us with this terrible crime against Enrico. We wish you the best and assure you that you are welcome to Seville and Spain anytime. I will leave you now with Luz Maria and Colin, who can help you."

Cristiano and Frik regrouped in his office. Frik spoke first, "that was very well done, thank you. We just have to hope the funding comes in soon. I will see if we can learn anything about it when I return to HQ. We need Harriet to offer the job to Oxana."

Cristiano nodded and said, "Please let me know when and if Oxana arrives in Dublin. I feel she slipped through my fingers, and I am not happy. I interviewed her in the hotel managers' office. She seemed extremely believable. If she killed Enrico and the beggar in Vilnius, then she's a cold-blooded killer."

"Do you know anything else about Enrico? What was his family history?

"No, we just know of an estranged wife and a daughter. Is there more?"

"We are not sure, but his grandfather defected from the Soviet Union back in the cold war days. He was an 'in-tourist' guide in Moscow, and he swapped places with a genuine Spanish tourist and escaped. It made quite some headlines back then as the Spanish citizen was stuck in USSR and the Spanish government did not want to return Enrico's grandfather to the Soviet authorities. It took years to resolve."

"It sounds like politics at an extreme level. You have extraordinary records in Europol!"

"It was, and yes, we do. It probably has nothing to do with this case, just some useless information in the Europol database. The AI algorithms join up all kinds of things. Sometimes useful, sometimes useless. Anyway, it was a real pleasure working with you. I will head back to Munich today. I am still officially on holidays. I look forward to meeting you again."

"And you," replied Cristiano, as his desk phone rang. He shook hands warmly and went to pick up the call. Frik closed the door quietly behind him and made his way back to Santa Justa train station.

CHAPTER 23: HARRIET BACK IN DUBLIN

Harriet took a deep breath as she put her hand on the well-worn lock to the laboratory doors in Trinity college Dublin. Safely back home, she thought, and time to put aside the unpleasantness of Seville. The last 24 hours were like a blur to her. After her release her from the cells in Seville, they took her to the embassy in Madrid for a de-brief with the Irish ambassador, and then brought her to the airport for a scheduled flight to Dublin.

As soon as she arrived home, she jumped into a long cleansing shower until all the hot water in her apartment ran cold. She happily put all her 'prison' clothes into waste bins. She knew these went to the city incinerator and that pleased her.

As she entered the lab, her team looked up and broke into spontaneous applause. She blushed a deep red. A few cheers of 'bravo' and 'well done' came from the girls on the team. They all crowded around her to shake her hand, hug her, and pat her on the back.

Harriet was not used to this closeness and moral support. The only daughter of a Church of Ireland minister in rural Ireland, her upbringing was sheltered and quiet. Her youth was a firmly settled series of formal events from Service on Sundays through the rigorously arranged social life of garden fetes, afternoon tea, church choir, bring and buy sales, jam making competitions, and school outings. There were expectations placed on her to be 'good' and to set an example for her community. As a student, she spent a great deal of time in her books and gravitated naturally to science subjects where the mysteries of life became her focus.

One habit from her childhood remained. She loved dolls. She stored a collection in her flat. She loved to pretend she was their teacher. They were all named and dressed for school. They were good dolls, like Harriet herself, and if they weren't she kept a cane ready for them.

Even as a young woman and student in Trinity, she shied away from rag weeks or loud social events. She was happiest when she was deep in study in the college's library. She loved to feel the sense of history of all the great achievers who went before.

This raucous greeting in her lab, was too much for her. The first time the sound dropped, she raised her hand and cleared her throat.

"Thank you. I feel like a prodigal son returning home after years away. You are all wonderful. I don't know what you heard, and I wish to put it behind me as soon as possible, but yes, they arrested and detained me in Seville. Yes, there was a man found dead in my room. His death has nothing to do with me. It was a horrible experience, but thankfully the truth came out. They released me without charge, and I am free to come and go as before."

Another cheer broke out from her team. The twenty students, researchers, also went through a tough time. From the highs after the keynote to the lows of WhatsApp messages about Harriet's arrest. It was a rollercoaster time for them all.

"I want to say we are in prime position to get the extension of funding for the next three years. The EU committee informed us by email this morning they are formally confirming the news next week when they complete all the pilot contracts and see the funding balances. In the meantime, I am going to work, and we are going to work as if it is all set, and they have granted the funding extension. We will be moving to our bigger larger lab in the next weeks also. So, there is a great deal to do and while I suffered a terrible day and night in Seville our work will not suffer and will move forward from here."

There was another loud cheer as all the team members contemplated new space, new funding, new opportunities and most important for academics and researchers a secure funding for three years.

"As part of that, when I was in Seville, apart from the keynote, I also met with a Russian lady. She is interested in joining us as our project manager and I have formally offered her this role. She has accepted and will join us as soon as they process and issue her European work visa. One of the good things from the horror of Seville is I now have a couple of great contacts in the Irish Embassy. They have promised to speed up the visa for Oxana, yes that is her name, Oxana Karpov. I expect she will join us in the next ten days."

Turning to her right-hand man on the team, she said, "I am sure, Jack, this news will be a great relief to you."

Jack smiled, and picking up a parcel of the lab desk, he handed it to Harriet. "Yes, it's great news. First here is a small welcome home gift from all of us," he said. "It's great to have you back."

Harriet blushed a deep red and took the soft package. Carefully pulling the wrapping open, she unfurled an orange tee-shirt. Holding it up, she rotated around the room with the words facing the others. They all cheered and finally she turned it around and read the words printed in bold and black on the front, *'I got out of prison- for this?'*. She read it out loud and laughed. They were such a warm, supportive team.

The mood in the room lightened. Harriet appreciated Jack. He could bring everyone together and take the focus off the individuals without affecting the group. That is why he was such an effective team leader. He was only twenty-eight and small in stature, but had the natural ability of a stand-up comic to read a room and lift the mood with a quick comment or gesture.

"Ok, we hope you like the colour, Harriet." Jack said as the room laughed. Harriet laughed also, which led to more laughter. The orange prison jumpsuit she was given in Seville now changed from a bad memory to this new, lighter memory.

"I am sure I will, eventually," Harriet responded.

"Ok, good, now you are safely back, can we do a quick stand up here and see what we are doing next? I assume we will have to consider a new bucket list of items and features we wish to develop. We have to set up new meeting schedules with our sponsors and allocate times, budgets etc to all the parts of this project. I look forward to meeting the new project manager as she will have a great deal to do to set us up nicely from the start. In the meantime, let us have a final catch up of where the pilot project is and what bits we will take forward."

The team of twenty were working on how to stop human ageing and ideally how to reverse it. There was a great deal of recent work in this area, since cheaper electron microscopes became more common. The skills of biological modelling with more powerful supercomputers and better prediction algorithms for biochemical pathways also added new skills to the research process. Using of Crispr-Cas9 gene editing techniques allowed labs around the world to delve deeper than ever before into how the human cell divides and how mistakes repeat and how telomeres shorten and how cells age.

Further advances and the development of reliable measurement methods sped up research in this area. Europe wanted to be seen as a leader in the development of a fresh wave of medicines and treatments which might come from this research. It uniquely placed Harriet, given her extensive background in genetics and biological research, in a lead position in a pan-European research and development programme. There was a great deal at stake.

The work of the team on the pilot boiled the research down to just two basic pathways. There were two other paths, but these were now eliminated because of the pilot and it was why the keynote was such a success.

They nicknamed the two remaining pathways the Avenger pathway or the Peter Pan pathway. Briefly, the aim of the Avenger research was to find out why cells age and stop whatever causes it. The Peter Pan pathway let cells age but promoted self-healing to repair any ageing errors or faults.

Both were simple enough to develop in modern science labs with plentiful resources. The key factor was guessing which one to develop. Part of the guessing process were questions like, what would be the most likely to succeed, what would be easiest to scale later, what would be easiest to mass produce, and how to administer the treatment into human cells. This followed rigorous testing, licencing, and wide registration with regulatory bodies. The development of both would take a much larger team and budget.

Harriet, her colleagues, and the team spent hours and days debating the relative merits of each pathway. Harriet knew the team she selected, and her personal background favoured encouraging life to repair itself and grow. She actively campaigned against Avenger strategies all her life as a researcher. Maybe it was her childhood and early years which led her to believe in the goodness of things and the ability to self-heal. Her life experiences taught her an Avenger strategy would, maybe years later, develop an unexpected side effect. An effect which made the first problem seem insignificant. As a result, she was firmly in the Peter Pan camp of research.

She looked around her team as they updated each other on the progress they made and the likely start off points for the next three year's work. She felt proud and pulled her new tee-shirt closer to her chest.

CHAPTER 24: OXANA PLANS TO MOVE TO DUBLIN

Oxana opened the latest email from Harriet. It confirmed the flurry that went before. It contained a formal offer for the position of Project Manager in Dublin for three years. They would provide accommodation on campus, or they would pay a fixed sum ex-pat living allowance for her to find accommodation.

She was to begin at once to get her work visa approved. Oxana noted with interest the last email concerning her visa contained a copy to an adviser in Europol and a member of the Irish Foreign service. She wondered who they were?

Oxana soon saw the benefits offered by these two additional names in the email. These two people, Frik in Europol and Colin in the Irish Embassy, responded to her request to help in the visa grant. Within minutes, a prefilled visa application form appeared on Oxana's computer and Europol sent a signed and sealed, *no reason to refuse,* statement to the Irish embassy on official paper.

Oxana finished a nice breakfast on the terrace of the dacha with her father. The sun was shining, and the room was warm and smelled of buckwheat porridge and Russian pancakes. He was still in the blue steel wheelchair, but they bought a special table so he could slide under it. Before that, they moved him roughly out of the chair onto a dining room chair and then back into the wheelchair again. This led to complaints and cold breakfasts, which lead to further complaints. She saw first-hand her father could be a very grumpy old man when he wanted to be difficult.

She went through the visa application form quickly; someone else, she suspected the embassy people, prefilled it for her in many sections. It asked for her sex, birthdate, passport number, etc. She made her declarations about health insurance and access to reserve banking funds. She completed it quickly and sent it back to Colin. She liked his name but needed to look up how to pronounce it. When searching, she saw many video clips about strange Irish names. She would meet them all in the next three years. She knew not to worry; she would adapt, she always survived.

What she didn't see was the email from Agent Frik in Europol to Police Inspector Cristiano in Seville saying the Irish Embassy was about to process her visa. She also did not see the email from Frik planning a visit to Dublin to meet with the police commissioner about her arrival there and what steps needed to be taken.

She knocked on the door to Gregor's office. He barked, 'come in'. She tried to decide, based on his command, what humour he might be in, but gave up. She would deal with him as she found him. He was a tough, greedy businessperson with an emotional and real hold on her. She sold her soul to the devil, and she would have to manage the devil as best she could. He smiled as she entered.

He rose and greeted her with, "Oxana, how wonderful! You look younger than ever. Is it the Russian air or is the new improved Rattler treatment working better for you?"

He seemed in good humour, so she tried to help him stay like that. "I must agree, Gregor, the effect of the patches is dramatic and good. After the second day, I could see an improvement in my hair and skin. It is a good deal better than the tablets. Did you change anything else? What other tricks do you have up your sleeve?"

"Thank you. I will tell the researchers. They are always making small tweaks. It is a pity we cannot test it on more humans. We could develop the product much more quickly and probably more safely. But no tweaks or tricks, well apart from the boring stuff about delivery. You know how we get it into the human customer. We have tablets, patches, but someone can also inject it. That is not something most people want to hear about. We probably will use such a method when we launch it through beauty clinics around the world. They like to have a specialised way of administering it to their clients. Botox gave them all wonderful business; Rattler will do the same.

But first we will sell Rattler to all the movie stars and models around the world. The rich playboys can have it too, for a rather hefty price. We cannot openly market it as it is un-licenced, but it is quite amazing what unregistered products humans will buy if it makes them look good. They are all so vain."

Getting into his stride, Gregor continued, "We will make plenty of money on this. We need every rouble. This has taken a couple of years and cost a great deal of money to develop. It works simply too; by helping a few telomeres to repair themselves. Simple ideas make the best products. We researched the idea of preventing telomeres from damaging themselves in replication, but it was a dead end. No, this works well. We will turn the rich of the world into Peter Pan."

"Gosh Gregor, you are in an excellent mood. Should I take the chance to ask you to give my Nana his own dacha and a permanent allowance to live on without me having to work for you?"

Gregor sat down, laughing. "Oh, Oxana, you can be so funny. I enjoy you and the splendid jokes you make. I must tell our friends. That is funny, Oxana. Don't be ridiculous, we love you and your father, and we will look after you. Look how young you look. At least 25 years less than your passport. All thanks to me and our research team."

"You can't blame me for trying, Gregor. But when you mention passports, Gregor, I want to tell you my passport is about to get a work permit for Ireland. I told you before that I was interviewing for a job there. I have formally been offered and accepted the role of project manager in a research project in Dublin at Trinity college. I accepted this morning. I trust that is, ok?"

Gregor looked up sharply at Oxana, and his brain was putting pieces of a jigsaw together. This new piece seemed to fit, and his brow unwrinkled. "Oxana, bad girl, you are leaving us, and leaving Mother Russia again. We will think you dislike us. You should have asked me first before you formally accepted the job. But Dublin, will be fine. I had expected your success. Who could resist your charms and skills?"

"We need you to go back and forth to the United States. There are many flights from there and they seem to be almost like the

51st state politically. That will be fine, but please ask me before you set off for new jobs and countries. You do not wish to make life difficult for your father now, do you?"

"What a stupid question, Gregor. Of course not. Dublin is good too as it allows me to visit here every couple of months to check on how well you are looking after Father. Hopefully, direct flights will resume in the next few years, and I can stop all this flying around the world to get to Moscow."

"Yes, and for you to get new patches, too. I am sure it is also important. In a new job, one must look one's best, eh?" Gregor was enjoying himself now. Meeting the needs of his new customers in America would fall into place easily now.

"Was there anything else Gregor, you hardly called me up to chat about the weather and tell me I looked good?"

"Yes, there is one more thing. I am delighted about the patches and their obvious success in making you look years younger. But in a few weeks, you will go to the USA. I think it may be from Dublin. That will suit our customers. We have a new M278 delivery method to try out for our American friends."

"As with Rattler, we have changed the method of delivery. You were lucky to escape in Vilnius and Seville. In the future, you won't have to put M278 into the drink of the target anymore. You can simply inject it when the person is sleeping. We have also changed the speed of affect. Nothing will happen for two or three days to the person. Nothing, they will not notice anything nor feel any pain. Then the drug will activate, and death will happen as quickly as it did before. There is no pain to the target. They just stop breathing, as usual. So it makes it easy for you to give the treatment, move away, and ensure you have a good alibi at the time of death. With good planning, you could be back in Ireland when the target passes away. Isn't that wonderful? Scientists are so clever! I love how they can make solutions to problems."

"I see. I must be close enough to inject them, though. I wonder, will they object to that? Most will. Not too many like a stranger walking up to them and injecting them. Have you gone completely mad?"

"Now, now, Oxana, take it easy. We will give you lots of sleeping tablets for them. They can be asleep when you inject them. They won't even know."

"You try it then—if it is so easy."

"I hope you will not be difficult. Our USA clients are very keen to try this new method. It will help them finally deal with a political hot potato." Gregor stood up and, moving to a side table, picked up a bag from an internationally renowned ladies' underwear shop. "I normally don't give my team, especially my lady team members, underwear. In your case, I make an exception." Gregor peered into the bag and licked his lips.

"I should get you to model these for me. You are still a 34D I trust?"

"I'd rather model for a stadium of lusty soldiers, Gregor. You don't respect any life, especially the life of women. Everyone and everything are for your enrichment. But to answer your question, yes, I am still the same size."

"Well, there are three lovely colours here. Each has one vial of M278 in the usual pouch over the under wire. The glass is stronger too. Each has a size 30G needle attached. These are tiny. You just need to get the M278 under the skin. You can buy or get syringes in any dispensary. Use a fine short needle if it breaks or you lose it somehow."

Oxana picked up one bra from the box. It was red, lacey, and carried a very high-end brand label. If anyone, especially any man in customs, looked at them, he was unlikely to think they contained a bio toxin. She always chose gates with middle age white men as customs officers when she went through immigration. They always reacted to her like the stereotypes they are. She expected the Americans would behave the same— especially if their president was any guide.

"OK, and the target? Will you send it to me in the usual way? I will send you a new drop point for messages when I get to Dublin. It will be a library as usual, but I don't know which one. I assume we will use the same chessboard code?"

Oxana was referring to the message deciphering system they used for many years. The standard chessboard has 64 squares. The Russian alphabet consists of 33 letters with ten vowels. A further ten squares made up numbers and there were ten unused and they used them for punctuation. The code was based on each square relating to each letter. The code related to a specific chess match and started at the position of the king when the loser lost the match. It worked right to left from there and back to the white side of the board wrapping over, if needed, to the black side.

A very complex message could look like a series of chess board positions, and they constructed every message based on a specific chess match. It was a pretty simple system, but complex enough to be difficult to break.

"Yes, Oxana. Send me the drop location in the usual way. I think Dublin has some magnificent libraries. I seem to remember the library in Trinity is extremely large. I am sure there are good places to hide messages there! Goodbye Oxana, we will look after your father until you return. Be careful in America, they are quite aggressive sometimes. Don't get shot by accident. They have so many guns and appear to be quite trigger happy."

CHAPTER 25:
GREGOR GETS THE
AMERICAN MONEY

Gregor stepped out of his office through a door hidden behind a mirrored wall with shelves holding many colourful bottles of alcohol. The movement of the powerful electric motors was smooth and silent as the door swung ninety degrees. Inside, the lights flickered on to reveal a bare room with solid grey concrete walls, floor, and ceiling. The LED lighting was garish and harsh and was typical of a prison or a cheap hotel room.

The only furniture in the room was a steel table with a large electronic laptop. The laptop seemed to be about the size of four normal laptops and, because of its bulk, was not very portable. Beside the table was a hard metal chair, made with thick, round black steel legs and a flat plate for the seat and back support. It was the chair a movie hero would use in a bar room fight if they were strong enough to lift it.

Gregor stood looking into the Faraday room as the hum of noise gradually rose. He waited. Soon pale pink streaks were visible in the concrete. They formed a lattice like structure similar to the panels in a soccer ball. The white light faded as the pentagons and hexagons interlinked, and soon the room was a pink hue. The concrete shone like a silk cocktail dress. The hum became more hushed as the equipment warmed up.

Gregor stepped in and pushed a button on the remote he carried in his large hands. Behind him, the thick steel door swung closed and gave a firm thud as it connected with its locking mechanism.

The sound of an air conditioner kicked into action, and he could feel a faint draft on his permanently dyed black hair. A mechanical computer voice said, 'Please wait for all systems to power up'.

He thought about the cost of this room and how seldom they used it. A few initial calls with his friends in the Russian FSB to test its operation were soon replaced by face-to-face meetings in open public, green areas. Covid led to more frequent visits to the Faraday room, because there were so few people on the streets any meetings were obvious to cameras. Cameras were more active than ever during pandemic times. Cameras appeared on more and more walls and poles. They were all put up in the name of security and protection of property. The development of face recognition software opened the opportunity for potential insidious use. He and his colleagues preferred to be as anonymous as possible in their work.

He rarely used the room since the Covid restrictions lifted. The general approach in underground work in Russia was paper, and face to face meetings. The use of electronic communication reduced due to the ability of hackers to infiltrate most systems. He hoped this call today would lead to more use, and more reliable export work, and lots more cash in his and his colleagues' international bank accounts.

'All systems are ready. Please access the laptop.' He stepped forward, sat on the steel chair, lifted the laptop lid and looked at the camera. He placed the thumb of his left and the index finger of his right hand on the designated areas of the keyboard. The camera opened with a small blue light and the screen said, 'retina scan, facial scan, fingerprint tests commencing. Please wait.'

He looked at the Tag Heuer Porsche edition watch on his wrist—he was still a couple of minutes early. If he delayed the secure connection at his end, then his new customers would not be pleased. He installed the best of equipment in the room at enormous expense but it was slow to start up.

'All systems ready,' the voice chirked. The screen showed a

small green square blinking in the bottom left-hand corner. He held down the control and c keys and typed in the instructions. After filling a few lines, the voice chirked again, 'Connecting, please wait.'

He sat back, and slowly the screen filled with the images of three heads. Beneath the thumbnail images, the facial recognition software entered their names in subscript. From left to right, he read, Sam, Bill, Fred. It sounded like the coaching squad of an amateur softball baseball team. The peaked cap with a NY Mets emblem on the head of Sam added to the impression. Gregor straightened his pale-yellow tie which was carefully knotted over his pale blue shirt.

"Good morning," he said. "Can you all hear me?"

The screen wobbled like the old 625 hertz television sets his father bought decades ago. Gregor was tempted to thump it in memory of his father's technique for adjusting the horizonal hold on those old sets. It eventually straightened, and under each name now displayed an icon of an open microphone. Sam spoke first, "loud and clear, Gregor, loud and clear. I assume you are in your Faraday room?"

"Yes, I am," replied Gregor.

"Hold please while we run security diagnostics from the satellite over Moscow. It will take two minutes at most as I already locked us onto your GPS coordinates. Are you alone?"

"Yes, you asked for a meeting with me and your colleagues. My systems are all green and tell me the Faraday room is secure and there is no electronic signal leakage from this room. The only way in and out is over the fibre cable and we encrypt this cable connection with a military grade algorithm. Encryption removal requires special equipment coded in the parameters of the formula."

"Yes, just have a bit of patience, please. We will know for certain there is no electronic signal detected from your coordinates in a few more seconds."

An Americanized female computer voice said, 'systems are secure.'

Sam continued, "Good. We are all clear and can talk freely. You can see my colleagues here; they are from various parts of the US secret service establishment. You do not need to know exactly what service, but I assure you they are all capable of agreeing and completing payment for delivery of product of interest to us."

"Greetings to you all," Gregor said, sounding as polite as he could. A murmur of American accents came back over the speaker on the laptop. Gregor nearly laughed as one voice, he thinks it was Fred, said 'Howdy,' just like the cowboys in the old black and white movies from the sixties.

Sam spoke again, "Until we get our relationship onto a more trusting basis, and complete some projects together, all contacts will come through me. As things develop, we may separate and deal with you individually. But we start with slow steps, one step at a time, let us see how we get on and how we can use your product at this end."

"That is fine with me," replied Gregor. "It is easier to deal with one person, but we can widen our interactions in due course. I prefer to have contact with one paymaster. I am sure we will grow our business together as the M278 product is excellent. Have you seen the results from Seville?"

"Yes, we have seen the results. We have just one question about that." This time, it was the voice of Bill on the speaker. "You must get very close to the target to administer the dose? I understand in both cases they administered it via a drink?"

"Yes, that is correct, but we have a newer version now, the same product—M278, with an additional delivery method —injection. It also now incorporates a delay mechanism of between 48 to 72 hours before the bio-toxins act. Once that time passes, the chemicals act as quickly as before. The activation delay gives the agent a chance to escape after they have injected the product. It will make it more difficult to trace the agent administering the M278. Plus the site of injection will dissolve with the rapid decomposition."

"Injection, well, it requires super close contact as well. Maybe more so than a drink. Your operative was clever in Lithuania. They got the M278 into the mark without standing around observing the immediate effects. They were able to administer, walk away and circle back to take the photos. That time gave them an opportunity to look for police or others interfering."

"Yes, it was an interesting idea. We were nervous here if someone else, or perhaps a dog or cat, might have also taken a drink. We agree, you need to be close to administer the dose, but it avoids collateral damage, and the associated risk of failure from a reduced dose or a misplaced dose."

Fred spoke up, "From our end of things, we like the idea of it being close. We have extremely specific individual needs. We do not want any collateral damage and prefer each target termination to appear as a mystery to the other parts of the State interested and investigating."

His country accent was so strong, it completely made a lie of his pale blue eyes and triple chin. The amount of fatty tissue on his cheekbones and face would feed a small army for a week. Gregor could imagine Fred eating several big macs every day with no difficulty.

Gregor moved to close out the sale. "So? What happens next? We are placing our operative in Dublin. They can reach most parts of the USA from there in 5-10 hours. We have four doses available immediately. We can move two doses with our operative with minimal to no risk. Are you ready to take delivery? Do you have the bank accounts set up?"

Fred spoke again with his chins rippling up and down like water in a swimming pool. "Just hold on to your hat there, Gregor. We need to see a sample in action over here. So far, we just see pretty pictures and indirect confirmation of the success. We want our guys here to get stuck in and see if they can figure it out before we order up a quantity. The equipment you have in Europe for post-mortem analysis may not be up to our standards. We want to check it out here first hand."

Sam stepped in and said, "Gregor, we do not doubt your bona fides. However, we need to see it in action over here and put our doubting Thomas fingers in the wounds."

"We propose to select a target in the Washington area, that's DC, so East coast USA. The target we have in mind is a Russian who defected to the US about twenty- five years ago. We think his death in suspicious circumstances will encourage everyone to believe the Russian secret service was involved. The media and police will target all suspicion towards the Russian government as the state actor involved in the defector's death. Does that present a problem to you back there in Moscow?"

Gregor said, "Any Russian who defected to the USA deserves all he gets from Mother Russia. I assure you it will be our pleasure to deal with such a target. Traitors are traitors. You will provide access to this traitor for my operative?"

"Oh yes," Fred spoke again, "we will do more. We will provide your operative with a full US passport so they may enter the US without so much as a second glance. If they are based in Dublin, it is a perfect location as the numbers of US citizens going through there are small but large enough for us to have tracing systems in place. We can follow their every move with our passport in their pocket."

Gregor sat back in the hard metal chair and wished for a softer seat cushion. He knew hard steel was better in a Faraday room, but it still pained him to sit for so long on such a chair. He was getting soft in his old age; he thought to himself. Looking at Sam, he said, "Even if it is a woman?"

They were all a bit surprised but quickly hid it. "Oh yes, equal opportunity fake passports. We are all for them." Sam laughed. The others laughed too. "Just send us a picture of her present Russian one and we will make up a new one. She can pick it up in a Parcel Motel we will rent for one night in Dublin in ten days. We will send you the details so she can get into the locker and get the goods."

Gregor smiled. He hadn't heard of this method of delivering packages, but it made sense. He preferred to use short term rented rooms in apartment blocks. This was one benefit of Airbnb. If you opened an account, you could book an apartment for one or two nights, leave a package there and the operative could collect it easily and at a time suited to their privacy. The delivery and receiving contacts never met, and the exchange is not traceable. Anyone with the login code can access the Airbnb account, so there are no messages other than an instruction to check the account routinely. They looked for rentals which provided access via a key in an external lockbox. The drop location could constantly move and look like an everyday transaction to any algorithms watching accounts. As he thought about this simple system, he reminded himself to talk about using this software with some of his other colleagues.

"And the target?" Gregor said.

"The details will be in the package, but the name is Luv Alburt."

"Ok, we will wait for instructions. Do you have the accounts set up? We will want a ten million US dollars deposit before we start, ideally in 4 different accounts so we know they are all set up and working. Is that a problem?"

"We will send you $9 million into three accounts. Each of us will send one third. The rest will come the same way when the work is done. We will pay the second amount when we are happy the death mystified the police. So, for the test it is $18million. After that we will move to full price of $20million and we will want two doses delivered to us on the East coast of the US within four weeks. As your operative will have a US passport, it should be easy for her to go there. There are many flights from Dublin. She can travel through Florida or Atlanta or New York."

This imposed discount annoyed Gregor. He was sure the two-million-dollar discount would end in some of their personal slush funds. But he could not refuse. Plus, Oxana would have a legitimate and legal American passport. This would open up markets to him he could not access with a Russian passport. The prospect of receiving $58 million dollars in the next two months left him salivating.

"You can make up the $2 million discount later when you see how successful it is. Ok, we will agree to this now. We await your instructions and passport. I will alert Oxana it is on the way."

"Pleasure doing business with you," Fred said in his comically funny John Wayne drawl.

The screen blinked off, and the faces disappeared. Gregor jumped up from the chair and danced around the table, pumping his fists into the air.

CHAPTER 26: HARRIET GETS A NEW LAB

Harriet decided she would walk from her flat in Harolds Cross to Trinity. It was a lovely Spring morning in Dublin and the Grand Canal was coming to life after the darkness and solitude of winter. Every day more cyclists took to the bike lanes as they headed to the city docks where the large IT companies set up their European headquarters. They whizzed by her riding gaily coloured electric powered town bikes with their computer bags in the basket in front of them.

It was years since she rode a bike. Her mother didn't approve of young ladies undertaking activities requiring physical exertion. She felt it would only end up with sweat and perspiration. These were not bodily functions a young lady should display. Horses, though, were another matter. Short walks were fine. For anything else, a lady should take a horse, or be driven. She smiled to herself as she remembered her mother's view of the world.

She envied the IT professionals their direct green route to their work. The greenway turned away from Trinity and by following it to the end, led her on quite a detour. The direct way meant she left the peaceful canal and walked in the crowded city centre streets. If it was raining or wet, she could jump onto a passing tram which brought her to the door of Trinity College, Dublin. But when she walked, as she did today, she ended up on a bus or on a heavy train to connect to college.

Not for the first time she planned and promised to buy herself an electric bike. She patted her ample hips and thought a bike might help to slim them down a few inches, as well. A bus turned sharply in front of her, waking her from her daydream as it mounted the curb beside her feet. She almost walked into it!

Her mind switched back to the message from the Provost of Trinity. They, the senior professors, mostly tenured men, wanted to see her this morning. It was an unusual request, but as the work was going well and they were likely to get the research grant extension, she was not overly worried. As she passed through the gates and up the stairs to the provost office, she felt good about her world.

Harriet enjoyed the presentation to the wider faculty. The provost announced the EU approved the research team for the full grant to continue the anti-ageing research. This was a quick confirmation. Harriet was confident it would be given, but not this quickly.

It thrilled her as the others applauded when she walked up to sign the acceptance of the official offer. The word spread around the campus she was awarded the full funding they requested. This was big news in the city centre university. They often regarded Trinity as top quality, but outdated. Working on the cutting edge of bio, genetic research would enhance the reputation of the college. This was the excitement around the campus.

At the end of the meeting, the provost called her aside, shook her hand warmly, and congratulated her on the success. She also intimated the university would advance her personal status to tenured. Tenure is the dream of many academics as it guarantees them a job, and income, for life. This was great news for her, but she also realised it was a set of golden handcuffs to tie her, and the financial benefits of her work, to Trinity for the rest of her life.

The meeting disbanded as each went about their daily work in this thriving, yet historical, University. They left her with her thoughts and the estate manager who stayed behind after the meeting ended. He was there to tell her where her new lab would be. Their old lab was too small and not equipped for the larger group and the type of research to be done.

The Estate manager explained where it was, but she didn't remember it. She would get Jack and Oxana, when she arrived, to move the existing group and their work. She knew where the new lab was vaguely but could not bring the details of it to her mind.

She built an image in her mind of computers, screens, plenty of people working, some experiments on the tissue cultures they would use in a side room and lots of drawing on boards as people tried out different ideas to solve the problems they faced.

After the theoretical lab work started, she would need to collaborate with her colleagues in the larger veterinary school. There, they would evaluate and prove the success of the lab work on animals. But that was some time away.

The estate manager coughed, and she returned to the present and could see he was holding out a huge keyring with dozens of keys on it. "You will need these," he said drily. "I understand your lab work needs to begin now. Here are the keys to the lab and all the rooms on that floor."

She remembered the sound of the spinning noisy autoclaves and centrifuges- plus the hissing, gurgling homogenisers. She would need a solid and reasonably soundproof side room. The 3-D printer could go in there also as it constantly whirred and clanked as it built the models designed for the storage of the chemicals they would develop.

She knew she would also need a cold room for the tissue cultures they would work on. Hopefully, the experiments would quickly yield results and they could move onto delivery methods and efficacy trials.

The new lab would also become full on every flat surface, having a supply of pipettes, warm plates, heaters, samplers, emulsifiers, glass trays, and the omnipresent microscopes. They would buy all these and add to them over time as the work developed. She hugged herself as she thought of all the challenges they would face.

The labs always installed an air extract, an isolation place, and a locked chemical storage space for the more dangerous acids and alkalis.

She wanted a nice corner office with plenty of light and space. There was a small desk for three of four people at right angles to her work top. She liked this arrangement as it could be formal or informal. Under the window there was a glass case covered in a brown baize cloth. She guessed it used to hold scientific specimens. She thought it would be a place for her to bring her dolls. At least the ones who were behaving well. She could give them a holiday as a reward. The bad ones could stay in her flat and think about the error of their ways.

To share the work, the team would use the university's online collaboration platform. Even in this modern age, whiteboards, glass boards, projection equipment and the old-fashioned but easy-to-use flip board would be available to the researchers. The fun of scratching chalk on a blackboard was no longer relevant.

Most of the research would require annotating gene markers after treatment with acid to get them to unzip and then reversing the process with alkalis. This work was only visible under microscopes, but in reality, the machines did the work and analysed the results and displayed them on a computer screen.

Once they loaded sixty sample pipettes in the tray, the machine made its sucking and whirring noises. The machine sampled each pipette until it moved the entire tray into itself and finished extracting and analysing the contents. After a few hours and lots of computations, it displayed the results on the screen. Another piece of software then kicked in and showed the likelihood of the likely success of the recombined biochemicals. They tagged the best sample and remixed into a larger sample for stability studies. Jack tracked these results and built an extensive database. Most of the differences in samples were microscopically invisible. The work was repeated many times to understand the nature of the difference in different samples. Jack was a master of these databases and, setting up the parameters of what to measure and keep, gave him and the team the information they needed to progress to a conclusion.

As they received a huge grant, then they could get lots of new equipment. There was a special new technique involving PCR gel. Using this new type of gel research would bring an added dimension to the work.

As the genes contained 165 rRNA proteins, they were pretty simple from a genetic point of view. That and useful software packages and methodologies developed to allow her team to do their research. A big part was their ability to break down the chemical and biological elements they needed to develop the anti-ageing product.

While it all sounded simple, she hoped they did not have to develop additional new lab techniques. That could add months or years to the work. As many of the team would work at a more intense and accurate level than before, the addition of training and management supervision to their work would help make it more likely to succeed.

As well as all that, a good lab manager was vital to keep track of all the processes and ensure a proper labelling system to find and tag samples and archive products as needed. Harriet herself knew one of her weaknesses was a lack of tidiness. It was a delight to her Jack was on the team. He was a genius at creating order from chaos and keeping scattered students and scientists on point.

It was usual to see papers and notes piled high on Harriet's desk. She was the largest user of post-it notes in the University, and they even made their way to her car dashboard and piled out of her coat pockets.

It was Harriet's first time running such a large project. At the preliminary stages, they included a project manager in the budget. Harriet identified Oxana as the best fit for their work, given her experience in bio genetics. As well as Oxana, they estimated at the grant submission stage they would need at least twenty researchers and a few other associated staff. It would be a crowded, noisy lab when all hands were on board and working. As the pilot finished, they assembled most of the team. The next step was to move lab and focus on delivering the results.

Later that evening, she took the heavy bunch of keys and crossed the quad toward the heavy brown door. It looked like a Church door with the stone pointed entrance. The keyhole was the size of a small football and the heavy black key fitted in smoothly. She prepared to give the door a heavy push but found it move exceptionally smoothly with the slightest touch. Her trust in the estate manager jumped.

As she went through the outer door, there was a locked, smaller inner door. She looked at the key and at the keyhole. The latter was marked with a stripe of purple paint. There was one key on the bunch with a purple tag. She slid it into the lock, and it turned. It was a simple yet clear system. It worked smoothly also, and she stood at the bottom of a heavy wood staircase rising from her left-hand side. This led to the first floor, and she could see the lights coming on in front of her as she climbed.

A thrill of excitement rushed through her. As she climbed the well-worn stairs to the second floor, she wished the Estate manager had come with her. There were so many keys. They travel agent in her hand as she took one timber stair after another to reach the landing.

It was on the second floor of the University building in a darkish enough corner of the Science block. But at least in the summer, it would not be too sunny and too warm. It was about the size of a large gastropub. The timber benches ran in three lines, dividing the space into four long rectangular work areas. When she opened the modern fireproof door inserted into an old timber panelled wall, she realised it would need some work to upgrade the soundproof qualities.

On top of the long benches, there was the usual water, gas, and other connections. In the corner were gas extract chambers. These had roll-up sliding glass doors. She smiled as every student remembered these from their school days as they tried to make explosions with phosphorus and water.

There were various pipes and tubes at points from the ceiling and some curly pipes with strange shiny metal ends on them. She would have to ask what they were for- hopefully just water!

There were plenty of computer connections as well, but no sign of any computers. The estate manager assured her there was cabling behind the outlets and it was all wired back to a central server. Wi-Fi was also strong, showing her full signal on her phone. But this is as you would expect from a city centre high prestige University.

One thing she noticed in the lab as she turned on the lights was the strips of fluorescent lighting. This would not be acceptable to some of the younger research assistants, not only for the substandard quality of light, but it was not eco-friendly. She would need to ask the estate manager to plan to change them to more sustainable and useful LED lights as soon as possible.

She imagined what it would look like in a few days and weeks. She pictured one corner of the room with ice boxes of tissue cultures waiting for a test. On another bench, she imagined her team working on different chemicals and compounds. A communal, collaborative space with glass boards, flip-boards, and a whiteboard where people could write and doodle and think about their ideas. There would be a couple of phones added into the mix somewhere along the way. There would be lots of computers and screens. She and her team's specialised equipment to unzip and re-zip the genetic material. Computers analysed the result using expensive, elaborate software coded by specialists. These were all linked to a central database and facilitated the on-screen result display. Various specialists made comments during the collaboration stages. This drove the next wave of book research and test design.

She was happy with the room; she would make it work. It seemed reasonably sound and reasonably modern. As she locked up with the big bunch of keys, she looked for the toilets. She really hoped she would not find them by smell! But no, they were modern and well located just down the corridor from the lab. Looking around, there seemed to be little else on this floor other than her lab. So that would give them a wonderful opportunity to work together.

The lab was also pretty close to the canteen, which is really important for getting supplies of coffee. She was doubtful about the air control and the climate in the lab. She felt it was damp, and there was no sign of any air conditioning or air purification. So, this and the soundproof rooms for the noisy gear were the only issues concerning her.

The work did not involve really dangerous chemicals. There was no need for fancy positive pressure air locks or fancy protective suits every time they went in. She could do her work without those all-white, sterile clean rooms. Her first impressions were great, and she smiled as she imagined a happy chattering team working together to achieve the aim of the project.

CHAPTER 27: OXANA MOVES TO DUBLIN

Oxana walked into the Immigration Hall in Dublin airport after a connecting flight from Belgrade in Serbia to London and then to Dublin. Three flights! She was already having doubts about coming to work here. How on earth was she to visit her father on anything like a regular basis? There were so many direct connections in the past and for many, many years, she remembered Aeroflot stopped in Shannon, Ireland, on the way to Havana. Now they all went through Istanbul. But she knew her travel agent had made a mistake. It was possible to fly to Istanbul and then to Dublin. She would book it herself the next time.

She approached the immigration booth in the airport, where a smiling young officer took her passport and placed it on the scanner. The picture looked nothing like her as her passport photo showed her with short blond hair cut in a bob style.

For her work in Dublin, she switched to a long red haired wavy wig. There were few countries that thought red hair was normal, or at least not unusual. Ireland was one such country. She felt this was a wonderful time to try out a fresh look.

As all redheads have a pale skin tone, she set out to avoid the sun and work on removing the years of tan on her skin. She avoided the sun and used whitening face masks for the time she was waiting for her visa to come through. That, plus a new brand of very pale make up and foundation, allowed her to lighten her skin. It was not chalky white but, for her, it was very pale. She often thought as she looked in the mirror, she might even look anaemic.

The immigration officer looked at her. "You will fit right in with your lovely head of red hair! How long are you staying?" Oxana kept her head down. She also changed her eye colour to green using lenses. Despite her lowered head, she spied his name tag and said, "A couple of years, Stephen, maybe three years."

Stephen, the immigration officer, picked the passport off the reader and turned the pages, looking for her visa. He found it and, with dramatic flair, picked up a big metal stamp and bashed it down onto the Visa.

"You have a work visa for twelve months from today. Be sure to leave or renew it before it expires. We don't want to deport pretty, young women. Please look at the camera here." The immigration agent pointed to a camera attached to the booth, and she looked up at it slowly.

"That's it, painless, wasn't it?", he smiled at her as he handed her back her passport. "Tell me", he continued, "is your family name the same as the famous chess player, Karpov? Any relation?"

Oxana was a bit confused by this question. Has something shown up on the computer? Was there some marker in her file about her father? She didn't think there would be, but she felt nervous about her father. She wondered if she lied, would he say something?

"No," she said, "There is an Anatoly Karpov, he is a very famous Russian chess grandmaster and world champion, but sadly, he is not a relative of mine."

"Ah, fair enough," the pleasant young man continued, "when I was in school, my best friend and I practiced some of the great chess matches. Karpov v Kasparov was one I remember. Enjoy your time here. Good luck!"

Oxana walked quickly away. Imagine, she thought to herself, the immigration officer played chess. She thought the Irish were only good at singing and drinking. She took it as a sign she needed to be sharp and alert at all times.

Stephen checked the camera behind him and saw Oxana moved into the baggage hall. Holding up his palm to the next person, he opened the screen to show Oxana's entry. Her passport result carried a yellow flag from Europol and a big comment box opened under it with the prompt—*anything unusual noted*? He typed in Long Red Hair, Green eyes and does not appear to know her chess-master father. Picture attached. He entered a smiley face and closed the screen and beckoned the next person to approach.

Oxana walked into the baggage hall to collect her luggage. As she waited, she sat on the edge of one of the luggage belts and took out her phone. Jack sent her a detailed instruction on how to register an Irish eSIM card on her phone. There were a lot of steps and long numbers to enter, but it seemed to work, and a welcome message appeared in English. This seemed to her to be the perfect solution, as she still kept her Russian Sim on the phone and people back home could message her on that. Plus, she now owned an Irish mobile number she could use here. The idea of an eSIM card impressed her and, she wondered, was it possible to add more than one to her phone? It would be useful, especially when she visited the USA. Little did she know that it was the perfect way for state actors to track her every move as the eSIM was active even with the phone turned off or in-flight mode.

Her bag arrived with no damage and heading outside, she encountered typical Irish weather, rainy, wet, and cool, very cool. A taxi rank had a small queue, and she finally climbed into the back of an available one and told the driver, "Trinity College, please." She sat back to take in the sights of the city as the car pulled out into traffic and made its way to a motorway and then into a tunnel to reach the city centre in twenty minutes.

CHAPTER 28: FRIK SHARES NEWS OF OXANA IN DUBLIN

Frik closed his laptop cover and rubbed his eyes. He was reading the file about rival drug gangs in Sicily. It was not an area of interest to him except the new gang was importing extremely strong versions of hashish. The street name was Skunk, and it contained up to fourteen percent THC. It drove people to experience severe anxiety. The plant breeders in the underworld were quite skilled at increasing the 'hit' from every gram of cannabis plant material.

The old days of using a single plant from Africa or somewhere are long gone. Now the sellers mix up plants with high THC and CBD to give longer and higher highs. Science was everywhere these days, Frik thought.

This was fine provided the clients knew and used less, but in reality, what happened was the price fell and then the gangs mixed the real plant with all kinds of other things. Even smuggling it inside their stomachs led to contamination with faecal matter. They mixed it with some other unsavoury things as well.

But he knew the old Turkish gangs needed to get a fresh supply, or the Russians would take over their market. Ever since the Russian army left Afghanistan, the Russians criminal world was far more active in the drug market. It was almost as if they were the main export agent for the Afghani warlords.

Frik knew the Turks worked with the Sicilians for many years. They would not give up their patch easily. Sicily was the gateway to Europe for certain international criminal gangs. He reckoned there would be a few more fights before it all settled down.

He sighed at the never-ending nature of the work he did and reopened the laptop. A message pinged him. It was from Dublin. Opening it, he saw the message details said it was from an Irish immigration officer, Stephen. It was a simple message with a picture of Oxana. She was in Dublin and the image showed she changed her hair and eyes. Frik dropped the picture into the electronic folder and printed off the picture. He looked at it and put it into his slowly growing folder for the mysterious deaths.

The picture surprised him. Cristiano had not said Oxana looked like a twenty-five-year-old. He said nothing about how she looked as he was too upset she escaped Seville. But with her red hair, Frik could see she was stunning!

Frik copied the message and the photo and sent them on to Cristiano, the inspector in the Seville police force. He was already online as he replied in a few seconds- *are you sure it is Oxana? She looks completely different!*

Frik sent him back a laughing face and copied the details to his boss, Henri. He asked, *when do we ask the Dublin police to help*?

In a few minutes, as Frik was reading the rest of Oxana's file, Henri answered. *Whenever you can, the sooner the better, do it face to face. I will clear the way. There is a Dr. Bowe I know there. I met him in The Basque country some years ago. I will introduce you and I suggest you go there next week.*

Frik was debating going to Sicily, and now Dublin was on the horizon, as well. It was his eldest son's birthday next week, and he didn't want to miss it. Maybe the conversation with Bowe in Dublin could be online. Or maybe Henri could go himself. He would chat to Henri about it over lunch. He really did not want to miss his son's birthday again.

CHAPTER 29: OXANA IN THE LAB

Harriet thought she heard, but actually she sensed a disturbance in the lab. Looking out through the glass partition, she saw Oxana cross the floor from the door towards Jack. Her panther way of walking was unmistakable.

But everything else was very much a surprise. Harriet met a nice fair-haired woman with a short page boy style cut in Seville. For her interview, Oxana dressed smartly in a business type grey skirt below the knee and a white blouse with a grey blazer.

Now, she sashayed across the room with flowing long red hair, pale skin, an emerald dress which ended well above her knees under a black leather jacket. She was wearing a pair of round black horn-rimmed glasses too with heavily mascaraed green eyes. Her eye colour was no longer the nice hazel but was now a deep cat like green. The front of her dress was a tad low for polite society and revealed pale but very well shaped breasts.

Harriet could not understand how she crossed the room so quickly in the stiletto heels she was wearing. They were at least four, if not five inches high. Oxana's entrance caused all the team to stop working as they looked up one by one. Many of the men lingered, while the girls took in the entire effect.

Oxana zeroed-in on Jack and was smiling and speaking with him. Harriet stood up and, leaving her office, she crossed the lab floor quickly to join them. As she reached them, she heard Oxana say, "I am so pleased to meet you, at last, Jack, the prof has told me so much about you."

Harriet was not too sure who the 'prof' was, but if Oxana was referring to her, it would have to stop. She was Dr. in formal conversation, but otherwise she was just Harriet. She noticed Jack was bright red in his face and was doing his best to look anywhere but at the front of Oxana's dress.

"Ah, Oxana, welcome. I wasn't expecting you until lunchtime. I thought we would walk the wider campus here together and then we could come to the lab in the afternoon. I want to give you a general orientation of the University grounds."

"Dr. Harriet, I am sorry, I know what you said- but I am awake now for hours, I am still in Russian time, and I have read all the papers Jack sent me and I simply couldn't wait any longer. I decided to come up and see the lab and get started. We will work together for the next few years, so it is better to make a start. Everyone here is so friendly. There were two men—I think they said they were porters. They couldn't do enough for me to show me the way here. Such charming gentlemen. When they showed me into the lab, I recognised Jack here immediately. He looks so competent."

Harriet was a bit taken aback by the enthusiasm of her new project manager. But what could Harriet do? There was work to be done, and Oxana was keen to get on with it. That was not a fault. Harriet was once again struck by Oxana's youthfulness. Harriet was sure Oxana's low-cut dress encouraged the porters to help. They usually ran the other way when she needed assistance. She thought back to their first meeting over coffee in Seville. Oxana looked young then, but now she seemed to have taken another couple of years off her looks.

Harriet glimpsed the two of them in a mirror across the lab. She jumped as she realised, she was the older frumpy woman standing next to a stunning red-haired beauty. A twinge of jealousy ran over her nerves. How did Oxana have it all? She seemed to have both brains and beauty. Was it real?

Oxana caught Harriet staring at her and responded by looking her up and down with a crooked smile. Harriet felt stripped as Oxana took in her flat shoes, her frizzled hair from walking into work in the soft rain, and her great black university lecturer robe draped shapelessly over her. Oxana tossed her head and said, "I think I may have overdressed? No? I did not know the dress code and I prefer to overdress rather than underdress. It is normal in Russia to dress nicely at work. It is always possible a VIP can drop in to work there. They train us to be prepared. I am embarrassed now."

"No, no worries, no bothers," Jack interjected, before Harriet spoke. Harriet was glad, as her voice might have betrayed her feelings at that moment. "You are fine," Jack stammered. "I mean, you look great. I mean, we are very casual here in the dress code. Some days I might even wear a bow tie! It is very informal here." Jack's voice tailed off as he also felt somewhat intimidated by the vision before him.

Oxana reached out and touched Jack on the arm, and he blushed even deeper. "Thank you for making me so welcome."

Harriet spoke up as she recovered herself. "So, Oxana, come, let us go get a coffee and I can give you a tour of the campus before lunch. Jack, will you set up a team meeting for this afternoon, please? I want to introduce Oxana to everyone at the same time."

Harriet pointed Oxana towards the door and followed the scent of Channel no 19 as Oxana glided and it wafted behind her. She must have used an entire bottle to leave a scent as wide and long as a jet trail, Harriet thought.

CHAPTER 30: JACK AND OXANA

The afternoon team meeting passed with no major problems. This was more or less what the team expected. Jack led it, as usual, and they followed the way of working they were using. This was now a familiar pattern to the team. They all stood in a semi-circle in front of a board and outlined what they are working on, what is holding them back, and when they might finish the deliverable. The power positions of the various team members changed depending on their stage in the project. As they came closer to being finished, they were more involved in the meeting and took a place more central to the group. The others challenged the active stage leaders more when their roles came to the deliverable schedule. The others pushed them harder as they waited for them to finish their bits.

As most were now switching to the longer project, they asked many questions and many 'finding out what we need to learn' type of deliverables. Jack was drilling into detail and asking members to commit to certain dates so others could carry on with their work. For him, the last year was a constant game of chase the ball. The ball was soft and fuzzy and represented each tiny step finishing and then passed to the next person to do some work on.

The longer project they were starting would present quite a challenge and require a few minor scientific breakthroughs. There would be a need to conduct detailed and exact work in the lab under microscopes. The aim of the project was to find and develop an anti-ageing supplement for human use. Its way of working was to help telomeres, those tiny bits at the end of human genetic code, to repair themselves or at least to reduce the damage they suffered in normal cell division.

Jack introduced Oxana to them as the new project manager. He gave an outline of her credentials and made a point of telling them she was not as young as she looked. That attempt at a joke drew a heavy scowl from Oxana. He stammered and stuttered as he realised his mistake and tried to make it about how experienced she was despite her youthful looks.

Most of the assembled team saw her earlier when she waltzed into the lab unannounced. Some noted she had now draped a pale blue silk shawl around her shoulders over her green dress. She also tied up her long red hair into a ponytail behind her head.

He asked them all to take an extra moment to outline their areas of speciality, where they were from and what they hoped to get on a professional and personal level over the next three years. This was to allow Oxana to get to know them. Oxana listened intently and made plenty of notes as each of the twenty-two people spoke.

At the end, Oxana outlined her hopes for their success. She spoke about how she and Jack would work together as he spent more time on document assembly and filing in the scientific literature, and Oxana spent more time in the day-to-day scheduling, funding, problem-solving role traditionally associated with project management.

She asked a couple of technical questions and seemed well versed on the science behind the research. Jack noted this and said, "Based on these questions, Oxana, I think you will fit in well with our little group. To have a project manager who is familiar with the science of ageing and telomeres will be quite helpful."

Jack thought his comments would bring Oxana back to the project management role he wished for her. She blissfully ignored him, however, and soon they were all in a very technical discussion about how they might do the work. Oxana asked a few leading questions concerning the method of application of the end product in the body. She spoke about injections, inhalers, tablets, and indeed some slow-release patches. That annoyed

Jack, as it was far down the line and near the end of the project. There was so much to do in the meantime. He couldn't understand why she was looking so far ahead.

Jack sat back and watched as the entire team became animated in this discussion. His brow furrowed as he pondered why she was doing this. It was certainly not what he expected and wondered when she would talk about timing, budgets, interim steps, and other aspects of the project.

She seemed to be big into the detail of how they were going to deliver it to the market. He told himself he should recheck her curriculum vitae, as she was deeply knowledgeable in this area. Jack was increasingly disappointed she didn't outline definite metrics. She did not ask for a single completion target date from anyone.

The conversation continued for over thirty minutes and became an extensive discussion about the philosophy of their work and the benefits to humanity. Oxana clearly was setting herself up as their guardian angel. She wanted them to come to her if there was something in the way of their work. She emphasised how important it was they felt involved and empowered in their role, even if it was repetitive and boring. A bit of friendly banter broke out between the boys and girls over the point of keeping one's looks and health.

The boys were much more interested in the health aspects of growing old. The so-called health span. Several of them quoted research about the truth of humans now living longer, but not better. The girls, mainly, were interested in how they might look when they added health span onto lifespan. Several laughed when one said they would rather not be 120 years old if they looked like a wrinkled linen shirt just out of a tumble drier.

Jack smiled as he realised stereotypes were easy to create and infer, with many using them for creating a sense of banter in conversation rather than genuinely believing in them. Some remarks were bordering on being politically incorrect, but he wanted to see where Oxana brought them. Being Russian, he felt she might have different value sets on this philosophy.

Oxana thanked them all for their feedback. She said, "It is so interesting to work with you all. After the next three years, the men and the women of the world can look forward to not only living longer, but to living healthier when living longer! We will develop a treatment to help human telomeres stay healthy, and this will then help everyone stay healthy. If we get lucky, we may also look better as we age. Now that would be a popular product! We have a lot of work to do! Let's get going!"

The group cheered, and Jack felt strange and oddly out of sorts. They never cheered him when he called them to go to work. They usually just grumbled and made excuses. But here now, with Oxana, they cheered. She was only in the lab for a couple of hours, and she was acting like a coach and leader rather than a project manager. Plus, she seemed to be surreptitiously adding in beauty to ageing and health.

Jack looked at her carefully, wondering, how did she do that? Amazed at what he was seeing, an earlier thought struck him again. How does she look so young? She must have amazing genes, he thought to himself. He knew from her CV she was forty-six. But the woman here going around giving everyone a high five looked only twenty-five, maybe even twenty-two.

Later that evening, Oxana messaged Gregor back in Moscow. She took care to use a Telegram app, one was more secure, and used their agreed code from the chess books.

Gregor received it and slowly transcribed the positions on the chessboard into letters. His face darkened when the entire message became clear. The message read:

This project in Dublin is working on an anti-ageing product exactly like Rattler. As a university they have little interest in the mega profits you are chasing. This is a bigger threat than I realised. I can block them and destroy their work, but you will have to reward me, and my father!

CHAPTER 31: FRIK IN DUBLIN MEETS DR. BOWE

Frik looked around as he stepped off the airplane and onto the exit steps. Dublin airport was busy, with planes taxiing in and out. The sounds of engines and the smell of aviation fuel surrounded him. There was a constant flow of baggage handlers with their trailers of colourful bags driving about. Planes, oil trucks, cars with flashing lights, food trucks, and passengers were all crisscrossing like fish in an aquarium. It all looked so chaotic. It was one job he would not like to have, trying to manage an airport.

As usual, whenever he landed in Dublin, he checked the weather. It was a habit he picked up when he lived there. Every day could have four seasons. There was some blue sky and some clouds. Frik had glorious memories of this city where he stayed as a young student learning English. He was only fifteen at the time and was staying with a family near the commuter train line, the Luas, which ran along the coast. It joined the city centre with the beaches and old fishing towns along the coast. With cheap youth fares he enjoyed exploring the different stops on the train line.

He didn't know what to expect as his parents presented the trip to Ireland to him as a reward for doing well in his school exams. The trip was not just a short trip but an entire month in Dublin. When he heard it first, he thought he was being punished. Why not a month in some place sunny and warm with plenty of young ladies on a beach, football and volleyball? That would be a reward!

But when the month was over, he wished he could stay longer. The people were incredible, and his English improved so much. He was even dreaming in English. The host family had two sons his age, Peter and Sean. They became his friends, and he was looking forward to seeing them again.

Of course, they were adults now, with children of their own. Decades passed since he was a teenager. He knew in the future; history would repeat itself and they would send their children on an exchange when they reached the age of fifteen or sixteen.

Peter arranged for him to stay with them for these few days in Dublin. The train line along the coast was a street or two away from where he lived, and it went straight into the city where the medical pathologist Bowe was based. It was a simple hop by bus to the train from the airport and then out to Peters' home. They would have a Guinness or two to celebrate and renew their friendship. He was looking forward to their special brand of 'slagging' as they called it. If you did not know, the Irish sense of humour; you think sure you were being insulted. They said outrageous things to each other, especially the men. This was the most special part of their friendship. He knew they were best friends as the slagging was quite strong!

He passed through the VIP lane with his diplomatic passport. A young officer waved from behind a glass booth as the automated gates opened. As ever, Frik wondered why Ireland was not part of the Schengen group of countries. He knew the official reason, as the UK was also not a member, but he hoped it would change after Brexit.

Quickly getting the green double decker 747 bus, he tapped his credit card and enjoyed the short spin into the city. There were many changes since he was a teenager here. They built a new tunnel into the city centre. The Irish people nicknamed it the truck wash as it leaked nearly every day and cars and trucks use their wipers as they went along the four and a bit kilometres. It was a small price to pay to save over thirty minutes stuck in snarled up traffic on the streets. It also kept all the big HGVs with their fumes and road busting loads off the city streets.

Darkness was falling as he rode the train out to his friends in Dalkey. The water and sea were exactly as he remembered them, with an inky-black look from the shadows of the sky. He could enjoy this night and then ride the train back to the city in the morning to meet with Dr. Bowe and his team in the Criminal investigation unit of the Irish police An Garda Siochana.

The next morning started slowly. That was the best way. Peter said. "Never hurry the morning", was one of his father's quotes and he used it now as well. They drank strong coffee. Frik was glad to see the ubiquitous cup of black tea from his youth was replaced by strong black coffee.

Frik arrived in the Police HQ just after 11 am. Bowe was a big man, over 1.85m tall, but added many more kgs as he aged. With him was a younger officer, Patrick, or Pat. A smiling red headed man from deep in the country, Frik struggled to understand his accent. Bowe told him that, too. Bloody culchies, he called them. Again, Frik could see there was a good camaraderie between them based on the cheerful way they abused and insulted each other.

Frik brought pictures of Oxana and the two victims. He told Dr. Bowe about Harriet, the body in Lithuania, the body in Seville, and the connection to Oxana. Bowe sat up straight when he heard Oxana was now in Dublin, working for Harriet.

"She only looks like a slip of a thing," Bowe said about Oxana. "How old is she? She looks about twenty-four? She is far too innocent looking to have killed two people. Why would she, anyway? What is her motive?"

Frik replied. "Yes, but looks betray her. We know she is forty-six years old now. She was in both cities, and we have her on CCTV in Lithuania beside the victim. Oxana was staying in the same hotel in Seville where Enrico was murdered."

"We don't know her motive. Her father was a world class chess player but he is retired now. He lives in a dacha in Russia, but we know he does not own it or if he is a prisoner there. He has not left the dacha for years and his passport expired four years ago."

"The paperwork suggests the dacha is owned by a company which is involved with research, gene editing, and pharmaceuticals. The so-called owner, Gregor, was an officer in Afghanistan with the Russian army. He has two remarkably close friends, Alexandr and Sergei, who served with him in Afghanistan. They are not the people you would want to meet in a dark alley, late at night. All in all, the whole thing smells to high heaven. It would not surprise anyone in Europol if it all linked back to the political rulers of the country. It would not surprise anyone if it was heavily involved in manufacturing some of the more modern opioids."

"But there is nothing definite, no smoking gun, no DNA samples proving her involvement?" Dr Bowe was listening intently to all Frik said. He looked puzzled, deeply puzzled. He was also frowning like a fisherman waiting for fresh bait. Clearly, the idea of having a serial killer in his patch did not appeal to him. "Nothing to tie her to the murders? Any idea of the murder weapon? And what caused this rapid decomposition? I am working in serious crime now for twenty-five years and I never saw a body decompose like that."

Garda Patrick turned pale when he saw the photos and Frik realised, he might not have much experience with death and murder.

"We don't know, Bowe," Frik replied, "it is still a mystery. We found traces of a strange biochemical liquid in the stomach of both victims. But it could be a natural product developed after death. The samples have gone to Interpol, and they have sent them to Switzerland and America to see if they can find out what it is."

"In the meantime, this suspected killer is running around Dublin, free as a bird, and working in one of our most prestigious universities?" Patrick asked somewhat incredulously. "And she might have access to heaven knows what kinds of chemicals in the research labs there. And we are to do nothing about it? The high and mighty Europol said so!" Dr Bowe shook his head in disbelief.

Frik slowly answered, "yes, that is the situation. It is not ideal, but we need her someplace where we can arrest her or at least monitor her. She was in Russia, and we will never solve this if she stays there. We have some chance here."

"Do you expect her to kill someone here as well?" Garda Patrick once again interrupted. His face was turning redder and redder as he was clearly getting into a state about the situation.

Frik shrugged his shoulders and raised his hands, palm up. "We don't know, we simply don't know."

Patrick looked at Bowe. "Can we not just take away her work visa and send her packing? Why do we want her here in Dublin?"

Bowe sighed, "I agree, Garda Patrick, I agree. But this is from higher up. There is a threat here of some biochemical or terrorist event. That is why I am involved. Other senior detectives will keep an eye as well. The commissioner has asked me to stay involved as it may lead to bodies dying and decomposing strangely. We need to be informed and ready for every eventuality. This can become serious quickly."

"Otherwise, we would not have such a heavyweight involvement as Agent Frik from Europol in our office in Dublin. They clearly think there are much bigger fish to fry here. You remember, Garda Patrick, Russian agents killed people on the streets of the UK with some kind of injected poison. Also, there was a Russian dissident rushed by private jet, into a German hospital, to receive treatment for some weird poison. Do you remember?"

Frik stood up, "Gentlemen, you are on the right track. That is what we do in Europol. This may or may not be something similar. So far, the people who have died are not of any political or financial significance. One was a homeless person, and the other was a down on his luck waiter. There is a tiny thread linking them to defectors and double agents from decades ago. That may be something, or not. We are still working on that in the archives."

"There is plenty you can do here to be helpful to us in Europol. We need you to monitor Oxana, Harriet and their activities in

Trinity. Also keep an eye for any possible anti-Russian people or protests. If there are any political dissidents, especially anti-Russian, visiting, or any speeches to be made at any college events, then let me know. We will watch her passport to see if she moves out of Dublin. In the meantime, you know as much as I can tell you. Please stay in touch."

Dr. Bowe stood and shook hands with Frik. "Will you be in Dublin long?" he asked.

"No, just a few more hours. It is my son's birthday tomorrow and I want to get home. There are also some fresh players in the drug market in Sicily. I must go there in two or three days to talk to the local police force."

Garda Patrick opened the door to allow Frik to leave. "I wish you well and a happy birthday for your son. We will watch things here. We probably have a couple of members of the force doing part time evening courses in Trinity. We can ask them to watch out for any political tomfoolery. The officer at the front desk will get a car to bring you to your next appointment. We cannot spare him to stay with you for the day, but it will help a little. Bon voyage, Slan."

Frik thanked Bowe for sending a driver and walked out of the room. He made his way to the front desk and the car which would bring him to lunch with Harriet.

Bowe looked at his colleague Patrick and said, "there is significantly more to this than meets the eye. Europol does not send agents across the continent for a ten-minute meeting. That man, Frik, would not miss his son's birthday to tell us so little. Pay attention, Patrick, this will turn into a drama. We are playing in the big league with this one. I bet you will be in plain clothes as a student in Trinity in the next few days. It will delight your mother. She always wanted you to be a nerd!"

CHAPTER 32
OXANA GETS HER INSTRUCTIONS

Oxana expected a more friendly response from Gregor. He should be grateful to her, she thought. But so far, he seemed to be quite angry. She transcribed his reply. *Don't try to blackmail me. You will suffer- not me. Go to locker number 27 at the parcel motel in FreeFlow oil in Ringsend Bridge. They delete their camera recordings on the 27th of every month at midnight. Go as close as possible to that time but not later. The locker code is 273216. Message me when you have the goods.*

She put the chess book back on the returns shelf in the Main Library in Trinity. She looked around at the towering shelves of books. The rows reached some 5m into the air. It contained the decimal filing system on manual cards in beautiful wooden drawers near the librarian's desk. It would be easy to become sentimental about who used them, about the historical research done here, and the overwhelming number of books and information stacked high on the shelves.

The shelves were high and special ladders rolled along on lateral wheels in front of each towering stack. These allowed readers to climb and access reference books. Porters were also available to aid the frail, the scared, or the bewildered.

She looked at the book, 'Secrets of Chess Masters' as she placed it back on the shelf. She knew the writer. He was a sort of godfather to her until he defected to the United States. They kept her father and the other chess-masters under tight security for many years after he turned traitor. They even sent her to a state school when she reached twelve years of age. At the time, it surprised her all the children of great sportsmen and intellectuals seemed to go to her school. How naïve she was, she reflected.

They used a chess book written in 1997 for this coded message exchange. In that era, the chess masters maintained their superiority over the computers. The masters were developing new moves and studying the responses from other games. Books were a source of income to them as competition prizes were small. Since then, it all changed. Now the game had no sense of quality, it was just pure computation and risk management. The player adjusted the risk on a computer-generated slider marked conservative on one end and aggressive on the other.

Everyone knew the best players could not beat the computers now. The game lost its status over the last decades. The grand masters fell from fame and fortune, as well. Why would any parent teach any child to study and master a game when a twenty-dollar computer program could beat them every day? The game now featured on twenty-second clips on TikTok as an activity played in a park by people with nothing else to do and with unfulfilled boring lives.

Even the philosophy behind chess, to win, to beat the other player, to outsmart them, to outmanoeuvre them, had become politically incorrect. In the modern generation, everyone is a winner. Everyone received medals, regardless of their competence. Society sees men who beat others as toxic. They force expectations of inclusiveness rather than success using honed skills and developed abilities upon employers and families by enacting powerful laws.

She was ruminating about the life of chess players as she took the bus to the dead drop site. She stepped carefully down the steps of the number 46 bus. It was, like many in the city, a double-decker bus with a stair to the upper levels. She loved sitting on top and peering into windows and gardens of Irish people as they went about their life. It was especially fun at night when lights were on, and curtains might not be closed. From her perch on the top deck, she watched as mothers made dinners and children did homework while fathers watch massive television screens showing some sports or other.

The FreeFlow fuel station was across the street. She entered its small shop and bought a coffee. She used the few minutes to watch the screen behind the barista. They positioned it nicely behind the till in the belief if people knew they were being recorded, robberies might not happen. She observed long enough to see if anyone followed her. In recent days, she felt there were two students on campus who seemed out of place. They always seemed to be near the entrance to her accommodation in the student's quarters. She couldn't explain exactly why they caught her eye, but they didn't fit into the general melee of the university.

The two tall, fit men on the screen, caught her eye as they chatted just outside the door of the shop. The camera was not great, but a very visible white line showed across their forehead as if they normally wore a hat. A hat stopped them from getting sunburned or weather-beaten. The line ran an inch above their eyebrows, just where a uniform cap might sit. As well as the line, they seemed to have rucksacks designed to carry clothes rather than books and computers. The rucksacks were new as well and the men carrying them looked as comfortable as sheep in a lion's enclosure. They were not comfortable at all. She chuckled as she thought about how easy it was to spot their amateur efforts.

While the shop assistant was preparing her coffee, she asked for the keys to the toilet. The need for a key always fascinated her. Was someone going to steal the toilet? As she entered the toilet area, she noticed the fuse board high on the wall in the privacy corridor separating the men's from the women's toilets. A large bucket of paint stood on the ground beside it. She stood on it and pulled open the fuse board door. An electrician had done a super job and labelled every trip switch. The top row was usually the lights, and the labels confirmed this. Number four along held a little hand-written tag, *par hotel, ext lites*. She interpreted this as parking hotel, external lights. She tripped the switch.

Bringing the toilet key back into the shop, she paid for her coffee, and sat in the window seat, looking across the forecourt to the blue parcel lockers on the same side as the exit lane. They were more or less in complete darkness. She could see a CCTV camera on the pole. The camera was on the same pole as the light Oxana just tripped out. Looking at the screen behind the counter, one square on the grid was black. Maybe she struck a piece of luck, and the sparks powered the camera on the pole from the lights circuit. No cameras made her pick up easier. They would be deleted at midnight anyway, but it was better if there was nothing recorded at all. Score, she thought to herself.

Oxana watched for a few more minutes as the clock ticked nearer to midnight. The two men were still there. They looked increasingly nervous and were stepping from foot to foot as they tried to make themselves invisible and on the job at the same time. She got up and carefully finished her coffee. Walking to the back of the shop, she hit the fire glass a smart tap with her bracelet. The glass cracked, and she pushed the button behind with the knuckle of her right hand. The lights all went out and the emergency lights kicked in. Immediately, an alarm sounded, a very loud piercing alarm, and she saw the two watchers run towards the shop. She knew their training to act in emergencies would overcome their mission to watch without being seen.

She pushed the emergency door, now unlocked by the fire alarm, and exited the rear of the building. Rounding the corner, she pulled up the hood on her dark fleece over her hair. Scanning the rows of lockers, she quickly found locker 27, opened it, took out the A4 sized padded brown envelope, snapped the door shut, and walked to the bus stop. As she emerged from the darkness of the space around the parcel-lockers, she kept her head lowered. She heard the distant sound of a fire engine siren as she paid the driver at the front of the bus.

The bus took her north of the Liffey but towards the train

station at Raheny. From her vantage point of the top deck of the bus, she watched her two shadows cross the street, looking up and down and scratching their heads. She left the bus after four stops and crossed the street to Raheny suburban station. As she rode the escalator to the raised track, she looked back to see if anyone was following her. Nothing seemed to be out of place and at this hour, there was no one on the streets and only three people waiting on the platform.

Changing direction and boarding the last southbound train, she got off at Pearse station and walked the few metres through the dental college and up the stairs to her room in Trinity. She felt satisfied her two watchers had not followed he. She chuckled to herself, they were probably trying to get a lift back with the fire engines as all the busses and trains had stopped for the night.

Opening the envelope on the bed, an American passport with her picture fell out, a single A3 page with a typed address, and a photo of her target. She gasped when she saw the image in the photo; it was her near godfather, Luv Alburt.

CHAPTER 33: FRIK MEETS HARRIET

Frik looked at his phone as he waited for the driver and police officer to bring the car around to the front of the police station. There were several messages, including one from Harriet. He clicked on this and read, '*I am still at home, busy working. Can you come here, and I will make us soup and a sandwich.*'

The rest of the message gave the address of a flat in Mount Argus in Dublin to the West of the city centre. Frik showed it to the driver and asked if they could detour that way. The driver looked at the address and said it would be easier as it was not into the city centre traffic.

Frik told him to take him there and texted Harriet he was on the way. As the car made its way through the streets, Frik thought about what he knew of Harriet. The Europol file was thin—very thin, and in Seville he only met her for a few minutes before they released her. She was very distressed because of being held overnight in a police cell. It was her first time to be arrested, and she reacted badly to forced confinement. Frik knew in certain cases arrested people have heard so much about the process and the cells from their friends and family they are almost macho about it. Harriet was genuinely shocked and scared.

The background check come up, showing her state records to be quite innocuous. A passport, a birth certificate, a PhD awarded for biogenetics 5 years earlier. She lived a normal life, invisible to the police. Apart from her academic qualifications and the background check before the university hired her, the police had no files relating to her. There was no marriage certificate, no mention of a driving licence.

The passport showed Harriet travelled to a few countries in Europe every Spring and Autumn. They all seemed to coincide with academic conferences. She went to St. Petersburg once about four years earlier and received a week's visa following an invitation from a Russian research university. The proceedings from that conference recited her PhD study. She returned to Ireland within a few days of the conference ending, so Frik imagined she visited the tourist sites for a day or two when she was in Russia.

The information about friends and parents was quite sparse. Nothing they did came to the attention of the police in Ireland or in Europe. They never seemed to attend any protest marches or written any letters to any newspaper.

He sat back in the car and wondered how he was to get her on his side. He needed her to trust him and to understand he was investigating Oxana. Their first meeting in a cell was not the ideal way to start. He needed to find some common connection with her. Something would allow them to communicate in the coming weeks and months. But what?

The car turned into a treelined drive with lots of greenery in shrubs and beds. It stopped in an extensive car park beside an old church. The driver looked at Frik in the mirror. "This is as close as I can get you. It is an old church, and they built the apartments on the grounds where the priests used to walk and say prayers. All the priests and prayers are gone now. The church buildings only open for Christmas and for special occasions, if someone, for example, pays to have their wedding here. The flats are all new and used by executives working in the IT sector. They all ride bikes along the canal to work. It is very modern and European. Little Amsterdam it's called."

Frik looked around at the apartments and the space. They built architecturally designed apartments in well-spaced square blocks, with facades of structural glass. It was low rise compared to most European cities, with only 4 floors in some buildings. The highest point in the area was the church spire and ridge of the main roof.

Frik thanked the driver and went looking for building 12. The signs along the footpath were clear, and he quickly came to a door with a series of buttons. One said Harriet Fischer PhD. He pressed it.

Harriet answered the door buzzer, "Yes, hello, is that you, Agent Frik?"

"Yes, Agent Frik here from Europol," he replied formally and was a bit surprised at how deep his own voice sounded. Maybe it was the sea air in Dublin or the Guinness he drank with his friend last night. The door buzzed, and he pushed it in. The voice of Harriet echoed over the speakerphone and said, "Come in, push the door, take the lift to the third floor."

As Frik came out of the lift, Harriet greeted him from a doorway about 5m away. "Over here," she called.

Frik felt foolish and waved as he walked over to her. She motioned for him to enter past her, and she closed the door behind him.

He entered a square hallway with 4 doors off it. One was open and led to the main kitchen living area. He could see a large window and a balcony. He assumed the other doors led to two bedrooms and a bathroom. She didn't offer to give him a tour.

He took off his shoes, and Harriet handed him a pair of slippers. She led the way, "Do you want a tea or a coffee?" she asked. He was feeling peckish, as it was lunchtime back home in Germany and his breakfast was small and he ate it quickly.

"That would be great, but to be honest, I am looking forward to the soup and sandwich you mentioned. I had a few beers with a friend last night and it is past my lunchtime now!"

Harriet looked at him like he was a creepy bug. He realised it might be unusual for her to encounter a man demanding food.

"Sorry, that sounded bad. Sometimes I speak without thinking." Frik said a bit lamely.

She looked at him for a moment, as if deciding something. "That's ok," she said, "I prefer to give my guests something they want rather than try to figure it out. There is soup here, but it is from yesterday. It's vegetable and will only take a minute to heat. Let's sit at the bar counter here and I'll get the makings of the sandwich. I am sure a big boy like you can make your own."

"I am happy to invite you to lunch in a pub or restaurant if you wish. If this is too much of an imposition?"

"Not at all. I am waiting for a delivery. It was supposed to be here hours ago. I can't go out until it arrives. So let me see," She turned the heat on under a pot sitting on her stove top. Harriet opened the fridge door and pulled out bread, ham, cheese, salsas, humus, crackers, milk, and butter. She reached into the back and took out a sausage wrapped in white skin- it was Spanish chorizo. She took out a knife and a cutting board, a couple of plates and handed them to Frik.

"That should do us. I bought the chorizo as I came through the airport in Seville, so I do not know if it is any good or not. The soup will be ready in a moment."

Frik put the plates on the counter with knives and forks and unpacked the cheeses and hams. He cut a few slices off the chorizo and tasted it. "It is good, not too oily, and a little spicy."

"So, Frik, I am wondering, what is it with your name? I looked online and there was no mention of it. Is it just a fancy way of saying Frank?"

Frik was surprised. He had not expected such a direct question and even if he expected it, to get it so early in their first conversation was startling.

"No, not really, it is an old German, Dutch, Freisen language version of Frank. Not fancy, more historical. It means freeman way back in the day of kings and serfs and when people were more like slaves to the local royalty than farmers or educated people."

"Ah, and are you a freeman or do you like doing what you are told?"

Frik pondered this and wondered if the drinks last night affected his understanding of English. He made a little joke, "Oh, I always do what my wife tells me."

"I bet you do," Harriet's eyes gleamed. "Tell me, before you joined Europol, were you a regular policeman with handcuffs and a baton?"

"Yes, I started as an ordinary police officer and worked my way up the ranks."

"Did you ever hit anyone with your baton?" Harriet continued, almost as if she was reading from a script.

"Yes, of course, if they deserved it. Sometimes my colleagues and I were dealing with aggressive protestors, and we would execute a baton charge." Frik replied.

Harriet seemed satisfied with this and served the soup in white bowls. It was a carrot-coloured vegetable soup. She added a dollop of double cream to the top. With the fresh bread, it was quite delicious. Frik complimented her on her soup. She answered, "it is a strange girl who cannot make a bit of soup for a wintry day," she said.

Harriet fidgeted in her chair, getting up and down several times before looking directly at Frik. "What was your role in my release from jail in Seville?" she asked before quickly looking down again.

Frik thought this would be explained to her in Seville. He sat back and debated with himself how much he could reveal. His memory of the physical reaction of Garda Patrick, a professional police officer, to the images of the decomposing bodies made him pause before answering. "Our algorithms found some information in another country which seemed to show another person was responsible. In the language of police investigation, it seemed unlikely you did it, and highly likely someone else did it."

"And have you arrested this other person?"

"No, not yet. We are building our case against them. When we do, we will, as we know where they are. As they say in English, we are monitoring their activities."

Frik knew Harriet did not know the police were watching Oxana, and he felt this was for the best. Until they could track down some motive or weapon, they needed to just watch and wait. If Harriet knew, then she might give the game away and

Oxana might vanish back to Russia.

He wanted to change the subject. "How is your research getting on? I remember you were waiting for a grant from the EU. Did it materialise?"

Harriet, too, seemed glad for the change of direction of the conversation. From the way she changed the slope of her shoulders, he could see she was more interested in the future.

"Yes, we got a full award for the grant we looked for."

He asked, "I know I am only a police officer, but what are you researching? Is it a secret? Can you explain it to me? Explain it to me like I'm a five-year-old?"

Harriet replied, and her manner was like a clock that suddenly sprung its coil. Words flowed from her, many of them heavily scientific about genetics, and gels, and recombining of genes. Most of it went over Frik's head. He simply did not understand, but he detected the passion in her voice. When she paused for breath he said, "Sorry Harriet, clearly you are engaged in this work, but I did not understand most of what you said. Could I say I think you are working on something that will help people live healthier as they live longer? Is that it?"

Harriet rose from the table and began clearing the soup bowls. She thought to herself, here is another typical man-only interested in outcomes. The work, the challenge, was the satisfaction. Outcomes in science might or might not happen as expected. She took all the little steps so perfectly. The outcome would flow and would be what it would be. Her focus was on the steps. The rest of the world only cared about success. She felt herself getting angry at this small-minded police officer and his colleagues who arrested her and taken away her freedom.

"Whatever comes out of our research will be useful. It may not lead to a final product, but it will add to the scientific body of knowledge. It will be something to build on. Put it like this: when you are building a house, the walls are not the house, but the house is not a house without the walls. So, we are building, that is what I see, we are builders of knowledge, techniques. When we get them all together, then we might have a product.

Like the house, when the roof, windows and doors all come together, it might be a house. We have conducted complicated but valuable research. You cannot distil it down to a simple sentence. That is so petty and unscientific. If we learn all about house building but say the locks on the windows don't work, your way of thinking means it is a failure. Whereas to me, it was a tremendous success."

Frik sat back. Harriet banged the plates into the sink. He stood up and went over to her, "Look, I am sorry, I am just a simple police officer. Everything we do is about catching bad people and locking them up. I am not at all creative. I did not think of research as creative either. I am sorry."

Harriet was about to speak when the buzzer from the front door rang in the hall. "Ah, finally, maybe my parcel is here." She went out and Frik could hear her talking. She stuck her head back in, "Hang on a minute, I have to go down and sign for this. I'll only be a minute." Frik gave her a thumbs up and said, "bathroom?" Harriet pointed to one door in the hallway and went out.

Frik went into the door Harriet pointed to but found himself in a small bedroom used as an office. It was filled on one side with a desk. Over it was a wall with several shelves. Harriet clearly worked here a great deal as there was a large, powerful looking computer folded closed on the desk. As well as that, there were speakers, a round light, and a large microphone on the desk. The microphone was impressive and looked like it might belong in a recording studio or radio station.

As he turned to leave, the opposite wall caught his attention. A clothesline hung between two wardrobes. Along the line were four dolls, attached by clothes pegs to the line. One hung by its hand, another by its leg. Two were facing into the wall. One appeared to be bent over the line, with its backside facing up and out. Each doll had distinctive features and hair, but someone dressed them in the same clothing. It looked like a girl's school uniform.

On the small shelf below them a cane, the old-fashioned

headmaster's rattan cane, with a crook at one end, rested. This caused Frik to shudder as he remembered a dreadful corporal punishment case all German police studied in the academy. It featured a school-masters cane like this one.

Behind each doll was a post-it stuck to the wall. Some had several hand-written notes. They were in many colours. Some were on the wall for a while as the writing was faded. He stepped closer to read them. Helen, late for school, three slaps. Mary, skirt too short, six slaps, Joan, no homework done, two slaps, Olive, stammering and writing with left hand, 12 slaps (only six given).

Frik stumbled from the room and found the bathroom, where he washed his face in cold water as the scene embedded itself into his mind. What had he found? How was this part of Harriet's life? What traumas had she endured in her life to build this altar?

"I'm back. Where are you? Do you want coffee?" Frik heard Harriet return to the flat. He quickly finished and went to join her in the kitchen, where she was opening a package.

"You will think I am silly, but I collect dolls. I ordered this one last week, and here it is."

She opened the package, and a redheaded, very well-endowed doll with high cheekbones tumbled out.

"This is my latest addition. I will make her some clothes now and give her an official name. I have called her after one girl from my class in school, Xena. What do you think of her name?"

Frik looked at Harriet and the gleam in her eye. He replied, "That sounds lovely. Excuse me now though Harriet, I have to go to the airport for my flight home."

"Xena was an exceptional woman for hospitality, you know. She was from Ancient Greece. It was both a first and last name. She will make you welcome. You can see her when you come back. I will have her fully educated and dressed by then."

Frik felt uncomfortable and wondered how a welcome from a doll and a headmaster's cane all fitted together. Blurting out, "We can stay in touch. Here is my card."

He handed her his police card and, trying to deal with all the images in his mind, walked backwards to the door. He shook her hand and left the flat. He leaned against the wall before going out on the street to hail a taxi and took a few breaths to settle his mind.

CHAPTER 34: OXANA KILLS IN AMERICA

Oxana nervously fiddled with her American passport. She looked at it a million times before presenting it to American immigration in Dublin airport. The fully armed and uniformed marines were quite threatening as they stood behind the immigration agent. As he placed the passport on the reader, she tried to see what it said on his screen, but a special film coating blacked it out.

He picked it up after a minute or two and flicked through the blank pages, and said "Welcome home, Oxana," as he handed the passport back.

She mumbled thank you and with lowered head, she passed by the burly marines into the waiting area at the gate. She realised she was holding her breath for the entire time and nearly broke down as she inhaled deeply. According to the departures board, the plane to Washington DC was on time.

She was not to know, but the scan of her fake passport triggered a message. This message went to the agency in Langley. A small notification appeared on a screen and the CIA operator clicked on it and followed the suggestion from the artificial intelligence to update the file and to message the handler for Oxana in DC.

While she was boarding, her handler in DC was making dinner. Reading the message, she made plans to track her movements from the airport. She uploaded Oxana's digital image into the face recognition software of the DC law enforcement area and selected the watch and track label for it. The picture and software combined with thousands of cameras made it easy to track people in the city. Satisfied, she continued with her dinner preparations, confident in the morning, the first report of Oxana's movements and up to the minute locations would be waiting in her secure inbox.

Oxana enjoyed the flight. Gregor paid for a business class upgrade, so she could sleep for a couple of hours after the airline served lunch. She thought it was about time he spent some of the mega millions he was going to earn from her efforts.

The last call she had with him was not pleasant. When she received the instructions, she was upset, far more than she realised. Before all the victims were complete strangers. They or their family hurt Mother Russia in the past, so she had no qualms about the work—but this time she knew her target. She pleaded with Gregor to send someone else or to get the Americans to change the target.

He was furious, and she gasped when he switched the camera to show Sergei holding her father on the bed while Alexandr pulled out a loaded syringe and held it over his arm. She remembers his chilling words, 'This is M278. Shall we treat your father? You decide, right now!'

She screamed into the phone and promised to do whatever he wanted. He switched the screen off and refused to tell her if his two army buddies injected her father or not. He just laughed at her and spoke. "Mother Russia trained them and me to be cold-blooded killers. They have no scruples. Maybe they did or maybe they didn't. Do your job and I'll let you know. I'll ask them later. Let me know when you have injected the traitor, Luv, and I will check the health of your father. Until then, maybe I will let the boys play with him."

He closed the connection and Oxana fell into a heap in her room. She knew they would kill her father and probably her, but she hoped somehow, she would find a solution to get out of the situation.

The air steward shook her awake gently, and asked her, "are you all-right?" Oxana sleepily said, "yes, why?" He replied, "you were crying out in your sleep. Maybe you were having a bad dream?"

Oxana didn't sleep again and was glad to be among the first to disembark. The arrivals hall in Ronald Reagan International airport was full of all of humanity. The queues for immigration snaked around it. She located the preclearance lane and showed her passport again, taking only a few seconds for the embarkation visa in Dublin to be confirmed. Another 'welcome home' from the agent and she was into arrivals and looking for a taxi.

She climbed into bed in her hotel room, exhausted. Even with business class, she found long haul travelling stressful. The time shift meant it was early evening, but her body clock told her it was nearer to midnight. The hotel room air conditioning was running as it was not possible to open a window. They were too high up, the receptionist said, when she asked for a room with an openable window.

After a fitful sleep, she went out to the university to listen to a Project Management conference for a few hours. This was her cover. The project management crowd was mainly into computer technology and had nothing in common with her work in a research lab. All the talk was of agile management, whatever it meant. She knew managing projects was about getting people to do what they said they would, when they said they would and somehow keeping track of it all. But she recognised the weekly meetings and the idea of backlog- things to be done in the future.

Following the closing speeches, she got into a taxi and headed across the city to meet her sometime godfather, Luv. If he hadn't defected, he might still be her godfather, but she had to denounce him, as did all his family as well, when he ran away to the United States. She remembered playing on his lap as a young girl. Her father and Luv were great friends privately, but publicly they were competitors, of course. They were friendly as they travelled together to represent the Soviet Union in chess matches around the world. That all changed after Luv's defection.

The authorities required her to attend a special school and monitored her father's trips closely. They stopped the days of freewheeling lecture tours and book launches. Yet here Luv was—an old man now, and here she was, designated to extinguish his life.

It surprised her there was a door attendant, or maybe he was a concierge, at the apartment building. He was tatty looking. He looked like he slept behind the desk. He made her open her bag and pass through a metal detector. She stayed back from him in case he demanded to search her. She did not want his grubby hands on her. As she looked away towards the entrance, she did not see him drop a small tracking device into her bag.

Oxana found the American's way of life and dedication to making more money to be unsavoury. But she knew to be nice to everyone, to be unremarkable. Every culture has its own values, and she was here for a purpose. Nothing could jeopardize that. In response to his questions, she told him where she was going, and he studied her carefully. When she explained she was an old friend from Russia and had a gift for him from her father, he seemed to relax and handed her bag back to her. She read his name badge, Moonan, and used his name to help smooth her visit. A ten-dollar tip helped him to wave her towards the lifts.

She took the lift to the 15th floor and went into her sometimes godfather's apartment. He didn't open the door himself but buzzed her in using a remote. She brought him gifts of chocolate and vodka. As they chatted, she poured, toasted, poured again. She wanted him to relax and to be happy. She wanted him to relax and to be happy as she added a sleeping draught when she poured another vodka, She succeeded as he fell asleep in midsentence telling her again about some moment of chess glory from thirty-five years ago.

She placed him carefully on the sofa so he could not fall and break an arm or hip. Lifting her blouse, she took out the vial from its place under the wires of her bra. Filling the syringe, her hands shook violently, and she controlled her emotions by thinking of her father. With tears in her eyes, she plunged the needle through his frail, thin skin and into the muscle below. He didn't move.

She looked around the flat. Luv was delighted to talk to her and tell her how great his life was in America. There was nothing personal about the flat. No family pictures, just some old newspaper clippings from the glory days of chess.

He bragged and showed her his shiny new American passport. He could go anywhere now, he said- except Russia. If he stayed in Russia all those years ago, he declared he would still be a prisoner. She quickly tidied up the glasses and the vodka bottle, now nearly empty, and put it in the bin. She picked up his passport off the TV table and, after a moment's hesitation, put it into her bag. With a last look around, she turned off the lights and left.

She knew, as he told her, his cleaner would be in tomorrow to make him breakfast. The cleaner would find him well with a small hangover from vodka and the sleeping draught. She would clean up the apartment as usual and dump the bottles and other traces into the apartment rubbish chute. The trucks would take it away the next day for incineration.

According to Gregor, it should be 48 hours before anything happened to Luv. She would head to Chicago now to leave a couple of vials of M278 in an Airbnb and fly from there and be back in Dublin with an infallible alibi. As she left the building, she waved at the door attendant, Moonan, who seemed to be half asleep and made a slight jerk of his head.

The agents watched as the device their colleague, Moonan, dropped in her bag, silently tracked and recorded her journey via taxi and through the lobby of her hotel. The device sent its data to the watching agents. The next day, it tracked her all the way from the hotel to the taxi and through the airport and registered her landing in O'Hare.

The arrival there was a surprise to the watching agents. Quickly updating the police in Chicago with her image they tracked her in a taxi to an apartment building. She was inside for a few minutes before continuing her journey in the taxi and returning to O'Hare. The files were updated with the address of the apartment building, but the agents were not able to identify what she did in the building or where she visited.

From there she joined the line for Dublin airport and used her Russian passport with its Irish visa to regain entry to the country. She half expected to see Stephen, the immigration officer, again when she landed in Dublin. Coincidences with people in Ireland were common.

CHAPTER 35:
CRISTIANO MAKES
A FUSS

Frik looked at the messages piling into his inbox. One was from Inspector Cristiano in Seville. He opened it and read the tirade of abuse. The inspector was not happy. They did everything to help Europol. They released Harriet. They heard Oxana was in Dublin. Yet they still had an open case, an unsolved murder, in the middle of the beautiful tourist city of Seville. The media and his boss were chasing him to arrest someone. His own feelings were hurt as he had a superb record in closing cases, especially murder cases.

Cristiano wanted to see Harriet arrested and returned to Spain for trial. They still had a great deal of evidence against her. There was nothing to suggest Oxana killed Enrico. He wanted to close the case and satisfy the tourist officials and his superiors that Seville was a safe city, and visitors and residents alike could be sure it would not kill them without someone being held responsible.

Frik understood his frustration. The media and the political heads of police forces all over the world expect immediate results. Since DNA testing became available and TV series like cold case or crime scene investigations aired, everyone was a detective and could solve every crime in a few minutes.

Technology made substantial progress and more and more homicides were solved than ever before. That was a fact. The days of depending on fingerprints and door-to-door enquiries were fast ending. The movement of people and tracking them using phones, facial recognition, public CCTV, cameras in busses, taxis, and trains, made it easier and easier to find people locations and movements. As the ability to solve and prevent crimes increase, the acceptance of this intrusion onto individual privacy was become more widely accepted and expected.

He copied the note to his boss, Henri, and asked him to write to the Inspector, and his superiors, assuring them everything was being done and as soon as they had a break or more information, they would inform them. The last thing Frik needed now was to be distracted by an extradition demand from Spain to Ireland.

CHAPTER 36: OXANA LEAVES A CLUE

Harriet watched Oxana carefully. She had received a package at her desk in the lab. Oxana looked around to see who else saw the delivery. Harriet was not surprised as the postal person delivered to the working offices of the team from time to time. The postal worker was an internal university employee, and he knew where everyone worked. He probably was just saving himself a trip up to Oxana's apartment on campus. Maybe he was just making sure she got it earlier in the day. Whatever the reason, the parcel was on her desk and Harriet saw it earlier.

The postage stamps were Russian, and the customs declaration said, '*chess book, gift*'. The same declarations said it was of no value. Harriet did not play chess, but imagined everyone in Russia probably did. It was their national sport, after all. Harriet remembered her father talking about how the TV used to broadcast live and recorded chess matches. She was never fond of them and often said they were interminably long boring things that ended in a draw or stalemate.

Harriet watched Oxana open the parcel and remove a book. She glanced at the cover before placing it on the edge of her desk. It opened about one third of the way in and there was a plastic sleeve attached to the page. Harriet struggled to see clearly but noticed Oxana remove something. Then Harriet witnessed the strangest sight. Oxana lifted her blouse from her waist and was fumbling under it. She then threw something in the bin, rearranged her clothing, put the book away, and turned to her computer. This behaviour struck Harriet as quite mysterious.

Harriet hovered all day like a hen on eggs, waiting for Oxana to leave the office. It was normal for her to go for coffee mid-morning. Eventually she saw her leave, and casually, but quickly, went over to Oxana's desk. She opened the chess book Oxana just received. It fell open at a page with a small plastic sleeve attached to it. It was similar to a a sleeve used to hold compact discs. It was now empty. There was no way of knowing what it held. Harriet carefully replaced the book on the shelf.

Harriet carefully hooked the wastebasket from under Oxana's desk with her foot. She watched the general lab through the glass partition, but no one was interested in her. The bin was about half full. She picked up a pencil and scanning the lab again to check no one was looking; she gave the top layer of papers a quick push. Lying just under the displaced paper was a patch- a skin patch- like the ones used to replace nicotine for people giving up smoking or ladies in menopause receiving hormone replacement therapy.

Harriet quickly bent down and, picking it up, placed it into an empty brown folder she found lying on the desk. Holding the folder tightly so the patch did not escape, she made her way back to her own desk. She opened the folder and without touching it, put the patch into a petri dish and put the cover over it. Her curiosity was at bursting point. What could it be?

She decided she would get it tested it later in the gas chromatograph machine in the lab downstairs. She wondered what on earth the patches were treating. They were an unusual delivery method for drugs or medication. Perhaps she was seriously ill? She opened the personnel folder on-screen and checked if Oxana mentioned any health issues. The declaration simply said perfectly healthy with no issues. The mandatory medical check-up for admittance to the pension scheme stated the same: healthy. It was a mystery for Harriet.

When the lab cleared out at lunchtime, she picked up the petri dish and, putting it into a small sample box; she carried it downstairs. The gas chromatography lab was huge, with machines purring and clanking away on every bench. Her old friend and technician Louise worked there. The two friends chatted for a moment and then Harried confided in her, "Louise, I have a bit of a favour to ask. I saw a new member of my team surreptitiously putting on a new skin patch this morning. I normally would not care, but the package came from Russia. The patch was concealed in a book about chess. This is the old patch; I wonder what it could be? Will our latest fancy machine be able to tell?"

Louise beamed. "Yes, as long as it is biological or biochemical, it will. This is a genius machine. It can test for anything and everything. You say it is a skin patch?"

"Yes, I saw her replace it on her stomach."

"It is probably just a hormone; she may have some problems with her balance? How old is she?"

"Officially 46, but looking at her, she could pass for 25."

"Hmm, you are not jealous, Harriet, are you? Maybe the patch contains the elixir of youth. You know—the Peter Pan magic formula."

"Don't even joke about that, Louise. We are working on exactly that. Our European friends have given me a big payday to find it!"

"Leave it with me. I will test it."

"Just send the results to me. I want to keep it low key. If it is just oestrogen, or something routine, then I don't want her to know I was rooting around in her private medical affairs."

"Ok, Harriet, you owe me a beer."

"Cheers."

Later in the evening, Harriet was packing up to go home when Louise dropped in, "hey", she said.

"Hey you."

"I think you have a problem."

"Really? What kind of problem?"

"The results came back from the patch you gave me today."

"That was quick."

"Yes, we were running a batch today in the machine, but I didn't have a full tray, so I filled it out with your patch."

"That was nice of you."

"I am not so sure; I got the results, and the computer automatically analyses it against all known compounds in the world. It checks for everything registered, or patented, or in use. The only thing it doesn't hold in its database are military compounds or new products under development."

"Yes, so?"

"Well, yours is like several others, but it is not the same. It does not match directly to any compound on our databases. It is like some older ones. You might know back in the 1980's there were a lot of companies working on Telomerase. That is an enzyme supposed to help cells from being damaged when they divided. It was the popular thing. All the developmental worked failed to yield anything. A couple of start-ups declared an enzyme called TERT was the answer to all their prayers, but it was not stable. The enzyme kept getting attacked and destroyed by another enzyme called PAPD."

"And? I know all this stuff; I have a PhD in it. You make it sound like a Thai restaurant menu."

"Well, this one is like that enzyme, but it is stable, very stable."

"That is not possible."

"Yes, I know. That is why you might have a problem. It appears to be stabilised by a spike RNA protein. The kind found in viruses, especially nasty infectious viruses. RNA detection has improved in the last ten years. The researchers back in the 1980's didn't have it."

"I see. What should I do?"

"After you run a mile? I think you need to get this looked at by someone with some serious computing power. We are good here in Trinity, but we are don't have the powerful computers needed to break this out and really work on the design."

"You say this is a designed biological?"

"Yes, definitely. It is very sophisticated. Even the slow-release mechanism which allows it to work as a patch has special biochemical markers and features. Ultramodern, or state of the next art, if you know what I mean."

"Ok, Louise, thank you. Keep it under your hat for now, please?

I think I know someone to talk to about it. And I owe you a night on the beer!"

"You surely do, cheers."

When Louise left, Harriet did some serious thinking. She took out Frik's card from her purse and sent him a text message. *I need to chat with you. Something interesting about Oxana just came up.*

He surprised her as he replied immediately. She wondered if he ever stopped working.

Ok, when? He bounced back to her, short and sweet.

Tomorrow at ten am my time, she replied.

CHAPTER 37: LUV
BODY FOUND

Gregor went into the room behind his office with the Faraday cage. It was the end of his day in Moscow, and he was looking forward to going home. His two best men were waiting for him inside. They both looked serious, but expectant. The CIA agent, Sam, requested a call from them. It was early morning on the East coast of the United States.

Gregor hoped it was good news. Oxana was already back in Dublin, and he hoped she had carried out her work. He was not in direct contact with her, but he would invite her to visit her father if all went well.

The screen cracked, and Sam appeared. Sergei and Alexandr sat forward in their seats.

"Good morning!" Sam beamed.

"Good morning to you as well," replied Gregor. He felt better when he saw the big smile on Sam's face.

"Your agent did a great job, super work! Luv was found this morning at seven am by his housekeeper when she brought him breakfast. Or I should say she found some of him. That M278 is quite an amazing product. It turned a perfectly healthy adult male into a pile of dust in a few hours. We love it. Our forensics teams are onsite now and will analyse everything they can. We will soon find out if it is as good as it appears."

"It is," replied Gregor. "We have tested it here now for over two years. Many countries and their experts have seen the results, but none can decode its secrets. Now we have shown it works, have you transferred the money?"

"Yes, we keep or promises, well most of the time, we are the

CIA. Our reputation is not always perfect. The second payment of nine million US is on its way to the different accounts you nominated. When can we get the next two treatments of M278? You promised them within four weeks. We need them on the east coast of the US."

Out of the corner of his eye, Gregor could see his friend's fist pump and hug each other. They were on edge now for months, waiting for this payday. The first tranche of money was in their accounts, but they didn't touch it, just in case something went wrong. With this second payment, they could believe it was really happening, and they could look forward to their life of luxury and wealth.

"The next two doses are already in the US. They are not on the East coast. They are in a flat our operative rented when she was in Chicago. I am sure you can get them collected there. She has an Airbnb account she set up using your nice American passport. We will send you the address and the code to the lockbox with the key. In the flat you will find she left her bra behind. Silly girl. The treatments are in it. I am sure you can find a well-endowed agent to go in, put it on, and simply walk out. There are five days to go before the owner expects her to check out. You can stake out the place if you wish but hurry the money transfer. We have many bills to pay."

Sam pulled a face- he was not happy. "We wanted them on the East coast, not in Chicago. Is your geography so bad? Do they not teach the location of American cities to children in Russia?"

Gregor laughed, "it is up to you. They are in your country, ready for pickup when the money hits our account. I wanted to be sure you paid me first before you got any more supplies. If I left them in DC then you might have just picked them up and not paid us. We can move them for you and get them to the East Coast, but it will take three weeks, maybe longer. You decide."

Sam flinched. "Gregor, we need to work together. I dislike surprises. I will send you the money and then pick up the treatments in Chicago. I like your idea of using an Airbnb. They are so convenient. Cheap, non-traceable. Many have lock boxes to access, so when you rent them, you meet no one. Leave a nice review and no one picks up on the use as a drop point. But please let us build trust from here. We will do business again."

"OK, Sam. Let me know how all the post-mortems work out. It will mystify your expensive state-owned labs. The European ones certainly could not understand the chemistry. Russia has super scientists and the best have developed this product for you. It works, it is easy to deliver, and it leaves no clues. When exactly was the body of the traitor found?"

"At about 07:15 by the house cleaner. That was on Tuesday. Today is Wednesday morning here. The papers are full of the mysterious death of the great defector and chess player. It is sweet for us as we now know Homeland security had one of their eccentric former military police, a guy called Moonan, watching. He was acting as a concierge. He is a bit of a loner. Your operative must be very genuine in her movements and behaviour. He didn't suspect a thing."

"Yes, she is quite good. So, they had a man at the door. She never said. We wondered why there was no camera security. They must have thought he was infallible. But never mind."

"By my calculations, he died about thirty-six hours after the injection. We know there is a twenty-four-to-forty-eight-hour time lapse depending on circumstances like age, weight, temperature. It is in the middle of our expectations. I will pass it back to our scientists. They use this information to develop further modifications and improvements. We will watch the news tonight with delight at our increase in wealth and the removal of a traitor to Mother Russia."

"Enjoy the money," Sam said. "We will use M278 to fix a couple of difficult political problems here. When the next two are done, we will probably need two more. I can see a long successful collaboration between us, Gregor. So let us be friends and trust each other?"

"Friends, sure, but as our great Lenin said, 'trust is good, control is better'. We will work well as long as our control is strong—and your payments prompt. Goodbye Mr. Sam. We will be in touch soon."

The call ended with a computerised voice announcing the termination of the connection. The three men looked at each other in silence for a couple of seconds and then jumped into the air, whooping and shouting together. They back slapped, hugged, cheered and celebrated. The tension in the room was gone. Pure joy of success replaced it. The walls of the Faraday room echoed and vibrated with their enthusiasm. They were being paid by the mighty CIA in America for a product that they owned and developed themselves as a side-line in their company.

They opened the vodka and toasted each other, M278, Airbnb, Chess, traitors, the American way, and many other things in between until the bottle was empty and they left the room, each with their own dreams and delights.

CHAPTER 38: OXANA WANTS HER CUT

"Gregor, I have done enough for you now. Have you read the papers? Oxana was talking to Gregor and she saw he was in his Faraday room. She knew he was alone and decided to raise the stakes in this call.

"Yes, Oxana, yes, I did. The traitor, Luv, is dead. The best forensics in the world cannot understand what happened to him. One minute there, the next minute, gone."

"So come on now, please bring me and my father into your inner circle."

"No, Oxana, you are a walking experiment for Rattler. We need to see how you are. You are our girl Friday. We can send you anywhere."

"I am fine. It is fine. Just sell it to all those rich Americans and movie stars. But you must upgrade our arrangement. I want to be part of the action, part of the shareholding. I know I can be valuable to you."

"What is wrong with you? We look after your father like he is our own parent. You have a great job. You look twenty years younger than you are. Why are you moaning? That visit to America has made you self-centred. I tell you what, as a special reward, I will give you a few weeks off. I have a delightful place in Sicily. In the capital, Palermo. You could go there. We could all go! Maybe you are tired?"

"I am not tired, but I want to make some money from all this work, and I want to get back to Russia. Do you have any idea how hard it is to live in another country and work as a project manager in a boring university? I mean, they think they are brilliant academics and scientists. But you and I both know they are far behind. They are planning to spend three years inventing a product like Rattle. You and the Russian scientists have it made, produced, done and dusted, and it is working."

"You are useful to us there in Dublin. You can fly nearly anywhere from there and you now have a visa, and the Americans gave you a passport. What more do you want?"

"I know I am useful, in Dublin or anywhere. I have learned how to work. But now I want to have money, lots of money. I want to move my father into a pleasant house with me. You know you can trust me now. I have proved my loyalty to you several times. There are dead bodies in three countries to prove it."

"Are you getting sentimental, Oxana? Surely an obedient servant of Mother Russia will do what we ask her to do? Those Americans have turned your head with all their wealth."

"I do. I just want to spend time in Russia. I want a Russian man, I want to drink Russian vodka, to be close to my father, to eat Russian food. What is the point of looking so young and attractive if I am stuck with boring Europeans? Don't patronise me, Gregor. I know what I want."

"Oxana, give me time. I will set up a little fund for you. I think you must be brooding. I will give you some of my personal money, say two hundred thousand? Does that make you feel better? And you can come visit again in the next month. How about that? Are you happy now?"

"Yes, send the money, and in dollars; but otherwise no, you know what I want, Gregor. You can do it. Please."

"Let us talk about it more when you are here. I must go, Bye."

Oxana looked at the phone in disgust. She knew he was a greedy bastard. All short men are, but she would find a way. She promised herself. She would find a way. She unscrewed the cap off the vodka and poured herself a drink. At least there is two hundred thousand dollars on the way. It is a start. She would make him pay more, plenty more.

CHAPTER 39: HARRIET TALKS TO FRIK ABOUT THE PATCH

Harriet put the call through on her WhatsApp on her computer. A distant Frik picked up immediately.

"Hey," she began.

A loud screech came from behind Frik. It was clearly a bunch of children playing. Harriet could not see how many, but judging by the sound, there was at least one girl. He said, "just hold on a sec, please. I've to get these rug rats out of here."

She could hear him speaking in German, and the noise levels gradually dropped. He must have closed a door too as he reappeared standing up in front of the screen. She could just see his midriff and a nice black belt around his waist. He sat down and his face came back into view.

"They are lively," Harriet said.

"Yes, they can be. It is the weekend, and they like to burn off energy. We will go to the lake after early lunch and help them burn off more steam. It is just 11 in the morning here. They are up for hours and are dying to get out into the fresh air."

"How old are they?" Harriet could see Frik frown. He did not really wish to share his personal life.

"Old enough," he said, "now what is the problem?"

"It is not so much a problem as a development. You know how Oxana always looks so young?"

"Yes." Frik looked over his shoulder at a sound outside the door.

"Well, she got a parcel, no something smaller, more like a

packet, from Russia. It was a book and there was a skin patch in it. I found her old one and had it tested. It contains an unknown chemical with an interesting base. We think it is something to make her look younger."

"Good, that explains it. I thought she looked young. What age is she really?"

"She is forty-six."

"Really! She looks about mid-twenties. But why is it a problem? She uses some beauty skin patch you think explains why she looks young. So what? I don't see why it is an emergency or why I need to know this?"

Harriet could see he was getting frustrated and wanted to get back to his family. "Exactly, it is a beauty treatment. Maybe I am not explaining myself very well. The developers, whoever they are, have not registered it anywhere. We tested it and broke down its chemical formula. The chemical formula is not officially on any list. Do you understand the significance?"

"No, not really." Frik said listening for distant cries of children.

"All treatments for human use must have regulatory approval and when they do, they list them in an extensive global pharmaceutical database. If nothing else, it protects them from being copied. But this chemical compound is not in the database."

"Ah, so maybe the Russians are not in the regulatory process? Are they sanctioned or excluded from being added to the database? Maybe it is something they have not yet filed?"

"No, it is not that. Science, especially biological chemistry is regarded as separate from money and politics. They do not mix, so it would be registered regardless of the state of the political world. Oxana must have taken this treatment for over a year for it to have reduced her physical age appearance by so much. If they have it in use for a year, then they have had plenty of time to get it registered. They have not even put it onto the provisional or pending list."

"Well, what can I do about it? What do you think I should do about it?"

Harriet wondered how people could sometimes be so slow. She thought she was making it perfectly clear. "Well, maybe you should get your labs to look at it. It is a biochemical substance. Maybe it fits with some toxic stuff somewhere. We don't know about those databases of military or toxic stuff. The Universities don't subscribe, but you in the police might have access. The chemistry originates in Russia. It is being used by a Russian living here in Europe. Who knows what nasty side effects it might have or if it has other uses? Is it not obvious? That biological space is your area of concern, isn't it? Aren't you interested in new biologicals?"

"Ah, I think I see what you are saying. Europol should look at it to see if it is something sinister? Do you think it might relate to the people dying and decomposing rapidly?"

Harriet smiled; finally, she got him there in the end. "Who knows, but you should look at it. We have good computers here in Trinity, but I am sure you in Europol have better ones. My tech, Louise, can send the chromatograph to your people. We have some of the original skin patch too if they want to take their own sample and analyse it."

Frik frowned, "Ok, this is way out of my league. It is over twenty years since I read or studied any biochemistry. We have heavy weight teams here for that. You are correct. I will find someone on Monday who knows how to look at a chromatograph, and skin patches and chemicals which are not on regular patents and chemical databases. Thanks. Now I am going to have an early lunch and then enjoy my family."

"Ok," said Harriet, "have a good weekend, chat next week."

Frik closed the screen and then opened his diary and entered; *Get a sample from Dublin to our lab.*

After the screen went blank, Harriet got up, smiled, and paced. The call went better than she hoped. Oxana had access to a new and unknown chemical which appeared to make her look younger than her biological age, far younger. That was the area she herself was researching and trying to develop a product. If she could find out more about it, she could fast track her research and maybe get a product to market, or at least onto the patent register. That could make her incredibly famous. The lab in Europol would give her more information. If she could see what conclusions they drew when they tested it, she might design a copy. That was the key. If she understood it completely, then she could try to build it herself, as a personal side project to the main work here in Dublin. That could make her rich.

Harriet knew from the postage stamps on the packet containing the book, Oxana's supplier was in Russia. She knew from Louise this chemical was not in the European patent database. So, the Russians had not taken out a patent to protect their product. The product was unregistered. That was a huge opportunity for her. Unless, of course, there was something toxic about it or if there were horrible side effects that would cause the regulatory bodies to refuse its registration. She would set up a small, close team in her lab to work on it. Just Jack and Louise and maybe one more- Nancy. She was a smart girl and only recently graduated. She was good with exotic stuff like RNA spikes. Maybe she didn't need Louise.

Harriet went into her bedroom and taught the dolls about chemistry. The latest doll was called Oxana, and she dressed her in the same school uniform as the others. Harriet picked up the cane, swished it, and said out loud in a stern voice, "right now girls, open your textbooks to page 124. I want to see if you are studying."

CHAPTER 40: BOWE AND DAKOTA IN CUBA

Bowe shook his tired head and drank the strong coffee. He tried to stretch his back as it cramped and the ten-hour flight to Havana took its toll. As the pathologist of a UN country on the security council, he allowed his name to go forward as a neutral observer of prisoner conditions. He didn't expect to be summoned to Guantanamo Bay to certify the health of prisoners about to be released.

He remembered reading the message from the Irish Department of Foreign Affairs. That was less than 24 hours ago. They asked him to go to Guantanamo in Cuba to assist the USA as an independent medical advisor on a delicate matter. He could have refused, but the task intrigued him. He would be one of the very few people, other than lawyers and US soldiers, to visit the prison there. It was a chance not to be missed.

The next leg was overland by jeep. A major in the Cuban army called him at breakfast to tell him to be ready to go in under an hour. Bowe thought, ready to go? He was still on Irish time in his head, and it was at least seven or eight hours ahead. So, he was mentally asleep. He brought some melatonin with him to help him get over the effects of rapid time travel and to get his circadian rhythms in line.

The countryside was beautiful, full of greenery. It reminded him of Ireland in the 1930's when he was a very young boy. There were plenty of working horses and even, this amazed him, working oxen. The fields were small and full of plants-he guessed many would be called weeds by the farmers back home. The weather was warm, and the humidity was high. He suddenly had a flashback to his father saying, *that's a great day of growth.* He hadn't had such a memory for decades. But he knew, between the heat and the moisture, all plants would grow strong and quick.

The jeep came to a compound surrounded by high security fencing and with several heavily armed soldiers on duty. The driver presented his paperwork, and they checked it carefully. The senior soldier at the gate recognised the driver and the jeep, but the check was still thorough. Bowe could see rows of huts and a parade area with a large American flag blowing in the breeze. The air was fresher here and as they were close to the sea, it was cooler as well.

They gave Bowe more coffee in the medical hut. They brought him to a mini hospital with all the equipment needed to treat day to day emergencies in a rural area. A sergeant introduced him to a Swedish doctor, Dakota Schmetter. She told him as they greeted each other that the Americans woke her quite early as well and sent her with great haste to this prison. She knew the Americans planned to release two prisoners. The State department and the US army wanted independent confirmation of the health status of the men. They were prisoners since capture in the early 2000's. They were now to be repatriated to their home country as part of the US plans to empty and close the prison.

They gave Bowe and Schmetter a handbook, outlining the tests and checks they were required to perform. It was straightforward. There was a file on each patient showing a detailed medical history, including x-rays of limbs and scans for suspected cancer. Blood tests going back several years were also included in the files. Both prisoners were male and were past middle age.

The past medical history was of no interest to the Americans. The importance of this health check to the Americans was the signatures of the people doing it and their good reputation as independent assessors. There were so many accusations of the ill treatment of prisoners the US needed this to fend off the expected attacks from the media. The set it up to get a clean bill of health for these prisoners.

The prisoners surprised him when they arrived. Both were in good health and spoke good English. They seemed to know this examination was part of being released and were co-operative with both doctors. The doctors agreed to examine them individually and then to compare notes afterwards. Further examinations could be undertaken if one saw something the other did not.

This method did not impress the Americans as they preferred to work on a four eyes principle of both doctors examining the prisoners together. There was some minor discussion about this, and the Doctors acceded to the American wishes. A key factor was the ability of the Doctor's to compare notes on old scars. There were plenty of old scars, especially on the head and backs of the two men.

The last part of the process was to upgrade the prisoner's protection against all kinds of diseases. They were to be vaccinated for flu, covid, yellow fever, tetanus. Bowe and Schmetter drew up the doses, administered them to each man and recorded them in the standard yellow world health passport. Schmetter told the men there was another shot they would need to receive in the next few weeks. They could only give four at this time due to risk of complications. Someone else could administer the fifth in the next few weeks.

Bowe noticed this simple yellow passbook gave the prisoners hope they were indeed going to be released. They became quite animated as this news took hold in their brain.

Bowe pondered his role in all this as they helicoptered him back to Florida; where they put him on a flight to Dublin. He had a few minutes to look up the internet history of the men he examined. The US government held them for years without trial but accused them of heinous crimes and justified the incarceration on that basis. Based on what he read, Bowe shuddered at the destruction the men seemed to have wrought in the world.

The world Bowe read about was so far from the gentle world of pathology in Dublin he wondered if the world of terrorists was a real world. But he knew how patriotism, often converted into extreme terrorism, could lead to death, mangled limbs, and insane cruelty to innocent people.

He fell asleep thinking he would give his wife and daughter the biggest hug when he landed again at home in Dublin.

CHAPTER 41: FRIK LEARNS OXANA WENT TO USA

Frik was back in his office in Munich. The day was promising, with blue sky creeping over the Englisher gardens. He promised himself he would go down and watch the surfers in the 'hole' just below the bridge. They were always there and always riding the river water. He tried it, of course, years earlier as a younger man. He was a keen athlete and was up for any physical challenge. But it was not to be. After several dunking's and a few bruises, he decided his best position was a cheerleader.

The emails and messages from the various Team channels were extensive. Normally, he would take an hour or two on Sunday at home to screen them out and mark the important ones. But this weekend was fun with his kids. They went down to the local snow-clad foothills of the Alps and enjoyed a couple of hours on a toboggan. His girls loved it, and the boys competed with him on the twists and turns, trying to overcome their fear of crashing. They would soon beat him. Boys becoming men he thought philosophically.

A couple of alerts in the Teams groups made him angry. One showed Oxana returned from the US through Dublin airport two days ago. The Irish police didn't inform him of her departure from Ireland. He assumed she was in Dublin. They assured him they were keeping a close eye on her. He typed an email to Bowe to ask what was going on. How did she get out of Dublin, through the airport and into the USA.

The other was a bit more interesting. It was a message from

Interpol to Europol about a dead Russian defector called Luv, in Washington, DC. Once again, the algorithms did their work and flagged it as worthy of mention as the crime reports mentioned another rapidly decomposing body. There was something odd about this in the attached police report. The first person on the scene was a cleaner who came every day to make sure Luv ate breakfast and to tidy up the apartment. She called in the local police once she recovered from the shock. The report mentioned two CIA agents on the crime scene. It did not say who called them and they were not apprentices or beginners. These two were senior members of the agency and familiar with dark arts.

Frik wondered how and why they were on the scene. Was it some sort of CIA covert action? Were they interrupted in a clean-up? Were they checking out a black ops team? Why would they travel from Langley in person?

The victim was an old Russian chess player who defected years ago to the USA. Why would he interest them now? He offered the Americans nothing new, Frik was sure, to add to their information. They held him as a prize and trotted him out when they needed a bigger budget or to show the members of congress, they were worth the trillions of dollars they cost the USA taxpayer. He was an old dried-up well. A relic from the cold war when USSR and USA played games to show who owned the biggest toys. Why had they attended the scene of this crime?

Frik read the report and quickly checked the dates for Oxana. No, she was back in Dublin before they found the body and before the time of death on the reports. In the other cases, she was on the scene in or around the time of death. She returned from Chicago not Washington DC, so it seemed it was nothing to do with her. Frik wondered about it all. Oxana suddenly goes missing from Dublin without her minders noticing. Then she returns to Dublin from the USA and then a body, a rapidly decomposing one, showing up in Washington DC two days later. A former Russian defector. Plus, the small matter of the CIA involvement. It all seemed strange.

He asked the artificial intelligence support to look for links and to investigate if this death was in any way related to the others in Lithuania or Seville. After a few moments the AI reported it found no correlation. There was a relationship but nothing it deemed to be causal.

It suggested the most likely reason for the death of the chess master was natural causes, as he was old and had no purpose in life. It quoted research to state loneliness and separation from family was the major cause of death in prisoners and people who left their homeland for causes of propriety or justice.

Frik did not like the answer, showing no causality, but he was learning to trust the AI. It was usually right. It accessed gazillions of research papers and data. He only knew what he learned on the streets. It didn't sit well, though. A dead body again. Maybe the Americans, with all their high tech, can throw some light on it.

His phone rang, and much to his surprise it was Dr. Bowe, the police pathologist in Dublin.

"Good morning, Frik, you are tasty in your emails this morning."

Frik wrinkled his nose, "tasty, what does it mean? I hope it does not have a good meaning as I am very annoyed. You lost sight of a person you were supposed to be watching."

"Yes, it is an expression, tasty, and I assure you, it is not a good one. We do not appreciate emails with overtones of incompetence on a Monday morning. In fact, we don't like them on any morning."

"Well, explain it to me then. How does someone you are watching end up returning from the USA and you did not even report she was gone?"

"Well, yes, you know Dublin is a busy city. We had a world-famous country musician here, Nathan Carter, last weekend. Plus, an international rugby match. So, it was all hands-on deck. Every police officer was working for the weekend. Your Oxana was, well, we assumed, going to settle into Dublin. We didn't expect her to leave. But then we didn't know she held an American passport."

"Nathan Carter? My wife loves him. Me too. He is such an outstanding performer. And he was in Dublin. I would have flown over to see that!"

"Yes, he played 6 nights to record crowds, over 350,000 people. I am surprised you did not know. His fans always know when his next gig is on."

"Enough about him. We didn't know. We like him but we are not depending on his every word to live our life. What did you say about Oxana having an American passport?"

"Yes, we have our contacts, too. When your friendly email arrived this morning, I asked to see the manifests for flights to USA. We saw her in Dublin last Thursday. And there she appeared, leaving on Friday to Washington DC on a flight, business class, Oxana Karpov. It was not too hard there are only a couple of flights a week to DC. She left Ireland using her American passport. So how come you didn't know that? Or at least alert us to watch out for an American passport. We were watching her Russian one and the computers would automatically flag it to us if she went through an immigration gate. Did you know she was American?"

"No, I did not, and she is not. She never lived there, she and her parents are Ukrainian. There is no reason for her to be an American citizen. This smells rotten. Really rotten. I want to know who gave her the passport and why?"

"You will have to ask your American friends then. I can only tell you what is on the flight manifest. What happened anyway? What has rattled your cage?"

"There is another decomposed body in DC."

"Oh, I saw that, the chess player defector guy?"

"Yes, Luv Alburt. An old man, who is not important anymore. But still a sort of interesting death. Did the Russians kill him to warn others not to defect? Did the Americans kill him to imply the Russians can do stuff on US soil and get a bigger budget? What was Oxana's role? If any. She was safely back in Dublin a full day before he died. She was not in DC when he was found. So, it seems she was not in his apartment or near him. There was an agent acting as doorman also. He made no report of any visitors on the day of death or the day before. But why did she go there? Why for such a short visit and with new identity papers?"

"I don't know Frik, that is why you get paid the big dollars, and I go to watch Nathan Carter in a quiet, peaceful, and green country."

"Bowe, who runs the best lab in your country? The one with the best gas chromatograph and computer resources?"

"I don't know. I would think that sort of equipment would be in the universities. We have a State lab, but they would prefer to spend money in universities and allow a sharing system if the state needs extra capacity. The universities have a joint resource. It is based in Trinity. The police one leans into the UK one as well. The EU one, well you know about that, I am sure. It too is in London in the medicines HQ. But the Yanks probably have the most advanced ones. They have all those startups in California and all the universities with huge grants and donations. It is unreal the stuff they have. Why?"

"No real reason. I just have a sample I want to run through the best machine with the best computer attached."

"Try London then Frik, go through Europol and get into the EU medicines people. That is where they spend the money!"

"Ok, thanks," said Frik. "Please monitor Oxana. I need to know what she is up to!"

"Ok, I will get you tickets for Nathan if he books again! Cheerio."

CHAPTER 42: TWO POISONED LEAVING GUANTANAMO

Sam was not happy with the arrangements to deport the two prisoners. He argued and fought to resist their release in the first place as they killed or helped to kill thousands of Americans in 9/11. As far as he was concerned, they should lock them in prison until they died.

But the decision was a political one. The US government could not start an open trial as it would lead to publicity for the alleged terrorists. They would create a circus and with money, the people behind the men, or those just against the US would create chaos all over the world using the trial as an excuse. It might turn into the biggest recruitment opportunity for all the extreme groups hell bent on changing the world to fit the image they sought.

He looked at the A4 page in his hands. He read again for the twentieth time the protocols for each step of the repatriation process for the two prisoners. It was complicated with several escorting forces, airports, planes, and documents at each step of the way. The diplomats spent many meetings agreeing all the fine details. The list included several steps.

Step one, transfer from Guantanamo by US military plane under guard of military police, hand over to civilian police in Chicago airport. Prisoners to get final medical check and civilian clothes on landing. Military police to escort with civilian officers to the loading steps of the plane on the tarmac.

Step two, transfer to Dubai by commercial plane from O'Hare

airport. Escort by 4 civilian police. Prisoners to be handcuffed only. Accompanying paperwork to be a deportation order signed by the US President.

Step three, transfer in Dubai airport to Pakistan police on the tarmac. The outbound plane provided by Pakistan government. Escorting to be a joint operation with US police until plane Pakistan doors close. US escorts then stand down. American escorts to withdraw but remain on standby until the plane leaves Dubai airspace. There was backup support from local troops and special approved teams. Dubai police not involved.

Sam continued to read the list of steps. Next up was travel by plane to Islamabad. Decisions on dress and restraints to be made by Pakistan escorts on board. Pakistan diplomats to decide on paperwork required for arrival.

The Pakistani diplomats told the Americans they would have Pakistani passports for them in Dubai. The Americans sent over passport sized photographs in the diplomatic pouch weeks ago. Sam really didn't care. He had other plans for them.

Sam went through it again. For him, the troubles were going to be over in 12 hours when the flight left Dubai. But until then, he identified so many weak points, so many places attackers could target the operation. There were so many things that could go wrong. He argued for a simple US military plane transfer to Pakistan and hand over there. If he had his way, he would push them out of the plane over Islamabad without a parachute.

He cursed the Russians as well. They were supposed to leave the M278 in a drop place on the East Coast. But being clever or just acting like difficult Russians, they left it in Chicago. Some of his earlier work was to switch the whole transfer to go via O'Hare airport.

Originally the media handlers wanted a big fuss in Washington DC. They wanted more prime-time coverage and pictures of the President signing the deportation order. In the end, the switch of location by Oxana probably worked out ok as he had a good paramedic in Chicago who was completely trustworthy. The drug was there, the person to administer it was there, and the prisoners were on their way.

Despite his objections to the release of the men, the political spin doctors got their way, and they arranged the release. Sam was furious. Most of them were children when 9/11 happened. They had no actual sense of the clear and present danger the United States was under. They wanted to have a public deportation with a perp walk up the airline steps in handcuffs. They wanted to wave the medical certs and clean bill of health and run media campaigns about how justice was being served.

Sam imagined the drama when the plane left Dubai and the huge welcome when it landed in Islamabad. The entire world would wonder where the so called 'soft power' of the American people had gone. There would be hours of media and TV speculation about how they could give alleged terrorists so much media coverage.

When Bill came up with the M278 plan, Sam was all for it. The test on the Russian defector Luv went well. They steered the media to blame the Russians. They made the implication and tied it into the various poisoning Russia wet work agents carried out in UK and in Russia itself. The articles in the news practically wrote themselves. Fred was more sceptical but after the test run, he was fully onboard with the plan. They could have both the prisoners die far from American soil. Let the media figure it out at the other end of the world.

The US media would be fed a line about Russian punishment teams wandering the world killing anyone they felt damaged Russia in the past. The two prisoners would feed the narrative as they were soldiers of Afghanistan freedom fighters when the Russians were there.

The editors of the newspapers and TV could feed readers and viewers with conspiracy theories about how the Russians were cold, vindictive, and never forgot. Long form radio and podcast programmes about earlier killings of those perceived to have damaged Russia would play on endless loops. He felt sure it would be a Netflix hit series within the year.

The papers and the agencies in the USA promoted the idea the Russians would kill anyone who betrayed them. They regarded defectors as their enemy. This could happen anywhere in the world. The agencies were happy about this message spreading around the world.

The Russians wanted all defectors and traitors to remember they would strike when they wished. This was the ultimate deterrent to those opposed to Russia. They helped the story by not denying they killed Luv- the former chess master and defector. The off-the-record chats the USA media handlers held with journalists shared many winks and nods to encourage this belief. They designed these to allow the journalists to think they were being told something special.

At some of their many planning sessions, Bill made the case the prisoners being released were in Afghanistan when the Russians were there and caused some damage to their troops and plans for the country. They selectively leaked this to the media. The US agencies were happy to see news stories about the poisoning of defectors. It would give the perfect cover for the results from M278.

As far as the prisoners, media and the diplomats in the countries around the world were concerned the men should be released. The media and political pressure forced the Americans into releasing the men. Sam and Bill put into action their super secret plan. When the M278 did its work, the watching would believe the Russians stepped in and killed the prisoners in revenge. The team in the CIA loved the strategy. Thanks to the Russian drug M278, they believed they could actually pull off this sleight of hand.

As far as the allies of America were concerned, the president could wave the clean bill of health issued to the prisoners when they left American care. The president could expound about other state actors who were not so magnanimous as the United States. The President would relish standing on the moral high ground and it would be a huge PR coup to turn the fiasco of Guantanamo into a good thing.

Time to move, Sam thought putting down the checklist. The final step of the plan was about to go into action. The prisoners will be passing through any minute. He checked the two vials of M278. He held the yellow vaccination passports in his hand. The prisoners were told they needed to get one booster shot before they left. This caused no wrinkles or adverse reaction from any of the prisoners or their advisors. They were all happy they successfully administered the first four shots. What was one more? Was America not continuing in its final care package for the prisoners after years of torture and detention. It all seemed innocuous.

The man administering the shots was not really a doctor, but a paramedic. He was trained by the Army and the services obliged him with support for his family in exchange for the occasional medical favour. That he was only a paramedic was not unusual. Sam felt to employ an independent doctor would be overkill and might even arouse suspicion. Felix owed them.

He knocked on paramedic Felix's door and together they went to the holding room where the prisoners were deciding what clothes to wear. They were offered the opportunity of wearing Western suits or more traditional dress in their home country. This incensed Sam. He felt sackcloth was too good for them. But he kept his cool and watched as the men calmly rolled up their sleeves for the injection. Sam watched as Felix injected the M278 into each prisoner. He watched as they updated and stamped the yellow vaccine passports. He counter signed all with a flourish and handed the paperwork to the administrative detail escorting the prisoners.

The passports vanished into the folder beside the deportation order and the medical reports. Sam took the chance to walk away and went back upstairs to wait for the next twelve hours to unfold.

CHAPTER 43: THE PAKISTANI MEN DIE

The US press secretary walked into the briefing room wearing her usual big smile. Her skirt swung as she walked, and everything about her gave an air of assurance and command. She was the White House, and therefore the world's, press secretary. Anything of significance came through her hands. Anything of significance and newsworthy, that is. Many lobby groups would disagree everything significant went through her.

"Greetings, and good morning. I hope you are all feeling wonderful. Today we have an unusual day as we have an unscheduled briefing by the President here in about thirty-five minutes."

"Before I start, I want to be clear we all know the ground rules. There were some fractious meetings here lately where disrespect was shown to this office and the speakers presented here. We will not repeat such behaviour today."

"These are the rules. The President will arrive and will read a prepared statement. We will release it to you all immediately he finishes speaking on the platform. We will grant you all access to the statement. That is so you do not misquote him. Some of you seem to have lost the ability to listen and write at the same time. That statement is six hundred words long and will take him five minutes to read it."

"When he finishes, there will be an opportunity for you to ask five questions. Five. No more. We will restrict the time to twenty minutes. The president will call on three US media journalists and two overseas journalists. The US will be one east coast print, one west coast print and one from the US pool. The international journalists will be two international TV, one of which will be a network with US coverage."

"There will be no exceptions. You know who you are. You have your own format for asking questions of the people you represent. The President has, as you know, an extraordinary busy schedule and will leave here on time."

"Afterwards you will have me and two representatives from the State department. We can, we hope, answer other questions you may have."

"Is all clear? If not, let me know. We will not have a repeat of the chaos of recent conferences. Two days ago, the invited speakers did not get to answer questions because of the press corps infighting. That does no one a service and your readers and audience will not be pleased to see such behaviour. We show it live on YouTube. The viewing figures for two days ago started extremely high. They then collapsed and the comments was full of complaints about the media infighting. We are here to report the news of the day from the White House. If you want to get clicks or eyeballs, then do it on your own dime."

"We are here to report to you what the US executive is doing and to answer your questions. We will not become part of a media spat. We can suspend these briefings; they are at the pleasure of the President and the Executive. Many presidents in the past did not meet the press. Some more recent ones ignored them and addressed the people directly. We can revoke your passes to attend here. I want to see you all behave with order and respect today. Clear?"

The assembled press corp. grumbled and shuffled in their seats as the press secretary delivered this tirade. It embarrassed some of them when they saw the behaviour of their colleagues earlier in the week. It resembled a junior school yard pushing session rather than the work of professional journalists paid to comment and share the news from the centre of world power. Some felt she did not go far enough. Some believed she should have revoked some of the press passes, but they prepared to adopt a wait and see approach.

The door at the rear of the podium opened and burly secret service men joined their colleagues. The president came in and acknowledged some of the more senior correspondents by lifting his hand and smiling "hello, good to see you".

The president opened a page in front of him. "I am going to read this piece here and then I will take questions. Ok?"

A few sounds of *I don't have it,* and *Ok Mr. President* broke out but at a very low level. The President looked up and silence fell on the room.

"Today, the prime minister of Pakistan, who is a wonderful friend of America, informed me two citizens of his country have died suddenly and unexpectedly. These citizens were released from Guantanamo in the last few days."

"The two men were held by the US for over twenty years. As part of my policy of closing down Guantanamo holding centre, we released these two people back to their country. Before this happened, there were extensive conversations with the people in Pakistan. They were delighted to have their citizens returned."

"As well as the arrangements and agreements leading up to the transfer two days ago, there was a medical check carried out by two doctors from countries on the United Nations Security council. The medical people came from Ireland and Sweden. They kindly, and at our cost, sent two of their most senior medical practitioners. The two doctors were given many opportunities to examine the two prisoners and were offered full access to their medical history since they arrived in Guantanamo."

"These two eminent doctors gave the prisoners a clean bill of health and certified they were fit for travel. Those certificates will be in the briefing pack released after this session."

"As well as the medical check, the doctors administered vaccinations. These are the standard ones available to all people travelling and include, Covid, Flu, Yellow Fever, Tetanus. We have administered these to many millions of people around the world. As part of this, the two doctors completed and issued the 'yellow passport' to the two prisoners. This yellow passport is a simple paper-based way of recording vaccinations. Many countries in the world require it to cross their borders."

"The two prisoners were in excellent health when they left these shores. They flew on a commercial jet from Chicago to Dubai. In this flight they were under American provided escort with observers from Pakistan."

"On the leg from Dubai to Pakistan, they were under Pakistani escort with American observers."

"The reports I have seen record both flights as uneventful. The prisoners ate and drank from food available to all on the flight. As I say, it was a normal scheduled commercial flight."

"I and the people I represent would like to take this opportunity to offer our thoughts and prayers to the families of the two men. We were sorry to hear of their death so soon after leaving our care."

"The world has changed since they were first brought into our care. We accused them of heinous and serious crimes beyond belief. We are slowly removing the last few prisoners in Guantanamo. There are today only twenty-three individuals there and we will release them over the next few years. It is our intention to do this as quickly as possible."

"I will now take questions."

As previously orchestrated, the East Coast print media representative asked the first question. This woman was a veteran of such sessions. She was at a disadvantage though, as she hadn't time to prepare a question and was thinking on her feet.

"Mr. President, I am sure my paper shares with you the sorrow at the loss of these two men. The US policy is not a success in this area and many Presidents have taken steps to close Guantanamo. When did these men leave and how many more citizens of Pakistan remain in our care?"

"Thank you, Marsha, that is two questions, but it is fine. There are now no citizens of Pakistan remaining in Guantanamo. The administration ensured our agreements and discussion enabled the return of all citizens from Pakistan to their homeland."

"Regarding the leaving date, they left O'Hare airport at 07:55 in the morning three days ago."

"Next question?"

The next person on the agenda was from the Pacific coast of the USA. A veteran also of many press briefings and indeed Presidents, he rose to his feet.

"Mr. President, thank you. It seems extremely odd the prisoners got a clean bill of health just before they left and now are dead. I gather from your statement the medical people certified them fit to travel approx. three days ago. Is that correct? And in keeping with my colleague, I will ask a second question, what caused their death? Do we know yet?"

"Thank you, Roger, again two questions. I think I may have to ask my press secretary to arrange training for you on how to count questions. That is a joke, by the way. You are fine. The doctors certified the patients fit to travel four days ago. After the vaccinations, we held them for one day to ensure there were no adverse reactions to the vaccination. Localised swelling can sometimes occur at the injection site. That was Friday, we observed them again on Saturday. They flew to O'Hare on Sunday in the afternoon. They flew to Dubai Monday morning early, as I have said. Now we get time zone changes to consider. They arrived in Pakistan Tuesday pm USA east coast time but Wednesday morning Pakistan time. The doctors informed us two hours ago today on Thursday at ten am. I should mention a paramedic attended them in O'Hare about three hours before they boarded the flight to Dubai. Neither the paramedics nor the prisoners expressed concern. The men seemed healthy and happy to be going 'home'."

"Regarding the cause of death, we have no information from the authorities about that. They will do their own post-mortem. They will bury the bodies quickly as is the custom in Muslim countries. We expect they will share the post-mortem results with us. One comment we received is the bodies are deteriorating quickly."

"Next question, please?"

The TV anchor rose.

"Mr President. Can you share with us pictures taken by us before the men left Guantanamo or in O'Hare? Our viewers will be keen to see what they look like after all these years in our care, as you so nicely called it."

"Yes Bob, we can. We will release a large media pack after this."

The President turned to his press secretary. "That is correct, isn't it?"

She replied, "Yes, sir, they will be on the usual press platform within the hour."

The President continued, "the pack will contain many pictures. There are pictures taken when they were first brought to Guantanamo. There are other photographs from last Friday. We photographed them at breakfast before they boarded the plane to go to Dubai. I think there is a video also as they waved goodbye to America. I should warn you their goodbye gestures in the video are not friendly."

"We will also supply the medical reports from the two independent UN nominated doctors. That includes pictures of the sites for the vaccination injections during the observation period. We will also supply a scan of the yellow passports issued after their vaccination. That has full details of what vaccinations the independent doctors administered, including brand and batch numbers. We all know the anti-vax conspiracy people will latch onto that as the probable cause of death!"

The assembled press corps laughed, and the mood lightened.

The press secretary called on the first of two international correspondents to ask their question.

A young man stood. "I apologise for my senior colleague not being here. We were not expecting this briefing."

The president smiled, "that's ok son, sometimes you get thrown in at the deep end."

The young man replied. "Indeed, thank you, sir. The question which is interesting to me is your comment about the bodies decaying quickly, leading to a rapid burial. Is there any further news about the Russian defector who died in Washington DC a few weeks ago? Are there any similarities? He too appeared to decompose rapidly."

The President responded, "thank you, young man. We are here to talk about the tragic news from Pakistan. I do not see Russia has anything to do with this. These men were active in Afghanistan when the Russians were there. But we will await the post-mortem results from Pakistan. The FBI is working on the loss of the great chess expert and friend of the United States. While it seems clear that state actors from Russia will take steps to kill people it no longer likes, and sometimes on the streets of our allies, we do not believe this is the case here. We may shed more light on the cause of death later when all the reports come to hand. In the meantime, we offer our sympathies to the leaders of Pakistan and offer our help if they need it."

"Last question, please?"

The young man sat down, blushing deep red from this encounter. The last speaker, a dark-haired lady from the Arabic based networks, rose.

"Mr. President, the sudden and unexplainable death of these men after decades of captivity in the US run illegal prison in Cuba will raise these men to martyr status in the minds of many Muslim people. My question is, has the US raised its military threat level in anticipation of what is bound to be a hostile and aggressive public display of loss?"

"No."

The president spun on his heel and left the podium with a wave to the assembled press, who tried to stand up and utter the traditional, "Thank you, Mr. President." The speed of his departure took many by surprise, including his press secretary. She jumped from her seat and took over the podium as the noise levels rose.

"Thank you all. We will stay here with my colleagues if there are any further questions. Otherwise, we will see you tomorrow."

The offices in Langley showed the watching agents the live feed from the White house. Sam, Fred, and Bill nodded quietly as the screen faded and the sound died back as the press conference drew to a close.

"I think this is one of our better ops." Fred drawled in his distinctive mid- west accent. "Two suspected terrorists are dead. There is a suggestion of Russian involvement. And our President can hold the high moral ground."

They nodded their heads in agreement. The apparent outcome satisfied them.

CHAPTER 44: HARRIET SETS UP HER NEW TEAM

Nancy, Jack, and Louise looked at each other.

"Do you know why we are here?" Jack asked.

"No, I don't," replied Nancy.

"Me either," said Louise. "It's peculiar she wants us to meet like this when no one else is around. It is decidedly odd."

"Yes", Jack said. "And here, where we are unlikely to be seen by any of the rest of the team. It is very mysterious."

"I hope she does not make a habit of this. I have a spin class in the gym in an hour, and I need to get home to change." Nancy pouted.

"What do you think of our new Project manager, the Peter Pan of project managers, Oxana?" asked Jack.

"Why do you say the Peter Pan?" asked Nancy.

Louise looked at her patronisingly. "You know she is forty-six, don't you?"

"Really, no I did not," Nancy replied. "She looks about mid-twenty. I must ask her for her beauty treatments. Whatever it is, it's a winner!"

Harriet walked into the room, looking behind her and killing the lights in the hallway leading to this old annex to the library. It was high above the lab, two stories and under the roof. They did not use it much as it was too hot in summer and too cold in winter. The new library in the quad replaced it, but it found no other use. Harriet used it as a kind of thinking place where she could go from time to time to get over her anxiety and fears of being found out. She wanted to meet this group here as she was sure no one would see them—no one came up here, and when they left, they would walk by the lab to the lower floors and would not raise any eyebrows.

"Why are we here, Prof?" Jack opened with what everyone was thinking. "Why not meet in the lab?"

"Yes, good question", the others mumbled and looked down at their feet.

"Ok, the reason will be clear in a minute, but first some background. Some of you know some of this and I want you all to know all of this.

"Our new project manager, Oxana, is a Russian lady and let me just say she has come to the attention of the police. I don't know why, and she is, of course, innocent until proven guilty, but the fact remains they think of her as a person of interest in at least two murders."

"The other day she got a delivery from Russia to the lab. Our postman was being efficient and brought it to her workstation, rather than to her room. She took something from it and removed a skin patch and threw it into the bin.

"I recovered this patch from a bin at and asked Louise to examine it."

Harriet could see she had their attention, but they were quite wide eyed at the idea of recovering a skin patch from a rubbish bin. She could almost read their minds and she was sure they were all thinking it was risky. Who knows what skin infections Oxana suffered from, or what chemicals it might have held?

"I tested it for Harriet," Louise offered.

"Yes, you did. And you also ran the results against the registered chemicals databases we have access to here in Trinity."

"And it came up unknown."

"Again, yes, and it set me to thinking. What could come from Russia in a book in a postal packet as a skin patch? Why is it used by our project manager, who also looks twenty years younger than she is?"

"It showed a couple of spikes of RNA type proteins," Louise commented.

At the mention of spike RNA, Nancy perked up and looked at Louise.

"Yes, Nancy, it is why I asked you to be here." Harriet said. "This is your specialist area."

"We are all scientists," Harriet resumed, "in keeping with our profession. Let me propose a little hypothesis to you all. What if the skin patch is a beauty treatment? A treatment which can make a person look younger- twenty years younger. What if it actually is more than just a beauty treatment? What if it reverses the ageing process?"

They all looked at Harriet. She could see pennies, or Euros dropping in their minds.

Jack spoke first, "and if it is, and we can break it down, design it here in Trinity, replicate it, and get it onto the register of chemicals first. Then we might just be onto a winner, financially." He quickly added, "and for the good of humanity, of course."

Harriet nodded as the idea spread around the small group. A babble of excited voices all spoke at once. The excitement went up several notches as the opportunity took root in their mind.

"Be certain, however, there are lots of ifs." Harriet continued when the chatter subsided a bit, "there are many steps from here to registration. But—and this is what I want to ask you. Will you join me and this small team in a subproject to see if we can fast track the work and copy what I have found?"

"I see a specific role for each of you based on your skill sets. I see Nancy can use her expertise to design the chemical. It will have to be designed using software here and then created using Crispr tech. We know it has a couple of spikes on its RNA protein, and it inserted these into the backbone of a long chain phenol. I can do the donkey work on replications and elimination. I will set up the trials and the control tests for the development of the product. Jack is the expert in registration and patents. He can make sure we quickly lodge the patent, and we fall under its protections as soon as possible. Louise has the equipment to test and compare what we make with the original sample from the patch I found in Oxana's garbage can. She can do all the testing as we develop the iterations of the product and the ultimate test to file with the patent."

"As a team, I think we have the skills and opportunity. If it works, it will be good for all of us. Financially, we can draw up an agreement with a four-way split. We might stretch it to a fifth split for later in case we need another person to join us in this endeavour."

"Over to you now. What do you think?"

"But we are contracted to the University? Are we not breaking that. Do they not hold intellectual rights to everything we produce?" Jack spoke with a worried tone.

"Yes, probably true, but we are not developing from new. We found a product and we are replicating it. So, it is not really an intellectual development. Plus, we do not know what, if any, the side effects are. It might not be a beauty treatment anyway. Maybe she has an STD or something being treated by some homeopathic unregistered chemical." Harriet replied.

"Sure, a homeopathic with a couple of protein spikes in a long chain phenol-based enzyme. That sounds likely. Not!" Nancy was quite sarcastic in reply.

"Look this could be worth mega millions, it is sensible to take some risks on it. Let us see what we have first and keep it to ourselves. It may come to nothing."

The conversation carried on for a while and eventually Harriet called for a vote. Harriet went through the small group one by one. They discussed many aspects of the plan. The funding, keeping it secret, what would happen at the end and the University discovered their work. How they might prepare the drug for administration to users. Which of them knew enough about patches as a mechanism for the delivery of the product into the body? In the end, the group went their separate ways with an agreement to meet again and get the project set up. Each promised to develop their role and decide if they would commit to the team.

CHAPTER 45: FRIK HEARS OF LUV. OXANA IN MOSCOW

The message blipped on Frik's computer screen. All day long, little icons pinged him on his screen or on his phone. This one was from the Europol immigration watch software. The automation software worked with scanners used at national borders. It picked up and reported flagged passports as they were read at an immigration point. He finished his email and pressed send, then he clicked on the icon to open the software for immigration.

He saw the report of Oxana Karpov passing through Dublin immigration. She was heading to Turkey and her final airplane ticket showed her landing in Moscow later that night. He would get another ping as she went through Istanbul.

He was curious how long it might take for Bowe or some of his merry men to tell him about Oxana's movements. The last time she left Ireland, she went to America. It was only when she returned that anyone in Europol knew she was not in Ireland. Bowe redeployed the team who were supposed to be monitoring her to general duties for a music concert. Frik hoped they were more alert now and were on duty.

A dead body was found in America also, but not until a day after she returned to Dublin. He gave Bowe a good stern reprimand and hoped some of it would change his behaviour. But maybe not. Maybe there was another concert or sports event happening in Dublin and the police were busy doing something else.

He opened the case notes on Oxana again. He was sure she was involved in the two murders in Europe. But there was no motive and no evidence. She was unlikely to be involved in the defector's death in the US. That looked like a section 12 wetwork job orchestrated from within the GRU- the old Russian CIA. The SPV- the Russian FBI were not effective for many years in executing such operations, so it was unlikely to be them.

There was nothing to suggest Oxana was a *Spetsnaz- a spy-* with the GRU. She spent too much time working in legitimate businesses and universities in Europe to be an agent. She was a real mystery. In the old days before AI and computers she could have operated freely for years without any fear of detection.

As he went through the file, he read a report about the chemical Harriet sent to him. She said it was a beauty treatment Oxana was using. Frik wondered at the time was it just jealousy by Harriet, as Oxana looked so young, or was it a genuine concern?

The report was terse and confirmed there was no chemical registered on any known data base that matched the sample results. It did, however, note their chromatogram showed similarities to the chemical found on the two victims in Seville and Vilnius. It was a fragment of a paragraph in the report. He nearly missed it. There *are similar spike markers at point 6 and 18 on the chemical extracted from the murder victims in Europol file number EUES223 and EULN171. They may, of course, be ghost peaks. We will need more samples to eliminate that possibility.*

Frik sat back and read the report again. He hadn't seen the detail even though the lab team filed it where he could access and read it. A similarity. What did it say exactly, he rechecked it, *Similar spike markers.* This could be the break he wanted. He didn't understand what it meant. He would need to meet with some of the chemical experts, or maybe Dr Harriet could help him. If there was a connection between Oxana's beauty treatment and the toxin that killed two people, then it might be enough for an arrest warrant. It was so far outside his skill set. He wished he spent more time in science studies.

He looked at the report and again at the graph full of colours and spikes. Two of the latter were highlighted by a computer pen circle round them. The second page attached to the file also had a graph with lots of colours and letters. There was a circle around two spikes on that image as well. He cursed his lack of knowledge of this high-tech science. In his mind, the spikes meant absolutely nothing.

CHAPTER 46: OXANA MEETS HER FATHER AGAIN

"Papa", Oxana ran up to her father and threw her arms around him. "It is so good to see you. You are up and about, dressed and looking great. You aren't using your wheelchair anymore. That is great. Did you have lunch?"

"Oxana, I wasn't expecting you. When did you get here? You look younger than ever. How do you do it?"

"Now, Paps, you never ask a lady her secrets. You just admire and enjoy." Oxana looked her father carefully up and down. He seemed to be the same as when she saw him last. His face wore a few more wrinkles and he stood with a slightly more pronounced stoop.

"Are you doing your exercises, Nana?"

"Sometimes Zolotko, sometimes. I am out of the wheelchair and that feels wonderful. But this old body is happy as it is. We are just waiting here."

"Waiting, waiting for what?"

"You know, to meet your mother, my Zaika, again. There is not much else I can do. She is in heaven waiting also. I think she is getting impatient."

Oxana wondered should she get Gregor to give him Rattler. What would the effect be on her Papa? Did it do anything mentally? He seemed to be resigned to a depressing future somehow, resigned but content with his lot. Would Rattler cheer him up and give him some purpose in life? How would he feel if he looked twenty years younger? Would that stimulate him to be more active and to have more hope?

She was taking Rattler since it was first developed. She did not think it changed her mentally, either for better or worse. When she looked in the mirror, she felt her actual age, but was delighted to see the young woman looking back at her. She wondered if Gregor checked the mental effects of Rattler.

"Come Papa, let's go for lunch. Out on the veranda. The sun is shining, even if it is still cold. We can hear the birds sing in the garden."

As they were sitting on the deck, Oxana said, "I met your old sparring partner, Luv."

"Luv, he was a dear old friend. I did not know you were going to meet him. Ah, that man was such a disappointment in the end. He and I were so close, you know. I wanted him to be your godfather."

"Yes, I know. He always sent me cards on my birthday and money from time to time. He seemed to be quite happy. He gave me something for you."

"For me, I don't want anything of his. He let Mother Russia down. He left her, he left me, he left you. What could he have that I want?"

"Freedom, Nana, freedom. He gave me his passport. His American passport."

"Well, you can give it back to him. I don't want it."

Oxana looked carefully at him. Was it possible he hadn't heard? Did Gregor not tell him? Was it not on the news?

"Nana, you know Luv passed away, don't you?"

She could see by his reaction he hadn't heard from Gregor or the news programs. She could see his sorrow at the loss of his old friend and his regret of speaking badly of him. She never heard him speak badly of other friends who passed away. She imagined it was an old Russian superstition. There were so many of those in the past. He looked forlorn, maybe he hoped for a reconciliation. But now that was impossible.

"No, Malyshka, I did not hear." Her father stopped and looked far away into the horizon. The kitchen girl bustled around unloading coffee, bread, eggs, meats onto the table. She chatted the whole time and did not seem to realise no one was listening.

"And he gave you his passport to give to me?"

"Yes, I told him you had not travelled for a while, and you found it difficult to get travel papers. He said we are all prisoners. He missed Russia, he said, and the people and the hardship."

"The hardship? He missed that. Did you hear properly?"

"Yes, he said it was something to made people strong. All the young people were too soft, he said. They wanted for nothing."

"He was a crazy old fool, then. No one should want to go back to the hardship of the past. Let me see the old fool's passport. What did he look like at the end? I only remember him as a younger man. He was in his prime when he defected to America."

Oxana drew the passport from her bag, after checking no one was looking. She knew the cameras on the veranda were looking at the wall and garden. "Here Papa but keep it down. I don't want Gregor or his cronies to see it."

"He looks like me," her father almost shouted as he opened the picture page. "The same hair and eyes. He is old, like me. Look at the great Luv, the most feared of Russian chess masters. He is old. And now, you tell me he is dead?"

"Yes, papa, I am sorry. I know he was your friend."

"That would be funny to travel on his old passport. To pretend I was him. An old joke. If he was alive and not a traitor, we could have fun travelling as each other. There are plenty of stories of twin sisters exchanging with husbands, we could do it as chess masters. That would cause great fun!"

"Well, I will keep this safe for you and if we want to go somewhere, we can. As you say, you look like him. No one would suspect an old timer like you to use a false passport. Now let's eat. I am starving."

Sergei appeared just as they were finishing lunch. They were chatting about chess and the computers beating everyone. Sergei looked at Oxana like a hungry wolf looks at a fat sheep.

"Oxana, Gregor wants you."

"I am having lunch with my father; I'll be there in about ten minutes."

"Now," Sergei pulled the back of Oxana's chair. Her father tried to jump up to protect her, but only spilled the drinks on the table. The serving girl rushed out with a bustling stride and a cloth.

"Sit down, old man," Sergei growled at him. "Now Oxana. No more food, let's go."

Oxana stood up. "I will be back soon, Papa. See you in a little while." Turning to Sergei, she said, "can you get him taken inside? He shouldn't spend too much time out here now. It will chill."

"I am here to get you. He can look after himself. I am not his minder. There are others here for that. Come on."

Oxana looked back at her father, who was crying, as he could not protect her from Sergei. She gave him a thumbs up and a smile. She saw one of the kitchen girls heading to the veranda. She knew they would look after him.

Gregor seemed relaxed as they entered his office. A small young man in a traditional Afghan Turban wearing Paizar footwear was cleaning around the floor with a bucket and mop. Sergei walked over the wet path he had just mopped, leaving a trail of dusty boot prints on the damp surface.

Gregor smiled and said, "Oxana, good to see you. What do you think of our latest recruit?"

"I don't know. Why do you ask?"

"He is a young Afghan prince. Look at how well he wields the mop. That is classic royal behaviour indeed. We are rescuing him from himself. He thinks Russians are barbarians after all the killing we did in his country. We are re-educating him. He will soon think we are the greatest."

"You are a teacher now, Gregor?"

Sergei laughed, and picking a plate off the desk, he threw in on the ground in front of the young boy. It smashed into pieces. Gregor laughed and shouted at the boy while closing his fist and hitting him on the side of the head. The boy reeled.

"Clumsy oaf", Gregor shouted, "pick it up. All Afghans are worthless. You can't even keep the floor clean. We should have killed you all when we were in your country. A nuclear bomb would be too kind to you. Clean it up!"

"We should have killed more of them when we were there, eh, Gregor? Especially the women. Then we wouldn't have vermin like this running around the world." Sergei spoke with some regret. He was a killing machine when he was in the army and missed those days.

The boy stumbled from the bash to his head and, kneeling down, picked up the broken delph with his hands.

Oxana looked at Gregor, "Come on, you are better than that. What is the point of being rich and powerful if you can only beat up refugees?"

Gregor's face turned red, and Oxana thought he might strike her, but he gathered himself and spoke. "Be careful, Oxana. Be incredibly careful what you say to me. This is not a human, he is scum. His people killed many of my friends and embarrassed our great Russian army. He deserves the worst treatment I can imagine, and believe me when I say, he will get it."

Sergei, meanwhile, grabbed the young man by the hair and dragged him to the door. Throwing him out on the floor, he threw the bucket and mop after him.

"Thank you, Sergei. I am sure I would have killed that snail if he stayed here any longer. Oxana, look how kind and how nice Sergei is—he just saved a life. Come, little one, let us go next door and talk. We have much to discuss."

Gregor led the way into the so-called Faraday room. They installed an electronically secure room at great expense a few years ago. It allowed Gregor to stay in touch with people, knowing he was not being listened to by eavesdroppers.

"Oxana, I am not impressed with your request to be part of our little group. I know you have done splendid work for us, and you have proven your loyalty. I am happy to recognise that, but I am afraid the spoils of efforts will stay with me and my two colleagues from my army days. You can never understand the extent of trust we have with each other and what we have seen and done together."

"I think I can imagine it," Oxana said as she remembered the smack the afghani boy just received.

"But I am not unreasonable. We are prospering. I will move to another house soon, a larger one, but not too far away. I will leave your father here with a carer and a housekeeper. I have already sent you money and as a special treat I will pay for you and your father, with a couple of my men, to mind you, of course, to go to Sicily for a rest. You may suffer from stress, and maybe you lost focus on what is important in your life. I will go there myself for a small business matter. I hope to buy a pleasant villa overlooking the sea."

"I assume you can organise a couple of weeks off from your work in Dublin?"

"Yes, I can. I will need to give some notice so I am sure I can go in a few weeks."

"Good, so this is the first step. Let me know the dates and we will bring your father to Sicily to meet you. I have a delightful house there, just in the better part of Palermo. I am sure you will love it there, nice old town, lovely sunsets, plenty of food and drink. It is a perfect place to de-stress."

"Thank you. He needs to see something different. I think he is becoming institutionalised here."

"Now, I need to know what progress the team in Trinity is making with their research? They are trying to create a product like Rattler. Is that correct?"

"Yes, but they are far away from that. They do not have the skills in the team. Although there is one girl, Nancy, who may steer them in the right direction. So far, she is quite quiet and is not making any impression on the direction of their research."

"Good. We might arrange for Nancy to have a minor accident if she seems to make waves which might damage us. The Rattler product is selling well. We brought it to Burning man in California and gave out free samples to the weirdos and highfliers there. They are all coming back for more."

"We are taking a stand at the next Gulfstream and Boeing air show in Farnborough in July and in Dubai in November. We will create a cover company for luxury goods from Russia, but we will give out free samples of Rattler. Once the women try it, they want it. We are changing the formula a little, so the effect takes two years to fully develop. The first effects are quite spectacular and are visible after two months. With this change in formulation, we have a customer for a longer time and if they stop using it, the effects will reverse in a matter of days.

"As a product, it is ideal. Non-physically addictive but completely psychologically addictive for all those rich, vain, and beautiful people. So far there are no side effects either, other than financial ones as they transfer their wealth to me."

Gregor chuckled to himself as he thought of all the monthly subscriptions rolling into their bank accounts.

Oxana said, "I'd love to help you with marketing and selling Rattler. Farnborough is close to Dublin; I could go with you? Am I not the perfect example of its remarkable success?"

"Yes, Farnborough, might work. But first, let us take a trip to Sicily, and get you and your father relaxed. I think we all could enjoy a vacation break. Some nice food and champagne and some nice weather. Maybe we will charter a yacht, or buy one, to sail around. Sea air is wonderful for the mind."

Oxana listened to this is some amazement. This was a different Gregor. Maybe he was changing now the money was rolling in. She thought, if only I could get access to his computer and see where it is going and how much. She knew there was a lab somewhere producing the Rattler product, and it also produced M278. But for now, she was happy she did not have to go anywhere to kill anyone. She would take the good news for now but remain watchful. Gregor was only interested in Gregor.

CHAPTER 47: OXANA EARNS A BREAK FROM HARRIET

Harriet enjoyed going to work. The trip along the canal towpath was green and filled with the sound of nature. She walked along it to the suburban rail system known as the Dart in Grand Canal Basin. It was a two stop hop from there to the station nearest to her lab in Trinity. She enjoyed seeing the diverse age and races of people as she commuted.

The most noticeable were the bikers and runners going towards the huge IT centre at Grand Canal basin. Then the city workers walking in waves into their offices. She enjoyed the bustle surrounding the coffee and food shops with staff working flat out from Monday to Friday. People were friendly and happy to greet her with a smile and 'good morning'.

Like most desk workers, when she settled into her workspace, she popped open her laptop and read through the messages and reminders. There was one in the calendar linking to an earlier message from Oxana. She looked up and noticed she was not at her workstation in the lab. As she read the reminder note, she understood why. *I go on a brief holiday with my father and Gregor Kasansky, a family friend, to Sicily for a couple of weeks. Sorry about the short notice. I will work on my laptop there. I hope you understand. My father is not very well, and it is his first chance to get some sunshine in three years. I will make it up to you.*

What could she do? She reflected the larger portions of the working teams were certainly running more smoothly since Oxana started as project manager. It was a pity they were not making any progress developing a working product. Harriet felt delighted in a way as it allowed her new, secret team to work on developing a functional protype sample.

Harriet typed a brief message; *I just opened this reminder. Have a nice break with your father. Please try to keep me in the loop on progress. The work seems to slow down here. Please ask the team to work quickly when you return. We need to get back on schedule.*

Harriet wrote a hasty and belated email to Frik- *à propos Oxana. You asked to hear if she was leaving Dublin. She just told me she will be in Sicily for two weeks with her father and family friends, someone called Gregor Kasansky. I do not know what sort of family friend he is, just she mentioned him specifically.*

Harriet closed the laptop and called Nancy and Jack into the office.

"Ok, Jack, tell me, what is the latest on the patent front?"

"It is easy enough," Jack said. "We file our data and forms in the patent office. That filing outlines what it is going to be and do. We claim the intellectual property rights to it. We must do that before we commercialise it."

"So, if we can get a design, you know, what it will look like chemically when it is ready, then we can file for that. The real question is how accurately we can describe it and if we can avoid it being copied. The largest risk of infringement is the day after you file. There are people who take every new filing and change it and then file the change under their own name. So, if you then develop it and it is not exactly as you say, then they may try to claim they have rights to what you develop. This is especially true if you are closer to their description than to your own original filing."

"Well, it hardly seems fair", Harriet replied. "We do all the work, and if we change mid-development, they might get the rewards. That seems outrageous."

"Yes, and it depends on what you are filing. If it was for a new type of toaster, for example, they would not bother, as they calculate there is no potential financial upside. But for us, a new beauty product to reverse ageing? That would make them all sit up and go cha-ching."

"We have two choices. Wait until we are on the final product or file dozens of patents to get as close as we can to the final product and hope one of them fits eventually to protect us."

Harriet's face looked more like thunder than sunshine. She was not happy with this news at all. She turned to Nancy. "How close are you to designing what we found in the skin patch?"

"I am not close at all. I have the chemical formula, but I cannot understand how it hangs together. There is an enzyme, there is an RNA double spiked protein from a virus. But there is something else. Some other glue holding it all together. It is probably bits of a bacterium. But there are so many of those and so many are not yet identified. A spoon of earth has more bacterium than there are people on the planet. Many of those are not able to be cultured and reproduced. So, if the people who are supplying Oxana have found and cultured one, I could be years trying to identify it. Years."

"Well," Harriet replied, "that is no good. We don't have years. Any suggestions on how to square this circle, people?"

Nancy spoke, "um, I might," she paused. Harriet jumped in, "yes, come on Nancy, out with it."

"Well, maybe my old lecturer could help. He is called Professor Vescusi. Do you know him? He is a genius at design of these long chain complicated multi carbon based biological chemicals. Maybe he would be willing to talk to us and suggest a way to help us get our chemistry design sorted. Even enough so we could patent it?"

"And who is this? Will he do it for free? If he needs money, it is coming out of your share!" Jack spoke with an edge to his voice.

Nancy replied softly, "I don't know if he needs money. He was always a bit soft on me. Maybe he will just help a former student. We got on well. The thing is, he is in Sicily, and rarely, if ever, leaves there. We will have to go to him."

"Sicily!" Harriet laughed. "You won't believe who is also going there. She emailed me a couple of weeks ago. I'd forgotten about it, until it popped up as a reminder this morning—Oxana—our project manager. Something about her father and a family friend and needing a break."

Harriet could see this might cause a problem. She did not want Oxana to see her in Sicily. The secrecy of her group was important. Yet she knew she needed to meet Professor Vescusi in Palermo. She'd heard of him. He was an expert before he retired. An expert in designing compounds using spike proteins. She was glad to hear he was Nancy's professor for her doctoral years. The time pressure was immense. The prize could be lost every day they delayed.

"Ok, Nancy, set it up, and quickly. Jack, you sort out the flights and the accommodation. We need to move this forward. The guys supplying Oxana could file for Intellectual Property or a patent any day, and then we lose our opportunity. Not only us, but the rest of the lab here, too. Our EU funding would vanish. Like a puff of a vape."

Jack looked at her and realised Harriet was extremely nervous and tense. More than ever before.

CHAPTER 48:
CIRCASSIANS PLAN
TO DEAL WITH
RUSSIANS

It was normally a noisy house. There were always people coming and going. They were mostly women and children. Going to the markets, bringing children to school. The general hustle and bustle of a big family house in a quiet, but exclusive residential street in Kabul. It was a perfect cover. So far, the leader of the extreme and violent Hadiya cell had lived there for five years. The entire world was looking for him and his face appeared on most wanted posters in every corner of earth. The US government put a price of ten million dollars on his head.

The house was downtown, in Qusaba, a nice residential area of Kabul. This was where the ambassadors, lawyers, and highfliers of the Afghan world wanted to live. In former times the citizens of the various colonisers and occupiers created a wide street with plenty of trees and shade. Owners of properties down through the years added flourishes and extensions according to their wealth and style. This made them larger and grander. The overall result was an exclusive and expensive atmosphere.

The more interesting part of the design was the security aspects. There was a chicane located at both ends of the street. There were no side roads onto the main stretch of this street. The chicanes were formed by huge concrete bollards that could be moved to open and close access. The chicane itself was made of heavy concrete blast walls. In the path were huge repeating ramps to ensure all vehicles moved at a snail pace. The materials to block the street completely, heavy trucks and pop-up bollards, remained ready to be moved into position. The street was always under armed guard. Within seconds, the street could be closed. The heavily armed troops made the street impregnable without a heavy military attack.

A few streets away, there was further back up support in an army barracks where a tank was always ready to roll into action. Every action plan by security agents protecting the residents living on the street involved blowing one entrance so it was impassible and escaping out the other.

Every plan designed by those wishing to attack needed sufficient manpower and weapons to attack both ends and also to close the air space above it. The calculations always required several hundred men and equipment. The mobilisation of such a substantial number guaranteed, so far, they never attacked the street in an ambush. Any attack would involve gathering troops and equipment and would be visible for many days in advance.

The leader of the Hadiya liked it here. This was the Paris of the East in the olden days. A place where natural beauty was present and where the borders of many countries met. This made it possible in olden days to collect taxes and to influence behaviours. In more modern times it made it easier for his messengers to travel and bring mission results and for him to send out strategic plans. He had one such plan in mind now.

He looked at his best friend from school. He had arrived quietly during the night. His arrival was carefully scheduled to ensure that the countries chasing the leader of the cell did not become suspicious. They were friends since they were five years old. Their families were close and intermarried with one of his wives being the sister of his friend. The trust they held for each other was absolute.

"So, my friend, what news do you have? How did our two martyrs die in Pakistan?"

"We do not know, for sure. They were fine and in good health. They were celebrating with friends and family and talking of coming to see you here in Kabul. Quite suddenly one of the cousins told his family he felt a bit tired. He went to lie down in a quiet bedroom. They all assumed tiredness was to be expected as he flew across the world in the previous twenty odd hours. Added to that was the stress and emotion of being released after years of imprisonment. His family wished him a good sleep and continued to chat and feel well about his return. The family talked about how he was exhausted with the emotion of release and being back in Pakistan.

When he did not come to prayer the next morning, they went into the room to look for him. To their horror, they found him dead and confusingly his body was decomposing rapidly. They buried him in a few hours."

"And his cousin?"

"His situation was different. He too was fine. He attended the funeral but somehow began to feel weak. Again, everyone thought the same journeys and then the sadness at his cousin's death was exhausting. After evening prayer, he ate with his family and then just collapsed at the table. It was all over in a few minutes. They carried him to a bed and when they laid him on the bed and checked his pulse, he was already dead. They sent for medical help and when it arrived, he was also decomposing. He too was buried quickly, beside his cousin."

"So, you are telling me that both men were both behaving normally; eating, praying, and then suddenly, both were dead in a few minutes."

"Yes, exactly."

They stopped talking and offered prayers for the souls of their fellow brothers in the struggle.

The leader spoke slowly again. "And the message I asked you to send? Did you have any success? Did anyone answer?"

"Yes, they answered. It took over an hour for someone to answer the codes you gave me. They were very cautious. It was clear they were surprised the satellite phone activated and worked. It felt like they were looking for older retired agents to come in and assess the message."

"Yes, that contact method was used in an old covert operation, called Mongoose. That was many years ago—when the Russians were here. I was a young soldier then. You were away studying English and law. I think you are correct, my young friend, the people who knew and used those old codes would be dead or retired now."

"Eventually an American came on the phone. His name was Bill. He sounded old. He checked everything very carefully and I imagine he was reading documents as we spoke. I waited many minutes in between questions. As I waited, I kept expecting a drone to arrive, drop a bomb and blow me to pieces."

"You are under God's protection. His plan for you did not involve a drone that day."

"Yes, it is true. But he gave me information. He would seek to get the Mongoose channel reactivated for a short time. We were to standby and wait. He told me someone from his side would be in touch. One name he shared was that of a man called Gregor in Moscow. Bill felt he would know the reasons behind the sudden death of our comrades. He told me to look at the papers about a Russian chess player who died suddenly Washington DC. His body developed the same rapid decomposition symptoms."

"This is news. Bill is giving good information. Of course, it suits him to do so. They have no love of Russians. If it is true, then our brothers did not die in vain. They have given us a chance to attack the Russians again. We spent many years driving them from this country. I want to keep attacking them and extracting revenge for all the hurt and for all the sons they killed."

"Yes, but they are in Moscow. We do not have many sources there. Or do we?"

"Leave it to me. The less you know, the better. We cannot do much in Moscow, but those dogs never sit still. They are covered in fleas and are always moving about the world. When they leave, we will learn of this from our American friends. We can than make arrangements to interview them. We will know about it. We can, God willing, deal with them then. We hope they go to a country friendly to us."

"Yes, I see. That is good."

"Let us eat and pray. We have much to do and much to be thankful for. Your contact was wise and inspired. Much revenge should flow from it."

CHAPTER 49: FRIK LEARNS ABOUT TWIN SPIKES

The message was from a new, unknown email address. One which was not in his contacts. It was the director of the European health agency in the UK. The message was simple. *There is a match between the skin patch sample to the bodies under investigation. The twin spikes are too similar to be chance.*

There was a lengthy article attached about designing chemicals using Crispr and RNA from virus sources. He didn't read it, as it was far too complicated.

However, the second attachment, titled, *extreme caution* and marked with a red flag, was more interesting. It suggested the best person to assist was Professor Vescusi, in Sicily. Either Palermo or Syracuse, the head of the European agency, did not know. The author included his contact and email details. Frik could follow up.

The head of the agency reported this was a very specialised type of chemistry, and one not associated with normal commercial labs. There was usually a state involvement in these exotic chemicals. The morals and ethics of its development were of grave concern to many scientists around the world. The research, if there was any, should only occur in highly advanced labs well-resourced with experienced scientists and extreme security.

In the food industry, the world banned the mixing of species at the genetic level. This was to prevent scientists blending the genetics of plants and animals to form the so called 'Dracula' combinations. These might lead to a horse crossed with a cow, or an orange crossed with a wheat plant. Scientists followed this ban in many countries of the world, but not all. The techniques could apply easily, once developed and thoroughly understood, to human embryos and reproduction. This could lead to creation of monsters and revival of the practice of eugenics.

The possibility existed some countries could develop the tools, techniques, and eventually—genetically changed products. The sample submitted contained bits of a bacterium, bits of a virus and a long chain biochemical. The design facilitated its ability to attach to the human body at a cellular level. The note from the head of EU Medicines did not speculate what might happen as a result, but the overall tone contained sufficient words of concern and caution to tell Frik the head of the agency was not happy to find this sample in his in-tray.

The letter highlighted this in bold, underlined text. *The European medicines agency does not recommend work on these types of chemicals without extreme caution, elaborate security of samples and oversight from competent and approved regulatory bodies.*

Frik read the message again, and wondered what they would say if they knew this chemical was already out of secure labs and was being used by humans around the world. He thought back to his own limited encounters with the dead bodies. They were in an advanced state of decomposition before he arrived on the scene. But he wondered about the interaction with Oxana. She was alive and presumably touching, interacting, and behaving as any attractive single female in western society. Was she a walking biohazard? Should she be isolated and quarantined?

Frik realised his life was about to get more complicated. He copied the email address and send a message to Professor Vescusi introducing himself and asking when they might have a face-to-face meeting. Frik offered to travel to Sicily if it facilitated a swift and urgent meeting.

When he finished the email, he read a message from Harriet telling him Oxana was going to Sicily for two weeks. He wondered if he could use the opportunity to arrest her.

He emailed Cristiano, *just informed Oxana will be in Sicily in coming days. I also have confirmation that a chemical in her possession has a unique and exotic double spike RNA protein that matches a similar one found in the dead bodies in Lithuania and Seville. I suggest you join me in Sicily so we can arrest her and take her to Seville under a European arrest warrant? Do you agree?*

While he was waiting for a response, he entered a *red flag, report urgently, do not detain*, for Oxana and her father in the Europol database. This update automatically transferred to border agents throughout Europe. The agent would ping him directly when they presented their passports to any border checkpoint.

He also entered the name Gregor Kasansky but could not complete the occupation section of the form, as he was not in their system. Frik and Europol did not know who Gregor was or what he did for a living. He added Gregor's name under known associates.

When Frik hit send on his Europol update, the algorithms went to work and copied the message into the Interpol system. The CIA linked its database into the Interpol system and the name Gregor triggered a message to the team of Fred, Bill and Sam in Langley. Bill looked at it with interest and remembered the call he recently had with an old contact in Kabul.

Bill searched, found and opened an archive file outlining the communication channels used in the previous decade. He hoped his colleagues had not decommissioned them. He expected another call from Kabul, but he thought he might reach out to them first. He found an old mobile phone number which appeared to be a Pakistan number and sent a message. This was using an old code system based on the daily newspaper.

He wrote *according to today's news, there is a movement of people from Moscow to Sicily. The news remarks the weather is better there and could get hotter.*

Bill did not know if this would reach the recipient. The communication channel was old and from a mothballed project. The last message was exchanged ten years ago. This channel was in use before the Americans were in Afghanistan. Since then, they activated and used other methods of communication. He was worried someone might replace and deactivate the old channels.

He called the embassy in Pakistan when it opened. He needed to find a channel to share this message. He was sure the people in Kabul would be interested in knowing Gregor's movement. Bill knew it would at least buy him a favour he could use some day in the future.

Frik read the rest of his emails, totally unaware his one message to Europol triggered the reactivation of an old CIA led communication network and would arouse interest in the Asian subcontinent. He was delighted to receive a message back from Professor Vescusi to say was at home in Sicily for the next two months and could see him anytime. He attached a mobile number and the address of his home in Palermo.

Now all Frik needed to do was to coordinate a meeting with Cristiano, the local Italian police, and then find and arrest Oxana. He felt good. He was sure the information from Professor Vescusi would develop the information from the EU medicines board. Together these should give enough evidence to arrest Oxana and extradite her to Spain for trial.

CHAPTER 50:
CIA SHARE INFO
ABOUT GREGOR

The car drove slowly up the dusty track. The driver was nervous as this was the second he made this trip within a month. Such frequent visits were against protocol. These visits could compromise his safety and of his host.

But he reasoned to himself, he had little choice. The information they gave him was for a fleeting time period only and if they were to act on it, then plans needed to be made and decisions needed to be taken.

The organisation operated as a cell structure where only a few knew anything about anything going on below or above them. At the highest level, there were no electronics, no telephones, no computers. Everything went up to the top did so by messenger, meeting face to face. Each level contained break points where the messenger did not know who was higher. They did not even know how many messengers were between them and the top level.

This structure was slow, but safe. The intervals between messengers and the level of control at the lowest level allowed the organisation to wreak havoc in the world with little risk of repercussions. Yesterday the Americans reactivated communications from Project Mongoose. It surprised the messenger as the organisation thought it was retired and decommissioned. It was a miracle anyone remembered the structure or its history or could understand the encoded message.

He stood in front of the men in a room without windows and with only one door in the basement of a house. He explained the Americans delivered a message over an ancient communication channel. "The project is ten years old and was called Mongoose. It was silent. Yesterday, a message appeared."

"Mongoose? I remember vaguely. That was a long time ago. That was when the Russians were here? Correct? We were younger and naïve. We still listened to the Americans as if they were our friends. We worked with them in good faith."

"Yes, it was a different time."

"So, tell me," The supreme leader sat, and bade his messenger to do the same, "Tell me, what message did they send you? It must be urgent to bring you here on this dusty day."

"The murderer of our two martyrs is on the move. He has left Russia and is going to Sicily in Italy."

"When? Are we sure?"

"We are only as sure as those American dogs want us to be. But it is a chance for us. We have people, good loyal friends in Turkey. It is a small trip to Sicily for them. They can be on the ground, and they can act! We could strike a blow for our fallen soldiers and also make Russia suffer. These men killed many of our brothers in the war."

"Yes, yes, your passion is clear. But let us deal with realities. Starting an operation at such short notice is risky. What do we know?"

"We know they will be in Sicily in a villa outside Palermo for two weeks. Gregor, the murderer, will be there. They are on holiday, so they will not be expecting trouble. They are unlikely to be armed as they fly from Moscow to Sicily."

"This is great news if it is true. It is a simple decision for me to take. I want to see the foul murderers punished. Please proceed, undertake reconnaissance. If an opportunity arises to take a strike, then do so. I authorise it. There are funds in Turkey. Instruct our administrators to release them. Put a small team of four in place. There are four good men who are recently trained. They can go immediately to Sicily, see what they can see and if possible, make a plan to extract revenge for our brothers. The higher the profile of the death of Gregor, the better. I sense we are being blessed by God with this opportunity."

You will have to ask another to carry this message. The infidels are constantly watching and will see you have visited here twice. They may decide to follow you. Find a trusted family member, your brother is old enough now? Get him to travel and bring the message. Do not write it down. Take this trinket from my bracelet, with this the supreme leader removed a bangle from his wrist, as evidence of the source of the message.

Travel fast and travel safe. Take yourself into a retreat for at least a month and do not come back here again for five or six months. There are spies everywhere and we must continue to act with caution.

The group were joined by a host of ladies bringing prepared fruits and meats. They washed and took a meal before the messenger left as dusk was falling. When he left the supreme leader called another lieutenant over. He spoke quietly from behind his hand, "the messenger was here too often and too frequently. He will have to be transferred to the training camp and sent on the next suicide mission in Europe. God willing, he will wreck extreme havoc and spend his after life in heaven surrounded by beautiful virgins."

CHAPTER 51: HARRIET TEAM PLAN TO GO TO SICILY

Nancy walked into the office and Jack quickly followed. It was early on Wednesday morning and most of the rest of the lab were at lectures or studying for their own degree programs.

Nancy smiled from under her long platinum blonde hair. She went into every room wearing a big radiant smile. She possessed an IQ over 135 but was completely happy in her mannerisms and behaviours. Harriet liked her a lot, and she knew Jack fancied her. But Nancy was a challenge. She was known for her sharp tongue. Harriet heard a man trying to ask her out once. He was doing a great deal of humming and hawing and saying things like *maybe we could*. She sliced him with a 'well if you don't know where you want to bring me or when, then I won't go. Get your act together before you waste my time.' The man scuttled off with his metaphorical tail between his legs.

But Jack was playing it calmly. He would bring her a coffee or straighten her coat on the chair behind her. Harriet thought this was a really interesting approach, as she watched Jack take Nancy's perfectly straight coat off the back of her chair and rehang it exactly as straight as it was before. It seemed to be working as Nancy radiated warmth and her special wide smile whenever Jack approached.

"How are you, Nancy?" Harriet asked.

"So good, I spent a super weekend at the Springsteen concert last weekend. He played all my favourite songs. I was buzzing after and still am."

"Really? is he still in fashion with you young kids? Bruce must be seventy years old."

"Oh yes, he may be that and a bit more, but he is so fit and energetic."

"And who did you go with?"

"No one in particular. There were a few of us from my debating team, and some of my old classmates came as well. So, we were about ten people."

Harriet smiled, "I haven't seen him since he was here in Ballsbridge fifteen years ago." Harriet and Nancy hummed, *Born in the USA.* They laughed as they realised what they were doing.

Jack turned away from the computer he was working on, "What's so funny?"

Nancy looked at him, "hi Jack, the prof and I were just dreaming of Bruce Springsteen. I was at his concert last weekend. It was brilliant."

"Ah, the Boss, he is great. I was there too! I didn't know you were going; I would have asked you to join me. I was with a bunch of rugby players and a few GAA lads. We were on the pitch just to the right of the stage as you look at it."

"We were up in the stands. It was great. We could see everything."

"Ah, we were jumping around all night. He is a class act and is still well able to belt out the songs."

Harriet intervened, "ok, ok you two, enough of the concert review." She dropped her voice and looked around. "What is happening with our little side project? Have we any new and innovative designs which might work this time?"

Nancy's smile ran off her face. "I have given you 220 designs for chemicals, Prof. All of them based on using the double spike RNA from the virus to bring the enzyme into the cells."

Harriet jumped in, "Yes, Nancy, I have pulled them together and created them in the lab here. They were all easy enough to create. Some of this new equipment here is simply amazing. Thanks to our European friends for paying for it all."

Harriet said, "I set up the screening and tests. None of

chemicals were stable. Once they were injected into living tissue cultures, they simply dissolved or burned down to their basic molecules."

Nancy shook her head, disappointed. "We are missing the base glue or foundation for these. Or maybe it is something else. At least one other something. There is something else in there and I do not know what it is. It may be RNA or a protein from another species. I thought it was just another long chain carbohydrate. Something that would act like a glue to the enzyme and the double spike. But what I think it is, is not working. My old prof in Sicily would say we need a pin, a dowel, something to hold it together until it gets into the cell and then the telomerase enzyme can work on the cell telomeres. But I can't find the pin. I need help."

They all paused and thought about the challenge facing them. If it was clothing, they were pinning together, they would just get a needle and thread or a patch and iron it on. If it was a house, they would get a nail or a screw or a staple. At the subcellular level in a tissue sample, they needed the biological equivalent of a staple or glue. There were none on sale in the local suppliers, so they invented it. Invent it, make it, and then test it for strength. So far, everything they tried had fallen apart.

They knew someone else had overcome the problem before. This was causing them immense frustration. Someone else had cracked it. They just needed some inspiration. They had Oxana's patch, and they could see every day the effect it showed on her features. They tested it every way they could, and it would not give up its secrets.

"Maybe it is a two-step process?" Harriet said aloud.

"Maybe it is, but what are the steps?" Nancy said.

"Well, if we make the enzyme stick to something else first and then stick the spikes to that. We are trying to put the enzyme in the middle. Maybe if we put it in the end?" Jack was talking aloud. As he was really an administrator, and a good one at that, he knew he was really out on a limb technically.

Nancy looked at him, "oddly enough, you may be right, if only my old prof would look. He can be brilliantly innovative. He is crazy, or, if I am kind, he is eccentric. But he might see the answer to our problem."

"Who is that?" asked Harriet.

"Oh, my old prof in Sicily, in Palermo. Antonio Vescusi. I told you about him before. He is as daft as a brush, but he has a brilliant mind. His speciality is designing chemicals with unusual bits added. He used to be an architect when he was young, then he became a famous pianist, then he became interested in biochemistry at the cellular level. He is a genius, but never leaves his house anymore. He is technically retired but as the university benefits from his name and prestige they try to keep him around. He even gives tutorials in his home now. He must have developed agoraphobia."

"And he was your prof?" This information impressed Harriet as she tried to remember their previous conversation about him. "I have heard of him. Everyone has. He is the Bruce Springsteen of the genetic modification business. He has forgotten more than most of us know."

Jack looked on mystified. "Will he see you if you ask? Can he help solve the problem?"

Harriet looked at Nancy expectantly. Nancy swallowed, "as Harriet says, he is like Bruce, you just don't rock up and see him. Plus, everyone knows he is super private. He just wants to be alone. He refuses people constantly."

"But?" asked Jack. "I sense a *but* there?"

"Well, he treated me like his favourite. He was always extremely sweet to me."

"You need help. I mean, we all need help with the design of the chemical. The missing piece. We need a stable chemical. Even when we discover it, it will take ages to get tests and patents, not to mention approvals. Did we not say we had to go see him?" Harriet spoke with an edge to her voice.

Jack looked at Nancy. "Did you ask to meet him? Tell him the problem? We have a shareholding left if he needs money."

Nancy said, "I didn't. Not yet. Keep thinking Bruce

Springsteen, Jack! My old Prof is like him, he does not need money. An offer of money might insult him. If you offered Bruce money to see you, he would probably tell you to talk to his manager and give you nothing. No, I need something else, something more personal. I will talk to him, but if I get it wrong the door closes."

Harriet and Jack looked intently at Nancy, "ok, let's make a plan to approach him gently. We don't want to lose the opportunity."

CHAPTER 52:
CIRCASSIANS
TO SICILY

The Circassian men gathered in a tight group outside the mosque as the motorbike roared noisily into the square. The driver kicked the stand down and removing his helmet, walked over and joined them. They moved to one side to let the messenger into the centre of their circle.

"We have approval to observe and if possible, to strike. They released the funds, the target is in place, and we are to be in Sicily in three days. Everyone here will be involved, but only four of us will undertake the mission itself. The captain will remain with the rigid inflatable boat to bring us back home after our victory. We need to complete our plans urgently."

"I have fuelled my boat, and it is ready to sail. We can make most of the journey under cover of darkness and land as daylight is breaking, so we can safely moor up for our return journey."

"I will access the weapons and materials we need tonight. I will bring them to the boat tomorrow in the late afternoon. We will meet here and drive to Kas. There is a large car park there beside the ferries. We can park in Otto car park and launch the boat. Be sure to buy a ticket for three days to park. It is not a problem as it is normal for ferry users to park and share a car across. Using this space is like hiding in plain sight. At night the ferries do not run so we have no danger from them."

"Our route will take us by Rhodes and Crete so we will have to look out for the Greek navy. They are always looking for migrant ships. Our little rib is too small to be interesting to them so we should be safe. But we are heading to a part of Sicily with a rough passage into landing. The Mediterranean Sea and the Ionian Sea meet there so it can be difficult."

"The landing at Porto Palo di Capo Passero is easy as there are some old fishing cassettas there. The contact will leave a big container near the old port, and it will be safe. Everyone will think it is for tourists or for something in the construction as the port is a bit old and crumbling."

"I have looked at the tides and God is kind to us; they are favourable for a night crossing. Coming back will be more difficult but we will sail with satisfaction for the revenge we have achieved in our hearts."

"I am ready to go. I want to seek revenge for the death of the martyrs of our friends in Pakistan."

"Me too. We will strike so they know our wrath for their taking of the lives of our brothers."

The men in the circle leaned into the centre with rigid backs. They clenched their fists in silent affirmation. Their voices uttered the words rapidly, and they spoke in deep, loud whispers. They prepared for this day and were ready to do whatever it took to deliver the mission set in motion days ago in Afghanistan.

They left Kas in high spirits. They brought two cars and paid the car park for three days. They unloaded the boat from the trailer and took the now empty trailer to the boat storage space in the Marina. They were confident it would be safe as there were many more parked in the boat yard. It was dark and the noise from the bars and clubs in the town was loud. A few people walked their dogs along the shore, and no one made any remarks as they loaded their sacks filled with their guns and explosives into the hold of the boat.

Their captain positioned them to be balance the boat in the water and slipped the mooring line. With a low rev in the engine, they moved slowly away from the land and into the inky sea. Gliding by large ferries dark and silent, they looked back at the shore wondering about their fate in the next hours.

The trip was endless. After passing north of Rhodes they were in Greek waters and the tension of encountering a passing Greek navy coast guard was acute. They rotated position in the boat, carefully, as they could easily tip it over, and took turns looking forward. Without lights and only the stars in the sky to light the sea, every shadow became a hazard. The captain was looking for nets, old floating shipping containers, illegal wracks of floating garbage and other people sailing at night.

The radio was set to mute, and they did not wish to turn the volume on. They moved to the north of Crete, into more busy shipping lanes, but they did not wish to accidently run into refugee boats moving from Africa to Europe. They crossed a fishing line once and as they hit it; the captain killed the engine so the propellors would not catch. They tipped the engine out of the water and cut off the thick line of the drifting net. They were sorry but one fisherman would have no catch when he returned.

The hardest bit of the voyage was after they left the northern shores of Crete. They felt comforted by the light from the island and the sound of music drifting across the water. After they passed there was nothing but wide-open water. Clouds came over the sky making it darker. The captain was steering simply by compass heading and became increasingly sharp as he spoke to the men. They were looking for a specific landing spot and he was afraid of missing it.

As they crossed the sea the going became rocky and two of the men quickly became ill and were sick over the side. This was dangerous also as the risk of turning over grew the more movement there was in the boat. The heavy guns and equipment helped stabilise the boat, but they were getting wet as water broke over the bow in the choppy waters.

Land appeared slowly as did the dawn and the captain relaxed. He was by the grace of God and a good compass in the right corner of Sicily and was able to quickly see the slope of the land and the crumbling old pier. The Cozzo Spadaro lighthouse greeted them with its three white flashes every ten seconds. The captain sighed and raced towards the beach only cutting the engine as he slipped onto the beach beside the mooring of the old fishing boats. A fat seal followed them in, hoping for some food.

The two sickest men dragged themselves ashore and threw themselves on the ground. The other two were busy unloading the gear and equipment. The two men on the ground slowly rose and washed their beards and faces. They laughed as they looked at each other. "You're paler than a ghost." The other slapped his friends' cheeks and said, "a ghost, is it? You are like white chalk. Even your black beard is silver.

The other men shouted over, "come on, we could see all night as you lost your food, you're not sailors. Let us see if you are donkeys and can carry this equipment. We walk to our rendezvous. It is not far, but you are useless so far with your seasickness. Come here and take this sack."

The men did as they were bid. Time was short. Food and prayers were high on their plans before they took the jeep to Palermo. Today would be the time to check their weapons and to complete the plan. They still need to travel over 200kms to reach their destination.

"Revenge will be ours," one cried as he heaved the sack of machine guns onto his back. "It will give me the strength to carry this forever."

"Or at least to carry it for five minutes," the eldest of the four joked.

The second man opened the waterproof pouch and extracted a small smartphone. He pushed the startup button with a shaky finger. His eyes scanned the screen repeatedly as it allayed his doubts one by one until the map opened with a red pin embedded. He uttered a silent prayer of thanks.

Reading the directions displayed on the small green screen, their destination was about two km east of their location. Taking the lead, he left the stony beach and the grey black rib that brought them across the Mediterranean during the night. Dawn was breaking in front of them as they walked in single file along a goat track. The captain waved at them and headed for another mooring to wait their return.

The map showed a road beside the beach and off it was a

minor road for the last few metres of their journey. He would split them into two groups of two for part of their journey so they would not be so noticeable. There were no car lights visible on the horizon, but the island would wake up soon. People might go to work early to get ahead of traffic. There were also illegally parked tourist mobile vans around.

The road appeared exactly as shown. The two men with the loads sat in the ditch out of sight while the elder man and the man with the telephone walked on. It was only five hundred metres. They expected to see a small fisherman's cottage, or perhaps an old farmhouse. But nothing came into sight. Just a small steel container used to carry freight on the high seas. It lay at a strange angle with one end in a ditch and the access doors about three metres into the air. They walked around it carefully and the red pin on the map was certain. This was it.

The angle of it made it impossible to enter the doors. They could see the combination lock holding the doors closed was still in place and snapped shut. A truck or tractor must have hit and pushed the container into its new position. But no such machine was there. The men looked at each other, puzzled.

"This is not good."

"The jeep is supposed to be inside."

"We have to get this out of the ditch to get the jeep out."

"We need a tow truck or a tractor."

"Here come the others. Could we push it back?"

"There are at least two tonnes of steel plus a bloody big jeep. There is no way to push it."

"We need a machine, a strong one."

The two waiting men were called forward and threw down their heavy loads and wiped the sweat from their forehead. The morning chill was gone, and the temperature was rising from the sun.

"Let me climb up and open the door and see what is inside. If the jeep is gone or damaged, then we will have to improvise. Here, push me up."

The lightest man climbed onto the back of his compatriot

and reached the ledge of the container. With some trouble, he opened the combination lock and pulled the door open.

His nose wrinkled as the smell of diesel came rushing out of the container.

He looked down at the others.

"It is here. It looks ok, but it has lost fuel. The smell is terrible here."

"Will it start?"

Turning back inside, the others waited. They heard an engine roar after a few seconds and a black plume of smoke came out of the door.

The engine died and their compatriot appeared at the door, "move away. The jeep is in the back. If I drive it towards the door, the entire container should tip over. When the weight of the jeep hits the front here near the door, then be ready to jump out of the way! "

The other men stood back, and their lips moved constantly as they uttered prayers. They heard a loud roar as the engine revved and the container moved. Slowly at first and then with a sudden bang as it tipped over. The jeep burst out through the doors into the space where they were standing. The driver was frantically pressing the brakes to stop its advance. It crashed to the ground about a metre from the rest of the men. It stopped in a cloud of dust. The springs creaked and groaned, the engine died, and they all laughed.

The men loaded all the equipment into the jeep and looked into the container. It was empty apart from some diesel fuel running out the door onto the earth. The jeep was mostly empty too except for bottles of water they sniffed, sipped, and then drank with some relish. They washed their hands and face, loaded themselves into the jeep. Finding the destination on the map in the centre of Palermo, they set out.

CHAPTER 53:
HARRIET AND TEAM
FLY TO SICILY

The three members of the special sub team, Jack, Harriet, and Nancy spent ages deciding who should go to Sicily and how long they should stay there. The decision was driven by the usual financial stress of life in a university. Despite receiving a large EU grant, there wasn't spare cash for hotels and flights. The cost of sending the three to Sicily and spending a night there would blow a big hole in their travel allocation. They know there were a few other conferences they would need to attend in the coming years. They did not wish to prevent themselves from attending those conferences as they would be important.

Eventually, all three decided to go as they found flights allowing a single day visit with an early start and a late return. It was risky though if delays to the flights occurred or if the conversation with the professor in Sicily took longer than expected.

Nancy knew the professor was elderly and unlikely to want to talk for very long, so when the flights fell in price on a special sale, they booked them for less than seventy euros return each. They could not get three seats together, but a two and a one. They felt this was not important. The most important was to prepare well for the professor so they could get his best ideas quickly before he fell asleep or became tired.

The day of departure arrived. They travelled without bags, but the flight was at silly o'clock in the morning. There were no busses running, so Jack collected them in his car. The cost of car parking for the day was much less than the taxi fare to and from the airport. In the early morning light, there was no traffic, and they arrived at the gate early.

Nancy and Jack soon became animated talking about their favourite music and the concerts in Europe they had attended. There were quite a few overlaps. As they did not know each other before meeting in Trinity, they were sure they were in many of the same places at the same time.

When they boarded, they sat together to continue talking about places and bands. Harriet brought her earphones and podcasts and was happy to let them chat. She was glad to move to a seat on her own, away from them. She even hoped she might get a few minutes' sleep on the three-hour journey.

As Harriet settled in her seat, a tall leather clad woman sat beside her. She was long and lithe with wide strong shoulders common to regular and long-distance swimmers. Harriet guessed she was around her own age, give or take a couple of years. But she seemed to be much more self-assured and physically strong for a woman of thirty-four.

They exchanged glances, introduced each other, and made brief hellos. The clothing of her companion immediately struck Harriet. She also looked exactly like one doll she had owned for over fifteen years. The doll was called Teresa. The long leather boots with the hint of stockings at the upper thigh where they met an A-Line skirt, again made of black leather. The white blouse was softer on this woman. The well-worn leather bikers' jacket had a patina about it that developed from spending many hours in sun, wind, and rain.

Harriet spoke first. "Hello, are you a good flyer?"

The lady looked at her with bright blue piercing eyes. Not old, but there was a keen, somewhat animalistic look behind them.

"I fly all the time for work. I have got used to it. Thank heavens for podcasts!"

The high quality of her English surprised Harriet. Her skin colour was olive and tanned a rich shade of brown. Harriet thought she was from Spain or even Greece. But there was a touch of an English accent to her voice.

"You have excellent English. I thought you were Greek or Spanish. Where do you buy your clothes? They are quite special."

"Thank you. My father was half Italian, half Spanish. My mother is from Northern Ireland. They met at the end of the war. He was a soldier; she was a cook. I spoke different languages with each parent. Then I spent some years living in Holland. There are so many polyglots there. I felt quite uneducated! But I learned some Dutch and German. "

"Oh my, you are so lucky. I am afraid mine only spoke English, some of it quite biblical too, as my father was a minister."

"I am not so good on the biblical unless it is swearing. Which I do best in Italian. As for my clothes, they are work related. I like leather, it is so hard wearing. I have worn this jacket since I was nineteen. I feel so strong and safe in it. It has travelled all over the world with me."

"It suits you. The black with the white blouse and then your lovely tan. It is quite an impressive outfit. You look like a powerful woman."

"Thank you, yes, it all comes together nicely. Plus, it is easy to keep clean."

"What do you do? You say you fly all the time for work, unless it is a personal question, of course."

"Hmm, you said you were called Harriet. Is that right?"

Harriet nodded.

Teresa continued, "ah good, normally Harriet, I make up a story when someone asks me what I do. But I feel I want to tell you the truth, right from the start. I am a high price dominatrix. I fly to my customers in the capital cities of Europe."

Harriet looked at her hands and then out the window and fixed her skirt around her legs as she sat up a little straighter. "Um, I see," she said.

Teresa spoke after a moment. "I know it is sometimes a shock. Let's forget about me. Do you like to fly?"

Harriet pondered the question and all the chat and said, "I am not sure. I do not fly too often. Mostly around Europe. I am usually going for a reason related to work, a bit like you, but not your kind of work, so I don't think about it. I never felt unsafe, but I know many are."

"Yes, it is so true. People just need a firm hand sometimes to get them to do what they should. What work do you do?"

"I am afraid what I do is not as exciting as you. I am a professor in a Dublin university and a research scientist trying to uncover the secrets to age well."

"Oh, I like the sound of your work. Ageing well."

"Yes, we all live much longer now, so we need to live as well as possible. I wanted to tell you Teresa, and it is something private to share with you, I have a doll at home just like you. I can't wait to go home and tell her and dress her in a white blouse. She has the leather trousers and jacket. She wears them when she is not in her school uniform."

"Really, that is so interesting. I keep dolls too. But all my dolls are male. Men in suits and gym gear and uniforms. What do you call my doll?"

"I always called her scrubber, but now I might rename her. Now I have met you!"

"You are funny. Scrubber. What a name."

"Oh, yes." Harriet pursed her lips. "She can be a handful. I have to be very firm with her. Very firm indeed."

Teresa fell silent at this remark. This was not something she expected from a university professor. The captain cut in on the PA to make his normal announcements and the coffee wagon made its way down the aisle towards them.

The girls plugged in their earphones and went into their own worlds.

CHAPTER 54: OXANA AND FATHER IN SICILY

Oxana looked out over the town from the second floor of the building in Palermo. It was impressive. She admired Gregor's taste in property. A nice dacha in Moscow, a pleasant villa here. She wondered what other properties he owned around the world.

This property was on Via Emerigo Amari and was a lovely penthouse. Just beside the church and at the cul-de-sac.

He was not too happy, though. He wanted a country house. The city was too noisy and smelly for him. He was looking for a nicer property in Syracuse on the other side of the island. He showed Oxana an image of a palace in The Giudecca on the island of Ortega. He impressed her once again with his taste in property.

She learned last night the business was earning good money and the dollars were rolling into their accounts around the world. The Rattler product launch, if you could call it that, at Burning Man in California, was a tremendous success. To their surprise more men than women purchased the product initially. The launch was two months ago and since then, the orders were off the scale. Sergei and Alexandr were over the moon with delight at the success. He sent them to the production factory to increase the production of the product, and to speed up the process. Oxana still did not know where the factory was, but they drove to it in their big black jeep from Palermo.

When the initial customers witnessed the age reversal effects after a month, there was a rush in sales on the app. This was helped by the family and partners of the initial users buying it for the first time for themselves. She learned Gregor charged five thousand dollars a month. The recent uptick in sales created a waiting list of customers. To get started Gregor gave them his preferred option of taking a contract for 12-month supply. She overheard one order for four treatments to go to one home in Silicon Valley. She calculated if there were one hundred clients, his income would be over five hundred thousand dollars per month. These figures made it simple to understand why he wanted more exclusive property.

The USA was his target market. With its twenty-four million millionaires and seven hundred billionaires, she imagined his sales would reach ten million dollars a month in a noticeably brief time.

She overheard Gregor talking about moving the factory to one outbuilding in the grounds of the palacio he was considering purchasing in Syracuse. She was surprised as she imagined a big industrial unit would be needed not an outbuilding in a palacio. But given his experience in drug manufacturing she did not doubt his skills. Rattler must be an extremely pure product.

He could fit forty-eight patches, enough for four people for a year, into a mobile phone box. A shoe box could probably hold enough for one hundred people for a year. A hat box would hold ten million dollars' worth of Rattler. She clucked and shook her head in disbelief as the size of the business became clear to her.

She couldn't keep the large numbers in her head. She understood Gregor would make millions every day, just in the US. She really wished to get in on this action. But she was stuck on the scraps, if even they were scraps from the table of these rich men. It was more like crumbs after the birds picked over the table.

The security Gregor placed around him in Palermo was intense. The building was large and there were only four apartments in the building. There were high gates at the access to the car park and cameras and double doors at the lobby entrance. Gregor rented all of the other apartments for his security team. That is where Sergei and Alexandr were staying.

She had the pleasure of staying with her father in the penthouse.

The cook and drivers stayed in the third apartment. She looked down at the cars parked in the space in front of the block; she counted twelve, including three big jeeps and two vans. A couple of powerful motorbikes stood there as well.

He certainly travelled in style. She thought Gregor was acting increasingly like a rock star than an ex-Russian army man. She saw several heavily armed men on patrol inside the grounds. These were probably former Army comrades of Gregor, Alexandr and Sergei. She imagined they had seen plenty of death and created their share of it as well.

But it was time for breakfast. She finished brushing out her blonde wig and slipped it on over her own pale, thin hair. She smiled at the mirror in front of her and took some lipstick off her teeth with a tissue. She was looking forward to breakfast on the balcony with her father. Maybe he would play a game of chess with her. Something from his glory days. She could follow the moves of his opponent using one of his books. They liked that. He often expounded on what should have happened at various stages. His mind was so great and strong.

CHAPTER 55: FRIK AND CRISTIANO IN SICILY

As Frik walked through Palermo airport, he expected to be stopped and challenged by somebody in a uniform looking for some document or piece of paper. They were in troubled times after all, and he knew he held a Covid vaccine certificate, and a declaration of movement, and a passport, and a boarding pass, and an antigen test result. The list made him tired as he thought through it. These were all scanned into his phone. Being a thorough German police officer, he also carried a paper copy of them in his carry-on bag. He hoped he was ready, but there was always this niggling doubt. Even with his list prepared, completed, and every item ticked, he still was uneasy.

He just kept walking and there was no sign of border or health control, or anything resembling a stop and show us your papers sort of place. He just kept walking and followed the signs for the train station. He knew he needed a train ticket and just before the stairs to the Metro, there they were a bank of three automatic ticket selling machines. The obligatory office was beside them but was, as seemed to be the norm, closed.

Looking around at what other people were doing, he approached the first ticket machine and found it presented instructions in six different languages. Using a credit card, he bought a one-way ticket to the central train station for six euros and ninety cents. As he was leaving, a Donuts shop flickered its neon signage. He bought a cafe espresso and a croissant, which cost five euros. He only took the croissant, as the train ride was nearly an hour from the airport to the city. He did not like the stereotype of police officers and donuts.

The train was sitting on the platform, ready to go. After finding a space for his luggage, he sat down and opened the window. A train with a window that opened— unusual, he thought. The journey to the central station was uneventful. Hardly anyone got on or off. The tourists had not returned and Covid was still impacting on travel. The scenery out the window was drab, rocky, and untidy. They arrived at a station, stopped, and left nineteen times in the short distance. Frik found these constant stops raised his blood pressure, and he paced up and down the empty carriage. He knew it was pointless as there was no express train from the airport to the city centre. Only this inch by slow inch suburban one.

It was, of course, great for the locals who wanted to get to town without a car. It also helped politicians. They could make speeches about how they arranged for the train to stop near the voters they were trying to woo.

Before he boarded the train, he checked the options on Google maps to get to downtown Palermo. He saw it was a thirty-minute car drive. But he did not wish to hire a car. He was only going to be in Palermo a few days and he hoped he would have a police car to bring him back to the airport—and if all went well— with a prisoner in tow.

As the train rattled despite its interminable slow pace, he reflected with a cheerful smile there was a real chance of taking a killer off the streets.

Eventually the train reached central station downtown. Palermo was enjoying a cool, damp day. It was early Spring and while the days were warm; the evening was cool, and it clouded over from time to time. The locals loved this kind of weather, as it gave them a chance to wear heavy boots and winter coats. These were items of clothing they rarely needed, but they loved to use when they got the opportunity.

Frik did not know this part of Italy but had heard much about it. From Mafia crime to ancient Roman and Greek history fused with Arabic influences, it was a mixed pot of culture, architecture, and history. The food, music, and the attitudes of the people developed from this cultural blend.

After stepping from the train and leaving the building, a whizzing electric scooter nearly struck him. These were a considerable success in Palermo if the numbers were anything to go by. The riders, however, showed a cavalier attitude and expected pedestrians to get out of their way. His first fifty meters walk was quite an adventure with at least three near misses. They were so silent they could hit you in an instant. The olden days of the noisy two-stroke scooters were failing fast. From an air pollution and global warming point of view, that was a good thing, but it made walking more dangerous.

He popped into one of the many phone shops and got himself a local data only contract for a week. The chatty man in the store set it up and gave him access to the Italian data networks if his German account didn't function perfectly. He had as a backup an Europol issued device that acted like a mobile Wi-Fi, but It was another piece of electronics to carry and keep charged. He preferred the virtual sim option, as it was cheap, quick, and easy to use. He then sent a WhatsApp message to his family back in Munich and one to Cristiano to see where he was and when they could meet.

Frik's flight was an early one, so he was tired. The hotel advertised a check-in time of 15:00. He asked at the hotel reception, and he was in luck. There was a room ready, and he could check in early. He took the chance to drop his bag and have a quick shower.

The hotel room was as advertised. It was nice and large and would do nicely for his two- or three-day visit. He connected to the hotel Wi-Fi and quickly checked to see for any new messages.

The reply from Cristiano said he was just boarding his flight in Seville and would be with him in three or four hours. Cristiano said he contacted the local police, and they were to meet around midday. The best part of the message was they might have an address for Oxana. Frik fist pumped the air. Things could go well, he thought.

He was looking forward to meeting Cristiano again. They could talk to the professor together to try to understand what was going on in the chemicals. They could get a chance to arrest Oxana and solve two murders. This could be a good trip. He stretched out on the bed for a catnap. He would get a few minutes' sleep and then go for breakfast and a look around Palermo until Cristiano joined him.

CHAPTER 56: HARRIET AND TEAM MEET THE GENETIC EXPERT

Nancy led the way out of the airport to the car-rental desk. The flight landed just after ten a.m. and they needed to transfer to Palermo, meet the professor, explain their situation to him, have a chat, and then get back to the airport for the return flight. It was all rushed. They booked an early morning flight out and a late-night flight back to Dublin. The risks were high as they might be delays due to air traffic strikes or planes just running late.

They spent hours discussing who should go and eventually decided all three would go: Jack, Nancy, and Harriet. The flights were cheap and if they sent one plus an overnight, it would nearly be the same cost. They hoped all three arriving at the professor would not put him off, but they thought it might flatter him more. They all wanted to meet him, as a famous scientist, and also bring him a cake, for his birthday.

Google maps showed a car parking space underground not too far from the professor's house. The street image of the house showed it was quaint with a nice garden, stone walls, and a dark slate roof. It was a lovely house and part of an ancient terrace of four. It was just beside a nice Catholic church and was part of the parish. They all looked at the images on the laptop and they imagined it was built around the same time as the church, given its style and colouring, and a stone façade.

When she saw the high walls and the solid gate, she was nervous he might even have security. They did not prepare for an interview with burly men speaking Sicilian. There was too much at stake and so much depended on getting the prof to help them.

After talking to Jack and Harriet, Nancy hit upon the idea of his birthday. It took her ages, but she found out it was two weeks ago. She messaged him and they chatted back and forth. She told him, even if it was not strictly true, she was going to Sicily, and she would bring him some cake.

He seemed delighted, so she proposed a date to him, and he looked at his computer and, to her great delight he agreed. Now she needed to get a flight, get accommodation, get a car, and get a nice cake. Plus, make her plan of how to bring up the problem they were having and getting him to help her.

It was all so manipulating. She did not like it, but the rewards were huge, and Jack kept on saying 'another week and the Russians did not file a patent, we must be running out of time.'

They walked to his front door and rang the buzzer. It surprised them when the professor opened it himself and greeted them with a huge smile and a rapid flow of Italian. Nancy allowed the traditional hugs and kisses and introduced Harriet and Jack to Antonio. She took care to introduce him formally to the others using the word 'professor'.

His reaction to Harriet was special. He must admire her work, as he bowed deeply and was very formal. He talked about how honoured he was to have such an eminent scientist in his humble home.

This display of admiration embarrassed Harriet, and they quickly moved into his front room. His wife waited there, and they went through the ritual of kisses and hugs and introductions again. His wife, Lucia, was quite frail with a steely look to her grey eyes.

She took the cake Nancy brought with her and went to the kitchen to prepare it and some coffee to go with it.

"So, thank you for coming and thank you for the cake. I am sure, though, there is another reason for this trip. You did not spend so much money to buy an old man a cake?"

"True", Jack said to the discomfort of the others. "Nancy has spoken so highly of you we also wanted to meet you and yes, there is a problem we have you could help us with, or at least it might intrigue you?"

Harriet also spoke, "my team of over 20 scientists, students, postgraduates are working with European funding to develop an anti-ageing compound that will help us all to live better now the medics have us living longer."

The spike expert professor listened and spoke easily, "but I am retired. I do not know of all the new techniques of gene editing and splitting. These are in your area, Nancy and you, Harriet. What do I know that can help you?"

Nancy spoke, "well you are being modest. Several of your published research papers are still the reference documents describing how to split genes. They are in use in labs and Universities all over the world."

"Thank you, thank you for these kind remarks. But can we be a bit more specific? What do you have? What do you need?"

Jack unfolded the chronograph and presented it. He marked it up with likely elements to make it clearer to read.

"This is a product we found that appears to be a success. It does not have a patent allocated to it, nor is it registered on the database of known compounds. We happened on it by chance. The problem is we cannot replicate it in our lab. We make the design, and Nancy does a great deal of that. We want it to lead to the product but when we do it, Harriet is the master there, it is unstable and collapses before we can analyse it."

The spike expert professor looked at the document and spoke about the bits that were combining to make it up. Their conversation became quite technical.

All were speaking at once and they barely noticed as his wife returned with a tray of coffee and cakes prepared on little napkins.

"Have you tried B. Necrophage? The professor asked.

"No," Nancy replied, "we did not. That is quite a destructive bacterium on human flesh, so we did not think it would work when we were trying to promote life."

"Well, try it," he suggested. "It has a strange on-off switch and I think in combination with the spikes, it may actually have a different effect on the cells. But enough talk. Let us eat cake."

Jack could see this suggestion of her old professor completely perplexed Nancy. The bacterium he mentioned was generally found in decomposing bodies, animals especially. The frown on Nancy's face told Jack this was a wild goose chase and the old professor was not as astute as he once was. It was clear she had no faith nor belief in his suggestion a bacterium known for its skill at degradation of flesh could possibly act in maintaining and enhancing skin cells. Harriet was strangely quiet and appeared to have dismissed the idea completely.

They all sang Happy Birthday to the professor and spoke of his early years and the people he knew. He was so interesting as he spoke of the advance of electricity and how microscopes with light were such an advance in its day. He wondered aloud and many others do also about what is below the next layer. Every time they find the contents of something, there comes along another new technique to reveal another layer below what everyone thought was the last one.

The discussion was over. That was clear. The spike expert professor gave them his time, eaten his cake, and was not to be drawn again on the matter they brought. He too perhaps sensed their disappointment and disbelief and felt he had spoken enough. He reminded them again he was retired. He went on to state their visit reminded him of the peace he now enjoyed and he no longer stressed or worried about the outcomes of bad actors splitting and recombining genes.

They were leaving and he had offered only one suggestion, one they thought was completely chasing shadows. If he thought of another idea, then he was keeping it to himself. It was a pleasant visit but perhaps a waste of time and money. None the less, they promised him they would try it and left the house with a flurry of hugs and kisses again. The time moved along quickly, and there was about two hours before they were due in the airport for their return flight.

CHAPTER 57: THE CIRCASSIANS ATTACK

They walked out of the spike professor's door, admiring his small overgrown front garden with amazing colourful flowers of all shapes and hues. The noise of the city was louder here as they reached the street. The sound of a heavy engine jeep made them all look up as it raced past them into a cul-de-sac with six steep steps at the end.

Jack was about to say something when the four-wheel drive crashed at speed into a heavy double timber door at street level that presumably led to a series of apartments. The door spilt from the impact. Two heavily camouflaged men with what appeared to be flak jackets jumped out of the now wrecked jeep and ran through the smashed door.

Jack saw two more men carrying machine guns run down the steps of the cul-de-sac towards the men leaving the jeep.

The sound of an explosion followed, and Jack watched in slow motion as a compact car flew and headed straight for Nancy, who was a few steps in front of him.

The blast hit him, and it blew him backwards into a row of parked motorcycles. Pain filled his body as his arm and leg collapsed on impact.

He saw, with amazement and surprise, Oxana running out the door where the jeep had opened a gaping hole, rapidly followed by three men carrying guns. They were firing into the hallway of the building where the explosion happened. Two latecomers arrived after the jeep opened fire from behind a car and two of the three men with Oxana fell to the ground. The third turned and fired a rapid burst at the men behind the car as Oxana darted away towards the church.

Harriet got to her feet, shaking her head and banging her ears with the flat of her hand. Jack tried to wave at her to get down, but his arm was not working. Suddenly a horse and wagon used by tourists galloped alongside Harriet and the man in front grabbed her and pulled her off the street. A hail of bullets hit the tail of the wagon, as it galloped away, causing splinters to fly into the air.

The men continued to shoot at each other and the one with Oxana made a dash for the church after her. Another tall, good-looking man arrived with a gun pulled and fired at the two men hiding behind the car. Their guns fell silent and then another explosion ripped through the air as Jack passed out unconscious on the road.

Jack awoke in a hospital bed with the sound of machines pinging and purring. His arm was in a sling over him, and he could see a part of his leg elevated and also in a cast. Pain was everywhere but was dull. His eyes looked around and saw Harriet sitting in a chair, looking at her phone.

She heard him gurgle, "what happened?"

Harriet looked at Jack and asked how he felt. He sat up and looked at his arm in a plaster and his leg suspended from a weight overhead.

"How do you think I feel? I don't remember much but a very fast series of noises and shots. I saw Oxana and poor Nancy. She was smashed by that car. What happened, what was it all about?"

"We missed the plane home," Harriet said. "I hope you have a credit card handy."

Jack tried to laugh at the face Harriet made, but his side was too sore. He must have a couple of cracked ribs too, he thought.

"You have to tell me Harriet, what happened? I was there but I must have blacked out."

"I am afraid, Jack, it is quite a story. We are all on the national and international news. The Circassians attacked some Russians today, some friends of our project manager, Oxana. Several Russians died, including their leader, a man called Gregor and Oxana's father. There were some other strongmen killed too. These were with the Russians."

"The four Circassian fighters are also dead. I am afraid it is sad news for us too. Nancy died under a car that flew through the air after the explosion and landed on her. I know you saw it happen. She passed away immediately with no pain. I spoke with her family, and they will fly out here later today. The embassy is being great and a young man I met before, Stephen, is helping a lot."

"Nancy is dead?" Jack shook his head. Clearly, he hoped somehow, she survived.

"Yes, I am so sorry. Such a waste of a young life. Wrong place at the wrong time. An incredible scene."

"What was it all about?"

"I am not sure yet. The Russians killed some comrades of the Circassians in Pakistan and this was revenge. We were just caught in the crossfire. The man who rescued me was a police officer from Europol. His name is Frik. I met him in Dublin after my troubles in Spain. They were tracking Oxana since she left Seville a couple of months ago. Frik was with a Spanish man, a tall good-looking policeman."

Jack interrupted, "I saw him, he shot at the, I suppose they were the Circassian, after the first explosion and before the second one. He is a brilliant shot; both Circassians fell when he fired. I blacked out then, that is my last memory."

"Yes, Frik and Cristiano were watching Oxana. They suspected her of murdering a waiter in Spain and a man in Lithuania. She was arrested with one of the Russian thugs, Sergei, in the church. She is going to trial in Spain for a murder there. They are trying to decide what to do with Sergei. They hope to find a warrant for him in some country. The police were here as I told Frik Oxana was coming here on holiday for two weeks. Frik used the info to come here to arrest her. No one expected this explosive situation to arise. The Italian police and ambulances are demanding an inquiry. The politicians, print and social media are saying the Germans invaded- Frik is German- and did not tell the local police."

"And the second explosion?"

"Yes, the Circassians ran out of ammunition, or their guns stopped working, so they detonated their suicide vests."

"Did you say someone else died?"

Harriet counted names on her fingers, "ah, yes, I said, Oxana's father. He was in the lift in a wheelchair. Oxana put him into the lift at the penthouse and was walking to the ground floor to take him out. But when the lift doors opened, the Circassians opened fire. They hit him with a blast of machine gun fire and died instantly."

The three Russians then shot those two as they came down the stairs, but then two of the Russians got shot by the other two Circassians as they went out onto the street.

You saw Cristiano shoot them and they detonated their vests. I was saved by Frik who jumped onto a horse drawn tourist wagon passing outside the church. He galloped up and picked me off the street. He stopped beside you so the ambulances could get to you and went with Cristiano into the church to arrest Oxana.

The windows of all the houses, including the professors were blown in from the explosion. He is a witty old man, he complained that his birthday cake contained shards of glass and wondered could we get him another one. That was before he heard about Nancy. He was very upset to hear she died when the car hit her.

"And you my dear Jack, seem to have survived. Such luck, you have broken a few bones, but the embassy says they will medivac you to Dublin in a day or so. I get to go with you."

EPILOGUE

Oxana sat in the Faraday room at the enormous desk there and opened the laptop of Gregor's computer. She copied his fingerprint onto a tape she took from a champagne glass the night before they went to Sicily. It was now or never. If it didn't work, her escape was all for nothing.

The computer gleamed into light, and she applied the tape to the reader. The screen opened and said, *Welcome Gregor.* She sighed and sat back.

After a moment, she opened the large looseleaf binder beside her and went through all the checklists. One by one, she opened the accounts with the tape and changed the passwords. She copied and renamed all the files and folders, the address book, and the vaults.

When she reached the end of the folder, she had about thirty-five windows open on the laptop. She went to the banking ones and quickly totted up the six overseas bank accounts. They held over ninety-five million US dollars.

Nearly enough, she thought, nearly enough to get revenge for her father's death and to buy the best lawyers to get off the extradition warrants.

THE END (for now!)

Step into the heart-pounding world of Professor Harriet, a brilliant bio-chemical and genetic scientist, as she leads a European funded research team in their quest to unlock the mysteries of ageing and health. Harriet's ambitions are thrown into turmoil when Oxana, a murderous Russian national, infiltrates their ranks with dual agendas and deadly intent. As the team races against time, a terrifying side effect emerges—a creation of a lethal product that reduces its users to dust. In a world where trust is a luxury and betrayal lurk around every corner, Harriet must navigate a treacherous web of secrets, power, and manipulation. Lives are at stake, and the line between allies and enemies' blurs as they all become pawns in a dangerous game with irreversible consequences. Can Harriet survive the deadly forces ranged against her?

Printed in Great Britain
by Amazon

26204338R00159